Hazel Stevens

Our

IKE

ISBN: 978-1-911424-64-2
SKU/ID: 9781911424642

Inside illustration: Vanessa Barbiero
Editor: Monica Turoni
Layout: Wolf Graham
Cover: "DEVOTION" by Vanessa Barbiero (Bibi)

Typeface inside: Minion Pro Regular, Palatino Linotype
Typeface cover: Zapfino Linotype One
Vector graphics, licensed for commercial use.
Publishing Company:
Black Wolf Edition & Publishing Ltd.
Scotland (UK)
www.blackwolfedition.com

Many thanks to my husband Andrew,
my family and friends for their encouragement and support.
My editor Monica, at Black Wolf Edition & Publishing
for her faith in me.

Prologue

I felt the bile rising in my throat as my anger increased. How could this be happening? Why was I letting it happen? Even more so why was my Dad letting it happen?

I felt a hand on my arm, turning I looked down at my girlfriend Alice. We'd not been together long, but she understood me, unlike my estranged wife Lily.

'Look,' she said, nodding over to the church doorway.

My eyes averted to the aisle, where my Dad, his face set with a hint of a fake smile, led my little sister, Our Ede, down the aisle. Turning back, I glowered at the man waiting for her arrival by the altar. Tom Lister! I seethed at how my Dad, upright and honest Alf Wagstaff, could allow this union. Without a doubt Our Ede looked beautiful, with her long, blonde hair cascading under her veil, she looked so grown up, a princess in her white, lace bridal gown. No, this couldn't be happening, she was too young, a child, she was only just sixteen!

However, I knew why Dad was allowing this debacle of a marriage to take place, no kidding myself there. It was to save face, save the family name and his daughter's reputation! Ede was pregnant, so she had to get married! It was the done thing in those days, a shotgun wedding folk called them.

'Look,' Alice whispered. 'See Tom.'

I didn't want to, but curiosity got the better of me. I gulped as I looked at him. There was no way, by the look on his face, had anyone forced him into this. His eyes spoke volumes as he looked at Our Ede, he was besotted with her. His smile couldn't have been broader. He held out his hand

and Ede took it as she turned to him, I caught the same be-sotted look on her face. They were in love, truly in love.

I sighed as I realised I'd never seen my Lily, not once, look at me with such adoration. I had been such a fool and I knew it!

Part One

Chapter One

It seems decades ago now, yet it was not even one, I'd left school as soon as I could and took a job at Leeds Station. General handyman, cleaner in other words, anything from trains to toilets. I thought it was great, earning my own money allowed me to buy all the latest gear a teddy boy, in those days, wanted to wear. Fashions were changing, but I'd always liked the style so stuck to it. Drain pipe trousers and winkle picker shoes. Mam always said I'd have bad feet with the long narrow pointed style of the shoe. I wore a long jacket, wages weren't enough for me to buy a red one, mine was black. I had an open neck shirt, with one of me Dad's boot laces tied loosely around the collar. My black hair slicked back with Dad's Brylcreem. I was sure women would fall at my feet. It worked, there was never a shortage of female company to be had, any time I wanted.

Shortly after my eighteenth birthday, I found London Transport had openings, I leapt at the chance and applied straight away, when I was told there was an opportunity to be a guard on the Underground. My aim, when I was old enough, was to drive trains. I'd always been fascinated by them and had hoped my menial job at Leeds Station would lead to something. I could see I was getting nowhere fast there! London might be my chance.

I was taken on, even provided with accommodation. London, here I come! I exchanged my moped for a bigger motorbike that would take me to and fro. Mam went mad as I recall. 'Death traps!' she called them. I assured her I was quite safe. But after a few visits back at weekends, I decided the train was comfier. At least Ede didn't have a chance to meddle with my new bike.

You will never believe that, when she was nine or ten, just after I got the moped, she only took the engine out of it. I know! I couldn't believe it either. I didn't know the full extent of what she had done till years after, when my mate Sid, from down our street, admitted he'd put it back together again. Of course, he was only an apprentice mechanic in those days, so hadn't known fully what to do. I just knew the brakes wouldn't work that night. I came home from footie, Leeds United of course, Mam asked me to go to the chippie. I didn't even get near the chip shop, when I realised something was seriously amiss. When I got home, Our Ede was hiding in the bathroom, so I knew she had something to do with it. Mam calmed me down, she could always wrap me round her little finger. I just admire and respect both my parents. Of course Our Ede was, well words fail me, but she could wrap me round her little finger too!

I went to London; accommodation was a room in a pub by Euston station. Pretty grim, I can tell you. A bed, chest of drawers and small wardrobe. The room was painted in a sickly green with curtains to match, draped across a grubby window. It was my place though and I was on my own, no more sharing, as I had to do with my brother Sam, after Our Ede was born.

My apprenticeship started. I only worked Monday to Friday so I was able to get home on weekends. I loved to go down our local pub and tell all my Leeds mates how wonderful life was in the smoke. I omitted telling them my teddy boy style was scoffed at, as it was going out of date fast. The Beatles were becoming very popular and their cropped hair styles and suits could be seen everywhere. The Rolling Stones with longer hair and more colourful flamboyant clothing also had an influence. But I liked my own style, dated or not. Of course, it was no good for work, we wore a uniform.

One weekend my work mate Vic persuaded me to stay in London and we went round the local pubs. It was there I met Lily. She was so delicate looking, even with her back combed hair and brightly coloured Kaftan, I could see how thin she was, her pale face enlarged her sad brown eyes. I was in love. Lily worked behind the bar in the pub down the road from where I was staying. The Prince Arthur soon became my frequent haunt. One night Lily agreed to let me walk her home. We meandered round the back streets to a square, surrounded by blocks of concrete flats. These had been hastily erected after the war, to replace the many homes lost in the Blitz. Lily told me her family had been living in a prefab, but had recently moved into the flats. She refused to let me go any further than the entrance to the square, mumbling something about her Dad not liking it.

I quickly fell into a routine of work, the pub, walking Lily home. Gradually Lily allowed our embraces to become more intimate. I was so in love and told her so. I took her home to meet my family. She hardly spoke a word to them whilst we were there. Mam tried her hardest to talk to her but Lily wasn't inclined to make conversation. Dad eyed her suspiciously, and my brother Sam blushed when Lily mumbled hello. He always was a shy one when it came to the opposite sex.

He's a queer one Our Sam, I could never understand his love of plants and getting his hands dirty on the allotment Dad kept. Why he even got a job working with plants at a nursery on the outskirts of Leeds. He always had his head in some gardening book or magazine. Too wrapped up in them for his own good, I reckoned, trying my best to encourage him to have a night out with me and the lads. No, he wasn't having any of it. Yet look at him, at Ede's wedding reception, dancing with a Lister! Another one had got to my siblings! That family! Dad always told us to keep clear as they were "layabouts and bad uns". Yet here were my siblings both obviously enamoured by the Lister charm. Okay I hold my hands up, yes I did have a bit of a go with Joan. By she was a flighty piece and still is by the looks of her. Joan was sitting at the bar, hair backcombed, a skirt so short you could practically see her underwear and her top so low cut, leaving nothing to the imagination. She turned, caught me looking, smiled and raised her glass to me. I turned away hastily. Yes, I'd had a lucky escape from that one.

Our Ede and her new husband were in a passionate embrace on the dance floor and I knew, somehow, I'd have to cope with that. It would appear that Our Ede was good pals with Sadie Lister too. When and how did that come about? I admonished myself, I should never have gone to London. I sat nursing a pint reflecting on that time and my own wedding.

One evening I went, as usual, to the Prince Arthur and Lily's hair was down. She always wore it tied back at work. That night there was no back combing, it hung straight partly covering her face. It was busy, the pub's darts team were playing at home. I got a pint and sat down with some of the train drivers from Euston Station, well you never could tell I might get somewhere. Sometime later Vic strolled in, with his bird. Vic was plain looking and could be always found in jeans and a tee-shirt. He was an apprentice engineer, who lived in the same pub as I did. His bird Kathy looked like she'd fallen out of a fashion magazine, short blonde hair, mini skirt and white boots.

Vic nodded to me then at Lily, he turned and grinned. 'Knew I'd find you here,' he scoffed. 'You got it yet?' he mouthed quietly.

'Shurrup Vic.' I snarled. If that's all he wanted from girls then let him get on with it. I would wait for Lily, as long as it took!

The away darts team won the match and left, Lily came over and whispered she was allowed to go home. I chucked back the remains of my pint and waited for her by the door. Vic and Kathy had gone a while ago and the pub only had their own darts team, and a couple of regulars, in. As she walked towards me I could see Lily's face was much paler than before and her eyes looked frightened, she nervously pulled her hair round her face and she shivered.

'Lily?' I ventured, not knowing quite how to ask if she was okay. I took her arm and we walked outside. 'Lily?' I repeated, knowing there was something very wrong.

Lily turned and threw herself into my arms. I lifted her chin and the street light caught the long black bruise down the side of her face as her black hair fell back. I gasped. She put her hand up defensively over the bruise, muttering how she had fallen on the stairs. I had no choice but to accept this. All the same, something didn't seem right. It hadn't for a while, as our embraces became more passionate, I could feel she was holding back. It was as if she was afraid.

I pulled her into the alley down the side of the pub. 'Lily, oh my Lily.' I murmured into her straight lank hair. She began to cry and I held her to me. 'Did you really fall?' I asked quietly. In the dim light I knew she was shaking her head. 'Tell me darling how did you get that bruise?' I tried to sound determined so she would not spin me a yarn.

Slowly and tearfully Lily told me how her Father had hit her that morning. I was shocked to the core that a man could be so violent to a woman, never mind to a member of his own family, to cause such bruising.

'We'll see about this, come on,' I wasn't afraid of anyone. The gangs round the streets in Leeds respected and looked up to me. I wasn't sure why but it gave me confidence.

'No, Ike no,' Lily cried. 'You...you'll only make it worse, he...he doesn't know about you.'

I was stunned we'd been seeing each other for quite a few months. She'd been home with me for the weekend. Where did she tell her folks she'd gone? To this she replied she'd told them she was on a work's trip with the landlady of the pub. I held her close, feeling my passion rising.

'You're coming home with me tonight and then we'll think about it in the morning. Look Vic is on about us getting a flat. I think he and Kathy want to move in together. We could all share it, what do you think?' I knew I was gabbling, my mind whirled, I was so angry with the man who had hurt my precious Lily.

Lily nodded, but refused my offer of staying with me for the night. I knew the landlady of the Queens wouldn't agree to it anyway, but I told Lily I might be able to sneak her in. This brought a little giggle to my darling girl and I relaxed. Tensing again when she was determined to go home. She told me she daren't do any other. She belonged to her Father, she added.

'Lily... Just what does your Father do to make you think you belong to him?'

'Why he loves me Ike,' Lily sounded so naive. I had to ask.

'In what way does he love you Lily?' I didn't really want

to hear her reply if she told me the truth. The truth, I was feeling, about this horrible man.

'In the w...way men and w...women love each other.'

'You mean you and your Dad...' I felt sick. 'Does your Mam know?'

'God no Ike, it's our secret, I shouldn't have told you. It's just well the last few months, it's well, as if he knows there's someone else. He has hurt me a few times Ike. I... I'm scared.'

'Oh God, my Lily, my Lily, it's wrong, so wrong.'

'He makes me, he says he loves me.'

'I know but it's so wrong!' I said earnestly, wanting to protect her and love her myself at the same time. 'You must tell your Mam. What if you get pregnant?' There I'd said it, the words I'd been thinking, but wondered how I could say that to her. She sounded so naive, as if it was every Father's right to have sex with their daughter!

'I won't get pregnant Ike, not with my Da' anyway, he's had an operation. But I don't want to love him like that anymore and I told him this morning, that's why he hit me.' She started to cry again.

'Lily, I love you. I want to protect you, look after you. Will you marry me?' What had I just said? Yes, I wanted to protect her, get her away from her Father, but marriage?

'He'll never let me go Ike, unless I disgrace him. He wouldn't like that but I think he might, if...if I get pregnant by someone else. He said that he'd throw me out if I went with anyone else.' Lily held me close and turned her face up to mine. I could feel the wet on her cheeks from tears.

'Come back with me, let him throw you out.' I took her hand and led her up the road to the Queens. We sneaked in through the back door. The pub was busy and noisy, so no one heard us.

I pushed Lily into my room and sat her down on the

bed. In the bright electric light I examined her bruising and spoke softly to her while removing her blouse, gasping at another great welt on her side and I was sure just above her right breast there was a mark like a cigarette burn. I touched it with my fingers, Lily flinched away from me. 'I will never, never, never hurt you Lily. Be mine, let's get you away from all this.'

Lily nodded and removed the rest of her clothes. Her shoulder blades stuck out of her back and I was sure I could count all her ribs. Gently I folded her into my arms and we made love. Looking back I made love, Lily just lay there motionless. She waved away the condom I offered.

'It's the only way Ike,' she murmured. 'The only way.'

Like a fool I trusted her judgement, believing I was in love with her and she with me. Also believing I could save her from the man she called Da.

After that night Lily received more bruises and I begged her to let me see her Father, I wanted to knock seven bells out of him. She refused point blank.

She started spending most nights with me and it was inevitable that it didn't take long for her to announce she was pregnant. I held her in my arms, half afraid and half pleased at her news. We discussed marriage and Lily agreed, it seemed the ideal solution to get her away from her Father, also to give our child a name and a home.

We moved to a flat, in a large Victorian terraced house, with Vic and Kathy. It had two bedrooms, a shared bathroom with another flat on the same floor as ours, a kitchen come living room. Not ideal, but I stopped going out, saving all I could, for the wedding and our own place. We would need one when the baby was born.

The wedding took place within weeks. Mam, Dad and

Our Ede came down. They stayed in the pub where I'd been living. Our Ede wore a dress of pink, lacy, silky stuff that looked like she was wrapped in candy floss. When I remarked on this, I received a playful slap off her and told to shut up. My brother Sam had apparently said the same. We laughed and Mam shook her head in dismay. I knew after having two boys she longed for a girl. She had lovingly made beautiful dresses for Our Ede. Somehow Our Ede always got them dirty or torn, Mam gave up, her little girl seemed happier in Sam's cut down trousers. Yes, Our Ede was quite a tom boy, with a feisty and sometimes fiery nature to match.

There had been quite a few ructions when Our Ede announced she wanted to go to college, to do engineering. Dad had her future all planned out for her, she would go to secretarial college, but Our Ede was having none of it. When she got pregnant, Dad's ideas had, of course, gone out of the window.

History repeating itself as I looked back on my wedding. Lily was three months pregnant, but it didn't show. Mam and Dad had no idea, or if they did, they made no comment.

It wasn't long after the wedding we were able to move into our own place. It was in the same terraced house, but up on the third floor, in the attic. We had one bedroom, our own bathroom and a sitting room with a tiny kitchenette separated from the sitting room with a shelving unit. At last we could start getting things for the baby. Friends of Lily's, who had family of their own, donated clothes, a carry-cot which had a set of wheels to double it up as a pram.

It seemed no time at all before Frankie arrived, I was mesmerised by this tiny person, my son. Lily did what was necessary for the baby but there didn't seem to be any love for him. I also began to wonder – did she love me? She'd never told me, even on our wedding night, she said she was tired and during her pregnancy we hardly ever made love.

She soon went back to work, in the evenings at the pub. I was on permanent day shifts, so she was able to do this. I would go home, every evening, to a flat littered with baby clothes. A bucket of smelly nappies soaking in the corner of the kitchen. Frankie not in bed, Lily would hand him over, say he was teething or something and she'd had a terrible time with him. She would grab her coat and be gone for the night. Frankie settled down after his bottle. So, I would set about washing nappies and tidying up. It was often nine or ten o'clock before I was able to get something to eat. I seethed at Lily's lack of home making and her going back to work. However, the extra money did come in useful and we were able to buy a small car.

Trips up to Leeds were easier, though we seldom went. Our Ede came down to stay and Vic was thrilled with her mechanical knowledge. I relayed this onto Dad but my words fell on deaf ears. His daughter was to go to his choice of college.

Frankie was just four months old when Lily announced she was pregnant again. I was thrilled, Lily was angry, very angry and told me she just couldn't cope.

We'd made friends with the old lady who lived on the ground floor. Ethel Black was in her eighties, bright as a button. She always wore a pinafore over brightly flowered dresses. The dresses had seen better days but were always clean, as was her pinny. Ethel had steel grey hair she put up in a bun. I only ever saw her with it down once, it was the first time we met her. One night there was a fire in a hairdressers three doors down from the house and the fire brigade insisted on evacuating us all. Ethel's hair, although tied back, almost reached her waist. I asked if she'd ever had it cut, only now and again she admitted. The brief conversation lightened the mood and brought a smile to her frightened face.

Lily was furious with the firemen, demanding when we could go back in as she was frozen. Yet it was summer and the night was mild and balmy.

Ethel smiled at Lily sympathetically, and tried to calm her down. Lily didn't want to know, she wouldn't even speak to Ethel, that is until Frankie was born and Ethel proved a very capable babysitter. Not that we went out much, especially after Lily started work again.

'What about me job Ike?' Lily asked angrily after announcing she was late and was sure she was pregnant.

I should have realised when she began getting out of bed in the morning and retching into a bucket. 'It's okay Lily, I'm due a pay rise before this little one is due.' I whispered, gently patting her stomach. 'Frankie will love having a little brother or sister.' I took Lily in my arms.

She pushed me away. 'Men that's all you think about isn't it. Sex and breeding offspring.'

I laughed out loud until I noticed Lily's grim expression. 'What do you want to do Lily? You...you can't be thinking of getting rid?' My voice broke over these words. I'd heard of back street abortions and knew they were far from safe.

'No!' she shrieked at me, her angry face turned to horror and fear. 'Been there done tha...'

I grabbed her by the arms and looked into her face. Lily put her head down and her lank greasy hair covered her eyes, but I knew she was crying. 'When?'

'It doesn't matter now Ike,' she murmured.

'Yes, it does!' For some reason I needed to know.

'When I was thirteen,' Lily said calmly.

I felt shocked, saddened. 'Oh, my poor darling. Who, why, how? Uh... Sorry it doesn't matter now. We'll be okay, I'm here and we can manage I'm sure.' I looked over her head at the flat and wondered just how bad it would get with another baby. Frankie would still be a baby himself.

Lily nodded. I pushed the hair out of her face and wiped the tears from her eyes. I was still curious how she had gotten pregnant at such a young age. 'Your Father?' I asked quietly.

Lily nodded again.

'I thought you said he couldn't!'

Lily looked up at me with such fear, I pulled her closer. 'He could then but after that he had an operation...' Her voice tailed off as I took full impact of what she was saying. I clenched my fists! How could a man? His own daughter? I wanted to kill him and if ever I saw him in the street, at that moment, I would. Trouble was I didn't know who he was. I'd never met Lily's parents. They hadn't come to the wedding and I presumed Lily hadn't even told them about it. I didn't ask where they thought she was living now or if she ever saw them or even if they might want to know they had a grandchild. The latter because there was no way I wanted my son near a man like that.

Until Conway was born Lily moped around feeling sorry for herself. Unlike Frankie the pregnancy wasn't easy for her. She had a lot of sickness. In the latter stages her ankles were swollen, she was finally admitted to a maternity home and Conway was born early.

Ethel was only too glad to help out and look after Frankie whilst Lily was away. The boy seemed to adore Ethel and his face would light up whenever he saw her. I got the flat in order too, even decorated our bedroom. I was able to get another carry cot with wheels. The first one being sold, as Frankie had outgrown it quickly, yet only a matter of days before Lily realised she was pregnant again. Ironic, really, but that's the way things go.

Lily and a tiny scrap of baby came home three weeks later. She still refused to feed the baby herself and I was terrified at the smallness of the child. Frankie had been a big baby and barely in first size clothes. Whereas these drowned Conway. Lily seemed to be coping with the two bairns, though she moaned Ethel was a daily visitor and always meddling with stuff. I knew Ethel was only too keen to help out, so did not rise to Lily's complaints. I just let her carry on, pleased that the flat was looking tidier these days and the babies clean and cared for. Conway was putting on weight and even Lily seemed more motherly towards him.

Our Ede had been down and though she spent much of her few short days with Vic at the workshop, when she was with us, she seemed to have a knack of settling both babies down.

My job was becoming more involved and I was training to be a conductor, the next step in my goal to being a train driver. Pay was better and though I told Lily she didn't need to go back to work, she insisted. Conway was only a month old when Lily went back to the pub. It was thanks to Ethel's help that I was able to cope with the little ones. She often went downstairs, after helping get them to bed, returning with a plate of hot dinner. She knew Lily never left me anything to eat after my day at work. Once my training was complete I would be on shifts.

'Don't worry lad, I'm here.' Ethel sighed and I knew what she was thinking, that Lily should be there. But she never uttered a word of her concerns to me. She would sigh and nod if I opened up to her about Lily.

The busy days sped by and in no time at all Frankie was walking and saying 'Dada.' It was a little easier, though the lad had been crawling for some time.

Lily seemed happier being at work and quite often we would enjoy walks to Regents Park on my days off. She still moaned about Ethel, now I was on shifts, I reminded her firmly that we couldn't both work if it wasn't for this seemingly tireless old lady.

The days went by, Frankie was growing into a cheeky young imp and Conway seemed a happy baby and keen to copy his brother. Even Lily and I were on better terms. Though now she was back at work, she still left a lot of the child care to me and Ethel. That old lady was amazing. How we managed without her I really don't know.

We had our name down with the council and it wasn't long before we got a letter offering us a place. It was a small terraced house, but it had three bedrooms. I'd never seen Lily so animated as she was when she saw the house. Although a bit of a way from Euston, that didn't matter. The underground would get me to work and back in no time. However, I had my concerns.

'What about the kids and Ethel?' I asked cautiously.

'What do you mean?' Lily snapped, 'I'll be glad to get away from that old bag!'

'Lily!' I was appalled and told her so, how could she be so ungrateful? All the help Ethel had given us, we would never have managed without her!

Lily looked shame faced and told me if we could afford it, she might consider giving up work.

'You mean that Lily?' I said, pulling her into my arms, 'Oh darling, to have you here in my own proper home, when I come in from work, it will be smashing.'

'Our home,' Lily murmured.

I nodded, our life was working out. I had Lily and two lovely sons, a job I was enjoying, what more could a man want?

We moved into 7, Walthamstow Road on June 1st. The weeks flew by, Lily true to her word gave up her job and spent the time decorating, with me doing the ceilings. The house soon became a proper home. On my days off we scoured the second hand shops for bits of furniture, it was a fun time for all of us.

Of course, Ethel was really upset by our departure, but I promised her she could come and visit any time. She said she would as long as I was there.

Ethel reminded me of my own Granny. I regaled her with tales of spending time with Granny and Grandad, and how, when Our Ede was born, Grandad made me a go cart. I do remember feeling jealous towards my baby sister. I didn't relay this to Ethel, she would never understand, she had seen the love Our Ede and I shared for each other.

My sister was, when she got into her teens, becoming quite a lovely young woman. She talked endlessly of her wish to become an engineer of sorts. Dad wanted her to do office work.

'But he can stuff that!' Our Ede told me firmly. She had come to stay again, not long after our house was almost ship shape.

I reminded her, until she reached twenty-one, she had to abide by what Our Father said. I fancied Our Ede's wish to go to college to study engineering would soon become a passing fad, once she got interested in makeup and boys. I left Ede with the boys and went to tackle the backyard, to make it more child friendly. First job was to remove the weeds from between the paving slabs. Later I planted up some pots of lettuce, radishes, and peas, vegetables my Dad had on his allotment. I very occasionally went with him when I was younger. Until I was old enough to go off to watch Leeds United. They were doing well and top of the league for some years, later on they even won the FA Cup. What's happened to them now? They barely get a mention, but I still remain a loyal supporter.

I preferred the time I spent at home with Mam, before my baby sister came along that is, we would bake and cook. I helped and watched how she did things.

Lily laughed when I told her that I could bake scones and cakes. She didn't believe me, but once we got the kitchen organised and I got used to the gas stove. I gave baking a go, Frankie helped in his own childish way too. Lily had taken Conway shopping but upon her return I presented a batch of scones, a chocolate cake and some buns.

She stared in amazement, looking round for Ethel. 'Has she been here?'

I shook my head and said proudly it was all my own work.

'Me, me.' Frankie chortled.

We all laughed and tucked into the cake with a cup of tea. Even Lily had to admit it was good. I remember feeling so happy, sitting in that yard, enjoying the sunshine, Lily by my side watching the lads play on a blanket we'd laid down. I felt content, wife, family, our own home, yes life was good, very good.

Chapter Two

Like all good things they have to end, I was shocked when our lovely life came to such an abrupt division with Lily announcing she was pregnant again.

I was overjoyed with the news, but she was angry.

'We'll have to get rid of it Ike, I can't stand any more babies! We'll have to find the money for an abortion!' she demanded coldly.

Grabbing both her arms I told her firmly we would be doing no such thing. Didn't she know the risk of these back-street abortionists? She could die, I reminded her of the room we had in our new house. I tried to reassure her all would be okay, wouldn't she like a daughter, I added encouragingly.

Lily slowly nodded, 'Yes... A girl would be okay, I... I guess. You're right about the abortion Ike. Sylvia Fisher died from one, guess I was lucky that time... But I just don't know, I can't cope.'

'Look I'll ask Our Ede to come down, once you're near your time. Will that be alright?'

Lily nodded and the following months were hard on us all. Her mood swings, forlorn looks of despair and as she grew bigger, she moaned about backache and swollen ankles.

Ethel came to see us one day, taking one look at Lily, she said, 'Lass, you're either carrying a lot of water or there's more than one in there!'

Lily was not best pleased and declared she needed a lie down. Ethel said she had better go, but she came to tell us her sister Enid would be moving in next door to us.

'Enid is younger than me and loves kids, I know she will help you out Ike.'

I protested and told her we were fine. However, if Enid was like Ethel then I knew she would be kind and helpful and she really was. Frankie was in a playgroup and Enid, bless her heart, would take him there and pick him up. Lily seemed to be grateful and she also accepted help from Enid, without the complaint of her interfering, as she had done about Ethel.

The last few months were hard. It was spring and the weather turned unseasonably hot. Lily took to her bed and when I was home I fell into the routine of washing, cleaning and cooking for us all.

The twins were born just after Easter and fine bonny babes, they were too. A boy, and Lily's longed for girl. However, they were both a bit on the small side, which was a worry and meant they all had to stay in hospital for a few extra weeks. Enid was a Godsend and even though I had a couple of weeks holiday, she looked after Frankie and Conway while I visited the hospital.

Finally, the babes and Lily were allowed home. After I went back to work, I knew Enid would be round at ours most days helping out, Lily didn't object.

Lily idolised Shirley, but would have little to do with Buddy. The twins thrived though and both had loud lusty cries. When they were quiet and the older boys looked at them adoringly, I felt content. Lily was really down after the birth and although she was pleased to have a daughter, Buddy seemed to rile her. Lily even breast fed Shirley something she had never done with the boys, Buddy had to make do with a bottle. It didn't matter to me. I enjoyed feeding my little baby and Frankie liked to feed him too, though I had to help of course.

Enid seemed to have taken charge of things and I will always be eternally grateful to this quiet, unassuming, mouse of a woman. She was small and dainty, unlike her older sister, Ethel was tall and solid. But their features were identical and they had the same colour of grey hair, in the same style too. They were house proud women and Enid seemed to have a natural way about her with the babies. Ethel had been nervous of holding the boys when they were little. I guess because she had never had children of her own. Enid on the other hand had raised four children, two were married and lived in Australia, with four children between them. Of the other two, one lived in America and one in Hong Kong. So she was glad to adopt our growing family, in place of the grandchildren she never saw.

As Shirley grew, Lily's infatuation waned and she announced one day she would like to go back to her job at the pub. I asked how did she know they wanted someone? I knew they had replaced Lily last time she left. She told me she had called in one lunch time and her replacement had handed in her notice. They asked Lily if she was interested in returning. It seemed Lily had already agreed to start back on Friday and Saturday nights. She would see the kids into bed and, when I was at work, Enid had agreed to babysit. Lily had organised everything, I felt angry we had not discussed it first.

Occasionally I would ask Enid to babysit and go down to the Prince Arthur. Vic and a new girlfriend would often meet me there. They never stayed long, preferring London's West End for a livelier night out. I would sit with the train drivers and watch Lily, she seemed to be a different person behind the bar, more animated and she smiled a lot at the punters.

One particular Saturday night an old man sidled up to the bar. He looked familiar but I couldn't think why? I did, however, see Lily's face pale when she saw him and I knew it was her Father. I couldn't hear what was said but he spoke a few words, turned abruptly and left before I had a chance to get to the bar. Lily stood staring after him, tears streaming down her face. I pushed up the bar flap and went to her.

'Lily, that man he was your Fa...'

'Yes,' Lily broke in. 'Ike, it's my Ma, she...she's dead. That's what he came to tell me.'

Phyllis, the landlady, beckoned us into the back room. After gentle questioning, Lily told us her Father had only come to tell her about her Mother, that she died and it was all Lily's fault, because she left home, broken heart he'd said. No matter what Phyllis and I said to Lily, it didn't seem to console her. How could that man be so callous! I was so angry, so very angry! Phyllis laid a hand on my arm and told me to take Lily home.

In silence we made our way back home, to be greeted by an ever cheerful Enid. She saw Lily and realised something was amiss, so left telling me we knew where she was if we needed her.

In the days that followed Lily stayed at home, she looked after the kids but just did the essentials and ignored Frankie and Conway's plea for her to play with them. I found out that her Mother had died two months earlier, from pneumonia, I relayed this to Lily saying it was not her fault. My words fell on deaf ears. Lily continued retreating into her own world, of what seemed abject misery. What could I do?

I rang home and talked to Mam and Dad, in return they sent some money down for us and I booked a caravan holiday on the South Coast. Hoping this would reunite us as a family. It didn't work. The caravan was small, the twins were fretful, only Frankie, Conway and I got any pleasure out of it. Lily was still consumed with guilt. She even told me she should be with her Dad.

'After what he did to you Lily? Are you mad?' I demanded. I was getting to the end of my tether. Nothing I did seemed to help her or please her.

'Yes!' she spat back at me. 'He loved me.'

'You think I don't! You think the kids don't!' I yelled back, my anger rising.

'Shut up Ike. Just shut up and leave me alone and take these Goddamn kids with you.'

I didn't need telling twice. I hastily got the twins into their pushchair, put Frankie and Conway's coats on, and dragged them outside.

'You'd better think where you really want to be Lily!' I yelled. 'Cos I can't take much more and neither can the kids, I'm telling you!'

I slammed the caravan door and took the kids to the playground. The older boys were delighted.

'Dad, why Mummy cross?' Frankie pulled on my sleeve.

'She's tired son, now go and help your brother on the slide.'

The twins had fallen asleep and I sat on a bench at the side of the play area, deep in thought. Did Lily really want to go back to her Dad? Surely not, not after he...

The sun came out from the darkening clouds and I watched my two boys chasing around with some other children. How could she not be part of this?

A young couple, with two girls about the same age as Frankie and Conway, sat down on the bench next to me, laughing together as they watched all the kids playing. We chatted about the weather and how well our kids were getting on and seemed to enjoy playing together.

'Look, I'm sorry to ask but would you mind keeping an eye on my two, while I go and...and get these two changed.' I nodded to the twins who were awake now and obviously restless.

'Not at all,' the young Mum said.

I quickly pushed the twins back to the caravan. I opened the door not knowing what I might find. Lily had been so angry, so had I. She must know I loved her though and the kids loved her too. We must matter to her! The van was empty. Lily had gone, her case and clothes with her. On the table a hastily scribbled note with the words 'Sorry Ike' written on it.

I sat at the table and tears fell down my face. How could she? How could she just go and leave us all?

I pushed the twins back to the park. The young couple greeted me with huge smiles.

'Frankie, Conway, come on, we must go. Now!' I shouted.

The boys ran up to me, Frankie complained he wanted to stay and the young couple said he was welcome to. I shook my head and pulled the boys away.

They both cried as I dragged them back to the caravan, telling them we were going home. When they saw Lily wasn't there, they began crying for their Mum. My heart was in shreds. I bungled them and our belongings into the car, left the caravan key at reception and drove back to London.

The house was quiet when we arrived, the kids were fretful. I managed to get them some tea and afterwards get the four of them settled in their beds. There was no sign Lily had even been there. I must go and look for her, but where to start?

I went next door and tapped on the window. Enid

came to the door, fear on her face at seeing me. 'Ike, what are you doing back here? What's the matter? You're supposed to be on holiday.'

In a broken voice I told her what had happened. She pushed me back home, sat me down and put the kettle on. 'Tea,' she ordered. It was something Mam would have done, how I wish she were there now. Enid however made up for Mam's absence in spades.

She gently asked me to tell her again what had happened. I told her everything, all about Lily, the abuse she had suffered from her Dad. Her getting pregnant so she could escape him. How she was consumed in guilt after hearing of her Mother's death and how she had said she should be with her Dad and finding her gone from the caravan.

'She took her clothes, I...I thought she'd be here, where is she? I love her, Enid.' I concluded, tears threatening.

'I know you do Ike,' Enid patted my shoulder and said very quietly, 'It's a pity the girl doesn't love you the same.'

'What?' I asked.

Enid shook her head and said it was nothing, but I'd heard her and I knew how right she was. Lily didn't love me, she never had. I had just been so infatuated I had never seen it or I didn't want to see it. I don't think she loved any of our children either. I think she just wanted to escape her Father. But now...had she gone back to him?

I asked the question out loud. Enid shook her head saying she did not think the girl would be so stupid. But I didn't know, I wasn't sure.

Enid pulled me up and told me firmly to go and find Lily and talk some sense into her. She thrust my coat into my arms and opened the front door.

'The kids.' I protested.

'The kids will be fine with me Ike; you have no fear of

that. Now get yourself away and find your wife.'

My first thought was the pub, the Prince Arthur. I went straight there, Phyllis looked surprised to see me. No, she hadn't seen Lily since the night her Father had come in.

I asked if anyone knew where Lily had lived; Phyllis and the customers all shook their heads.

'She worked here Phyllis, you must have an address!' I demanded.

'Well, of course I did Ike, but I don't remember what it was and when she gave me her new address, after she moved in with you, I chucked the other out.'

None of the customers, in that night, knew either. I left feeling lost, where should I look next? I thought I knew the block of flats where Lily had once lived, I couldn't be sure. I'd only ever walked her to the entrance of the blocks. I went round and knocked on a few doors in one block. No one seemed to know, or if they did, they weren't telling me. I went to the next block and the next, knocking on doors again with no result.

I crossed the paved area in front of the flats to the last block in the square. The first door I came to had wood nailed over the part where glass should have been. The paint was peeling on the lower half of the door, I rapped loudly on the wood. The door opened and an old man peered at me through the door.

'What do you want?' he said. 'I've no money.'

'I don't want money; I just want to find my wife Lily.' I knew I was looking at her Father. 'Is she here?' I spoke quietly, rage bubbling, I was ready to flatten him, but he was an old man and looked like a puff of wind would blow him over. 'Well, is she here?' I asked again, putting my foot firmly in the door before he could close it.

'You!' he whispered. 'You took her away from me! NO! She is not here!'

'Are you sure?' I asked quietly, trying to control my temper.

'Of course I'm sure! Why would the slut come back here, after being with you?'

I moved my foot and the door slammed. This man, her Father, how could he speak about his daughter, like that? If he hadn't slammed the door shut, old or not, I would have punched him in the face.

Where to look now? Would she go to Vic's? No harm in asking? Vic and his new bird Janice lived in the same flat we had once shared. Wearily I made my way there. Going over in my head who Lily's friends were, not that she had many, Lily always seemed to keep herself to herself.

I pushed the flat doorbell. 'Vic!' Janice cried, pulling the door open. 'You came ba...' Her face fell when she saw me. 'Ike.' She opened the door further and beckoned me in.

'Janice.' I nodded, noticing her dismay, she'd been crying. 'Janice are you okay? Have you seen Lily?'

'Ike...' Janice threw her head back and gulped in the air before a low laugh grew in her throat. It broke out of her like a volcano erupting.

I grabbed her by the shoulders and shook her hard, she was hysterical. 'Janice, what's going on here?'

'Like me Ike, you don't know, do you? We are always last to find out. They've gone.' She began to laugh again, high pitched and out of control.

She wasn't making any sense. 'Gone, who's gone? What are you talking about?' I shook her again and pushed her down into a chair.

Janice sat down and began to cry. 'Oh Ike, what are we going to do?'

'It's Vic, isn't it? He's left you?' I realised then the reason for the hysteria. I felt sorry for the girl, but I needed to know if she had seen Lily. How could I question her when she was going through the same turmoil as I was? I knelt down in front of her, wrapped my arms round her shuddering body and let her cry. 'It's okay Janice, Vic will be back, he adores you. He'll be back, don't worry. One little tiff isn't going to keep him away long. I came because I...I wondered if you had seen Lily?' I felt bad but I had to know.

Janice pushed me back, 'One little tiff, one little tiff. Have I seen Lily? Oh my God Ike, you have no idea, have you? He won't be back and neither will Lily.'

I grabbed her hands, 'What do you mean Lily won't be back either?' My mind whirled as slowly, I realised what she was saying even before she said it.

'They've gone Ike! Gone together, my Vic and your Lily!' Janice cried.

I sat back on my haunches trying to make sense of it all. How come? How? When? Slowly Janice explained. Earlier that day Vic had a phone call from Lily, she told him she was leaving you and getting the train back to London. Vic met her at the station, Janice said she thought it was to talk some sense into her. When Vic came back, he hadn't spoken to Janice, he'd gone into the bedroom and packed a bag. He looked round the flat, before telling her, Lily needed him and he needed her, they were going away together.

'Where, Janice, where are they going?' I demanded.

Janice shrugged her shoulders. 'He wouldn't tell me. Tell Ike I'm sorry is what he said before he left. Tell Ike I'm sorry, no apology to me. Nothing, Ike, nothing!'

I knew she was getting hysterical again but I couldn't help her. I stood up and left.

Lily and Vic, why? Why hadn't I noticed anything? How

long had this been going on? How could they do this? How could she do this? Leave me and the kids, no, she wouldn't leave the kids, would she?

I went home in a daze. It couldn't be true. Vic wouldn't just go off with Lily. He must have taken her somewhere to talk, try to make her see sense, persuade her to come back to me. Yes, that's what he would be doing. I'd go to his work in the morning and ask how he had got on, that is if Lily hadn't come home by then.

I fell into bed, sleeping and waking. The twins woke about five and the rest of the morning saw me seeing to the kids. It was almost eleven before I could get away. Enid had a doctor's appointment, so couldn't look after the kids any earlier.

I went down to the engineering works, where Vic would be. Looking round I couldn't see him anywhere, so I asked some of the blokes there. Vic's mate Fred came up to me and beckoned me into a shabby, tired staff room.

'Ike, I'll make us a brew. Now then Ike,' he said slowly, pressing a mug of tea into my hand, his expression made me wish it was something stronger. 'Ike, I...I had a call from Vic last night. He isn't at work and won't be back, he's gone...'

'Gone where?' I said, slamming the mug down on the table, splashing its hot contents over my hand. 'More so... with who?'

'Lily, he told me...' Fred said quietly, his voice trailing off. 'I'm so sorry Ike.'

My face fell, I sat down on the bench. 'Where have they gone Fred?' I mumbled.

Fred shrugged, 'I don't know Ike, honest I don't. He just said Lily needed him and he needed to be with her.'

'What about her kids needing her?' I spat, standing up

pushing the bench over.

Fred stared at me not knowing what to say or do. It wasn't his fault. I apologised and left. So it was true, Lily and Vic had gone off together and I felt, at that moment, such a fool for not having seen it, not having suspecting there was anything between them. How could I have been so blind?

I needed a drink and was glad to find the Coach and Horses, near the works, open. Ordering a pint and a whisky chaser, I sat down determined to drown my sorrows and numb the pain and the humiliation I was feeling. How and why could I have been so stupid? What about the kids? Would she want them with her? These questions flooded my mind over and over as I downed pint after pint and whisky after whisky. I felt easier as I stumbled my way to the bar for yet another round. The barmaid flashed her long eyelashes at me. She was being very friendly. I started feeling much better, even forgot, for a while, about Lily, my misery and my kids. The barmaid beckoned me outside when she was going for a break and I followed. I needed comfort and knew she would happily provide it.

Chapter Three

I stumbled home in a daze, drink fuzzing my head. What had just happened? Fumbling for my key, I opened the front door, our front door, the one I'd carefully painted in the bright red Lily wanted. I opened my mouth to call her name, but the house was empty and cold.

Nothing had changed, toys littered the front room. Pots lay in the kitchen sink unwashed. A bucket of nappies stood in the corner of the kitchen soaking their contents away. Seeing that bucket, I turned and collapsed on the sofa in tears. I tried to shrug them off but the more I tried the harder they fell. A grown man crying, what would my Dad say and my mates? I fell into a fitful doze waking and rousing myself sometime later.

The kids, I must see to the kids, I told myself firmly. I couldn't leave them with Enid much longer. I stumbled out into the fresh air, taking great gulps of it as I struggled to come to my senses, ignoring the knife slicing through my heart as it hit me. Lily, who I worshipped and adored had gone, leaving me with four children. Why? How? Questions invaded my thoughts with every step to my neighbour's house. I tapped on the door and Frankie opened it shouting, 'Daddy, Daddy's here!'

'Ike?' Enid looked at me questioningly. 'Come away in, you look terrible, tell me what's happened now?'

I shook my head not daring to speak.

'Ike come in, I can see by your face something is amiss, come on Ike tell me?' Enid shooed Frankie into the living room and taking my arm she led me into the kitchen.

She sat me down at the table and busied herself making

some tea.

'The kids, I... I...have to get them home for their tea.'

'It's okay for now Ike; Frankie and Conway are playing and the twins are asleep.'

I took a large swig of the warm, weak tea and knew I would have to tell her what had gone on. Very slowly the words came out, as I told her, it looked like Lily had gone for good.

Enid laid a hand on my shoulder and whispered, 'Oh Ike, I am so sorry. What will you do now?'

I wasn't at all sure what I would do and told her so. I thanked her and gathered up the children. Taking them home was a comfort, I kept busy unpacking things and preparing them all beans on toast, well the twins had bread and seemed quite happy to chew away at that. Frankie was good and said very little. Conway however, after a few mouthfuls, demanded to know where Mummy was. I told him she had to go to work. He nodded and accepted this. It was a struggle, but I managed to get the four kids fed, bathed and bedded. Standing for a long time, I watched them sleep. Conway and the twins sucked on their dummies, Frankie had his thumb. My tears fell at first then anger took over. How could she? What sort of Mother left her kids? If she could dismiss them so carelessly then we were all well rid of her. We really were. With those thoughts in my head I went downstairs and spent the evening tidying up, getting the washing done, anything, just to keep busy.

I finally fell into my own bed about midnight and lay there staring at the shadows on the ceiling, cast by the street light outside. Where were they? What were they doing? Thoughts kept going round and round, and nothing would take away the pain I was feeling.

I soon realised I could not cope. When Mam arrived I felt so relieved and grateful for her taking the twins and Conway back to Yorkshire. I promised her I would be up there as soon as I could. Frankie was at school and Enid quite happily took him and picked him up. Somehow, I got to work, but the days seemed endless and the nights too. My pain just would not ease.

It was one Saturday Enid looked at me and said I needed a night out. I shook my head, but she insisted and said Frankie could stay with her for the night. In fact, we both could move in and give my house up. If I was, eventually, moving back to Yorkshire then I would need every penny. Did I need to pay rent, when we could both stop with her? I agreed and set the wheels in motion, I also agreed to go for a night out.

I steered clear of any pubs Lily may have frequented, preferring to go further into the East End; this was the real East End where dockers and market traders drank after work. I felt I didn't really belong there. They turned and looked at me curiously when I asked for a pint in my Yorkshire accent.

I sat down at an empty table and supped my beer, trying not to make eye contact. I was surprised when a young girl came and sat opposite me.

'Lovely to hear a bit of old Yorkshire,' she gushed.

I looked up and stared at her. 'What?' I queried.

'Bit of old Yorkshire, I'm from theer messen,' she said broadly, emphasising every word.

Curiosity got the better of me and we spent the next half hour discussing our home towns. She was from Halifax, not too far or dissimilar to Leeds, both expanding cities, growing from cotton and wool mills.

'You look down in the dumps,' she whispered.

I nodded and suddenly the whole sorry saga came pouring out. What the hell was I doing telling my woes to a stranger? But Angie didn't feel like a stranger, true there was something distant about her that I couldn't put my finger on. But she seemed kind.

'Come with me,' she rose from her seat and held out her hand. 'I know a place, well, it's where I live. There you can forget all your troubles and I can get you something to ease your pain.'

'Nothing will do that.' I declared.

'Oh yes it will,' she said softly, in a voice as smooth as silk.

I took her hand and we walked out of the pub and down the street, turning into an alley, out onto another street and down another alley.

'Hey, where are we going?' I asked, feeling a little fearful not knowing where I was.

'Just here,' she said, indicating a doorway with no door just a piece of brightly coloured cloth hanging over the entrance. She pulled me inside. I stood firm for a moment, taking in my surroundings and the smells. I was standing in the hallway with several darkly coloured rooms going off it. I could see bodies in these rooms, some asleep, some staring wide eyed at the ceiling. One couple were actually having sex. The air was thick with a sweet smell, along with the stench of unwashed bodies.

'Sam, you got something for my pal here?'

A tall skinny lad appeared at Angie's side and held out cigarettes and a packet. 'Got any money Angie's pal?' he slurred.

'A fiver should do it Ike,' Angie whispered.

I obliged and pulled one from my pocket handing it over to the lad who melted into a room. Angie nodded and pulled me to the stairs. 'I ain't like this lot,' she said, nodding to the people in the rooms downstairs. 'Got me own space, here.' She drew back a curtain and pulled me inside what was little more than a cupboard. A mattress lay on the floor covered with an assortment of brightly coloured blankets. We sat down, and she lit one of the cigarettes, inhaling deeply on it. I realised the sweet smell downstairs was from the cigarettes. She held it out to me, I shook my head telling her I didn't smoke. She laughed and pushed it into my mouth and said, 'Take a puff.' Sitting astride my legs, I felt a sense of stirring. Angie lazily drew a finger around my mouth and took the cigarette away, inhaling the smoke deeply again herself. Pushing it back into my mouth I took a puff. Wow, the sensation I felt as the smoke filled my lungs, my body. I just wanted to take more and more and I puffed away on the decreasing cigarette.

'Hey, leave some for me?'

I lay back watching as she finished it, her emotions rose and she giggled as she stripped herself and then me. Through the fog I knew it was all wrong, but still.

I fell into a sleep, waking suddenly as dawn spilled into the room. Looking around I could see the filth and squalor Angie lived in. I wanted out. True the pain had left me last night, now it hit me like a thunderbolt, so much so I moaned loudly. Angie woke and put her arms round me. 'Ike what, what is it?' she slurred.

I pushed her away, 'I can't do this! What am I doing here?'

'Forgetting, easing the pain. I have something else you could try.' From under a cushion Angie withdrew a packet of powder. It was then I noticed her bruised arms. I held one of her arms in my hand and could feel the bone through the purple skin.

'What is this?' I nodded to her arm and the powder.

'Oh Ike, it's amazing, you will forget all your hurt, this

will really help you. I will help you.'

'Really?'

'Yes Ike, really.'

I was sceptical but curiosity made me wonder if it would stop the pain as Angie promised. I watched as she carefully prepared the substance. Producing a syringe, she drew the substance up into it, then held it towards me. Holding my arm she gently inserted the needle into the vein and I watched, mesmerised. A feeling, I can't describe, coursed through my bloodstream.

'There you are, my turn now, just lay down Ike and enjoy.' She injected herself and lay down beside me, holding my hand as we both went under the influence of this white powder. I felt woozy and colours appeared to fly round the room. I looked at Angie, she lay beside me, a smile on her face, her eyes wide and staring. My pain eased, she was right, it made it disappear. The room started revolving and I sat up but she pulled me down again. I started to panic, I felt I was losing control of my senses. I tried to get up again. Angie urged me to lay back down. Begrudgingly I did, in the knowledge that the way I felt, if I stood up, I would almost certainly fall back down again. The colours swirled round and round and round. I felt the panic going and a sense of euphoria filled my body. This was good, if only the colours would stop spinning. I felt good. I closed my eyes to shut out the colours and felt my body rise up. I was floating, wasn't I?

'Ike, Ike, wake up!' Angie's voice filtered into my head. I felt her shaking me. 'You have to go! I shouldn't have! I'm sorry... I...'

I stirred myself, opened my eyes and reached out my hand to wipe the tears off her face. What shouldn't she have done? I asked her.

'Given you smack.'

'What smack?' I laughed. 'God, I feel good, you were right, the pain, it went and I feel great. Look, I better had go now, but can I come back tonight.'

Angie shook her head.

'Please, I'd like to see you again and we could well you know.'

The tall lanky youth, from the night before, drew back the curtain. 'Yeh Ang, let the geezer come if he wants, no skin off our nose, as long as he brings pennies.'

Angie looked from him to me and back again. She put a protective arm round my shoulders. 'I'd like to see you again Ike, but let's meet for a drink.'

I nodded, 'Okay, just for a drink then and maybe well, you know, that was pretty good last night.' I staggered to my feet arranging to meet Angie in the same pub. I felt dizzy and disorientated, once in the fresh air, I felt better and even whistled as I made my way back to Enid's. Angie may not be God's gift but she was interested in me and that was all that mattered right then; yes that was all that mattered.

Enid seemed quite content to look after Frankie, taking him to school, picking him up and days would pass before I saw my son. One look at his anxious face made me half question what was I doing. But I was happy, days passed in a haze, somehow I kept my job going, mainly to earn money to satisfy Enid, but also my own cravings. Nightly visits to the squat became more frequent and soon most of my weekends were spent there in a delicious haze of euphoria. I was paying for Angie's habit too, she was regularly on smack. I contented myself with smoking weed and just the occasional hit. Angie kept me straight on Sundays so I was able to get to work on Monday mornings. However, as the days went by I began going into work later and later. I didn't care, work held no interest to me, Frankie and the others became a blur, life with Lily was well and truly behind me.

I skipped work for a few days, told them and Enid I needed a break. They seemed to accept this and Enid said she would look after Frankie. She was concerned, she said, adding I looked terrible, so a break might do me good.

I went to Angie's, she seemed unsure about me staying but as soon as I gave her the cash we were enjoying ourselves, oblivious to the world around us. We'd even gone to a café somewhere, new singers and bands played there. Angie told me Cliff Richard had played there before he became famous. She longed to see him, she'd heard he often came back for a visit down memory lane, not the night we went though. I was eager to get back for something a bit more than a smoke. The rest of the nights passed in a blur, I felt content. I didn't love Angie, guess she just made me feel good in more ways than one.

A few days later, one morning, I lay back in Angie's bed, she'd gone off somewhere and I dozed. Suddenly, I felt myself being lifted off the bed and thrown against the wall.

'Isaac! What in God's name are you doing lad?'

I blinked trying to clear my vision, only one person called me Isaac – Dad.

He physically dragged me out of the squat, where did Dad, my gentle kind Dad, get his strength from, left me even more bewildered. He thrust me into a cab and out again. When we got to Enid's, Frankie wasn't there. Ignoring Enid's protests, he pushed me upstairs into the bathroom and into the bath which he filled with cold water. Splashing it over my face, I could feel my body shivering and shaking. After what seemed like an hour, he left me. I heard him telling Enid to pack my things, would she also fetch Frankie, as both of us were going home with him.

The mention of home reduced me to tears and I sat fully clothed, in the freezing water, weeping.

Dad returned to the bathroom, not saying a word, he held the towel and helped me out of the bath. Eventually my teeth stopped chattering and I mouthed, 'Home?'

'Aye lad, I am taking you home, God knows what you've been doing down here!' he held up his hand. 'No! I don't want to know, just know that it's taken me long enough to find you and I am glad I did.' His voice lowered as he softly said, 'Ike, you've bairns lad, who need you. Not to mention a Mother worried to the bone. No lad, no more tears, get yourself dried and here's fresh clothes. These can go in the bin, when Frankie gets home, we'll get going, okay?'

I nodded, I knew I'd have no alternative and right then I wanted nothing more than to see Mam and my other kids. How selfish had I been? How cruel too? I had done just what Lily had done, abandoned my kids and that would never do. I would make it up to them, I really would. 'Yes Dad, let's go home and Dad thank you, I... I...'

'Get on with you lad, it's what you, as a Father yourself, would do!' was his reply.

I wanted to tell him how much I loved and admired him, of course I couldn't. A Yorkshire man of his age and standing didn't talk about things like that, no matter how they felt, or did they? He must have told Mam he loved her or she would never have married him. I couldn't see it, I really couldn't. Of course, I could have fought him but I didn't have the energy. I knew the habits I got myself into were no good to anyone. Why I had indulged I had no idea, except to forget the pain, the pain of Lily leaving. Yet I had left my kids. I shook myself out of my misery, reminiscing about what might have been.

Enid cried as we left, I didn't know what to say. Words of thanks seemed not enough. I heard her tell Dad she was sorry, sorry she hadn't seen it. I hugged her to me and told her we would keep in touch and to give my love to Edith. I knew that there would probably be no contact between us again. I was just glad I had given the house up and that wasn't to sort out before we left London. In the broad light of day I knew I was a fool. I'd make it up to them, all of them. I was certain of that. A new Ike dawned and it took a stern Yorkshireman to make me come to my senses.

It wasn't long before we were on the train. If I heard Frankie ask once, he asked a dozen times, what was wrong with me? My Dad just kept telling him I was ill and needed to go home, where we could all be looked after.

'You're going home, you're going home,' the train whispered as we bowled along.

It sounded good, I couldn't wait to see Mam, the kids and Our Ede of course.

Chapter Four

The next few weeks passed me by, I slept a lot, ate Mam's meals as best I could. She said I was skin and bone and seemed determined to fatten me up. I hazily remember the kids coming into the front room to say hello. Also Ede, she seemed to have altered. I suppose she had grown up. After all, she was leaving school at the end of the summer term. It barely seemed five minutes since she was a baby playing in the coal scuttle or an inquisitive child wanting to know how things worked. I heard her gasp one morning when she came in. I'd taken off my tee shirt, to put a fresh one on. Yes, I knew I had lost weight but hearing Ede gasp made me realise it must have been quite a lot. Yet she seemed to be filling out in all the right places. I'd have to get myself up and around so I could warn off all the, would be, blokes lining up for her. I'd show them, I knew what the blokes round our neck of the woods were like, out for just one thing. Well, I had been one of the lads what seemed like an age ago, yet only a few years now. Mates called to see me, but I had grown away from them when I got married and became a Father. Half of them were still going out on a Saturday night on the pull. Well I'd make damn sure one of them didn't pull Our Ede!

Dad got me a job at the Mill, driving the lorry taking shoddy (unwanted remains from the woven cloth) out to farms, which they spread on the fields as fertiliser. It had taken me several weeks to get over the poison I'd been injecting and the stuff I'd smoked. I suffered terribly from withdrawal symptoms the doctor said, after Mam insisted I go and see him. The doctor prescribed some pills he thought might help, but all they did was make me sleep. Mam always maintains, the best healer for all ills, is sleep and how right she was that time.

I enjoyed my new job, out in the fresh air and sunshine, the farmers around Leeds were very friendly and jovial. I even drove as far as York some days. Between Leeds and York the land is very arable, just right for growing crops, so my delivery was always welcome.

Through my work I met Alice. She seemed a shy lass, small and rounded with rosy cheeks. Alice worked in the distribution office and I would go there to collect my instructions of where to take the shoddy.

Once you got to know Alice though, she was quite bubbly and outgoing. Always making me laugh, she adored my children and they adored her.

As our friendship grew, from more than an evening out at the cinema, or a drink after work, I realised I had feelings for her. I never imagined I would feel for anyone again after Lily. One evening, we were sitting in the park and I told her I thought I loved her. Alice turned to me, her eyes wet with tears and told me she felt the same, she said she'd loved me from the first moment I stepped into the office for my list of deliveries.

I got my life back together; Alice and I rented a flat. Between us and my Mam, we looked after the children. I never imagined I'd be almost happy again, but I was. I knew Alice was old fashioned and really believed in marriage before living together. As I had no idea where Lily was, I could not file for a divorce. It would have to wait, I told Alice, it would be five years before I could divorce Lily. It seemed an eternity, but if Alice loved me, I knew she would wait. She kept me from kicking off at Ede's wedding, telling me they were truly in love.

'Ede's just a child Alice! What does she know about love?' I growled.

'Look Ike, look at them dancing together, they are besotted. Ede is no longer a child Ike; you have to accept it. That will be Shirley one of these days.'

I stared at Alice, what was she saying? I knew she was right, however, I knew for certain there was no way my daughter would ever have to get married. I also knew I could not do anything about Ede either.

'Just let us be there for her Ike if it does go wrong.' Alice whispered and put her arms round me, I folded her in mine and thanked God for this wonderful, sensible girl.

~~~ 50 ~~~

Part Two

Chapter Five

Tom looked down at me, his eyes full of love. 'Ede, thank you for becoming my wife.'

I giggled and told him I loved him. I had to pinch myself earlier that morning to see if it was real, I was going to become Mrs Tom Lister. I held Tom closer as we danced round the floor, gazing over his shoulder, I saw my brother Ike staring at me. His face full of, what I could only describe as, disgust. I shakily gave him a smile. He met my eyes for a brief second then turned away. I gulped back the tears. Ike, oh Ike, why couldn't he be happy for me? I knew why, he felt much the same about the Listers as my Dad did.

They hadn't thought I would be listening to their heated arguments about my marriage. Dad was adamant that I should be married. Ike argued no, it didn't matter these days, I didn't have to get married. Much to my relief Dad was, or seemed to be, on my side and agreed to the wedding. I loved Tom and wanted to be his wife. The fact that I was pregnant only came as an added bonus. Tom and I, once over the shock, were thrilled about the baby. He had bought all kinds of things for it, except the pram. Tom's Mam and mine were adamant and would not allow this, unlucky they said, we had to wait until the baby was born before we got that.

I buried my head in Tom's shoulder as tears fell. I just wanted Ike to be happy for me. He was the one person I looked up to. My brother Sam was always busy gardening, I couldn't really talk to him. But for as long as I could remember Ike and I had a bond, a very special bond. I could see from his face that bond was broken, it broke when Tom and I told Mam, Dad and Ike our intentions, and I was pregnant.

'Hey darling, come on, why the tears?' Tom whispered.

I shook my head, not daring myself to speak. At that moment I just wanted to run to Ike, beg his forgiveness, ask him to be happy for me.

'This is supposed to be the happiest day of your life Ede. I know it is mine. I never thought...' Tom's voice trailed off as he kissed away my tears.

'It...it is Tom.' I found my voice, 'These are tears of joy. We will be okay won't we, the three of us?'

'You bet my Ede, we're going to be just dandy.' Tom picked me up and swirled me round. I was soon laughing, the wedding guests cheered and clapped at his actions.

I wanted that moment to last forever but in no time at all we were spending our wedding night at the Queens Hotel in Leeds. In such a plush place, at least it was to me, it was very posh, I felt a bit dowdy in my plain going away suit Mam had made me, but Tom reassured me, he told me even in my overalls, I looked gorgeous.

The last few weeks had been wonderful. I spent every day at the garage helping Tom. In September I was going to enrol on a motor engineering course at night school. Tom wanted me to wait until after the bairn was born. No way, I wanted to show Dad I meant business. I was going to college and I would pass my exams and become a first class mechanic. Our baby, Tom had protested, where would she or he fit into my plans?

'He! Will fit into our plans perfectly.' I told my husband.

Tom smiled away the troubled look on his face. 'You are so sure it will be a boy?'

I nodded as we cuddled into the crisp white sheets in the huge hotel bedroom that night. 'Oh Tom this is wonderful.'

'Aye shame it's only for the one night.' Folding me in his arms, still a little unsure if making love would harm the baby. On Tom's insistence I'd asked the doctor, who assured me no, all would be fine.

Breakfast next morning was delicious. I could tell Tom felt a little uncomfortable and out of place in his jeans and tee shirt. I reassured him as best I could.

'Ede, we'll soon have our own place. It might not be as plush as this but it will be ours.'

I nodded happily. Later we went back to the Lister's to begin our married life. It wasn't ideal, but I knew Dad would not relish me asking if we could move into number One Congleton Terrace, though my Mam had hinted at the idea.

Ike and the kids had moved into their own place, with Alice too. Dad may have begrudgingly agreed to my wedding, however, I knew there was no way could we start married life under his roof. The very thoughts of being intimate with Tom, if we had moved in, was out of the question.

Tom had his own room in the Lister household. The house belonged to the council so was rented, and as the family grew the council took an extra bedroom from the house next door and incorporated that into the Lister home. It was this small room Tom had previously shared with his brother Harry, who had moved out, leaving the room for us. Tom had originally found a flat for us near the garage where he worked. When he revealed to the landlord, he would be getting married and we had a baby on the way, the landlord was very abrupt and refused Tom the tenancy, saying he did not want children in the place. Tom's room hadn't enough space for a double bed, so we made do with a three quarter bed. It was very cosy and lovely to be sleeping so close to each other.

I felt nervous going back there, Sam had already dropped off two bags of my belongings from Mam and Dad's. Mrs Lister, Margaret as she insisted I call her, made me feel very welcome. Tom's Dad enveloped me in his arms and squeezed me tightly in a bear hug.

'Niver thawt I'd see this day lass, ee me welcome a Wag-staff into me 'ome.'

'Well, she's a Lister now Dad and you can put her down thank you.' Tom remonstrated.

The days passed by so quickly, I soon became used to the loudness of the Lister family, as they gathered round the table for their meals. There were a few arguments but a lot of laughter too, amongst the siblings. Mostly however when their Dad wasn't there. He often rushed his food down and then was away to the pub. I was thankful Tom seemed quite happy to spend his evenings with me, even though he had once gone out most weekends, with his mates, I told him if he still wanted a night out he could. He refused saying he wanted to spend his evenings with me.

He bought a tiny television with its own aerial, it ran off a car battery, so we could have it in our bedroom. We would cuddle up in our bed and watch the grainy black and white screen. My favourite show was the Beverly Hillbillies. It was about a family who lived in a wooden shack in the backwoods of America, until they struck oil. They bought a mansion in Beverly Hills, but couldn't change their way of living. How we laughed at some of the antics Jed Clampett and his family got up to. We both swore if we became rich, we'd be just the same as they were. There'd be no airs and graces on us.

I thought about the palatial surroundings of the Queens

Hotel and the Clampett mansion. Even though I was young, I felt grown up and realistic, quite down to earth, I just wanted a small flat or anything I could call our home. I began collecting items for the baby and our 'bottom drawer'. You're supposed to have one of these, after you get engaged, before you get married. It's stuff collected for your new home. I just hoped it wouldn't be too long before I could put my towels and tea towels to good use.

I didn't mind being at the Listers, Sadie was good for a laugh and I enjoyed her company. The lads, Billy and Dennis, were too noisy and I often pleaded tiredness so I could escape their constant bickering.

Even when Mam arrived home with Ike's kids, after Lily left, the noise level at home grew with little ones in the house. However, it wasn't anywhere near as bad as at the Lister's, the lads would often argue over who would have the last slice of bread. Who should answer the door and as for watching TV! I was glad my pregnancy gave me a reason to go 'for a lie down'.

Phyllis was totally different to all her siblings, she was quiet, and more often than not she had her head buried in a book. She was slight and pretty, Sadie and her other sister Joan, were tall, ungainly and rather plain. Phyllis, was her Mother's double at least, when Margaret was the same age as Phyllis, from photos I'd seen.

What would my Dad be saying about Our Sam courting a Lister? Bad enough one being married to a Lister! I could see Sam and Phyllis were becoming quite an item. To think it all began with a dance at my wedding. Who knew what the future held?

September came round quickly and I began night school. Of course, the other students were male and they often teased me or scoffed at me, until I proved I knew my way round a car engine much better than they did. It didn't take long for them to come and ask me what to do next. My expanding stomach gave the game away that I was pregnant, but no one made fun or innuendos, I had a wedding ring and I was respected. As time went on the lads helped me and our tutor said we were the closest, friendliest class he'd had for a long while.

I would go home euphoric and eager to relate to Tom what I had learned that evening. I talked about the lads in the class, at first reticently in case he got jealous. Tom was okay and enjoyed listening to me rattle on. Commenting often I would soon know more than him! I doubted this as it was all pretty basic stuff we were learning.

It was good to see Ike settled with Alice, she was a smashing girl and had become a close friend and ally in the days leading up to my wedding.

Before the wedding, Mam kept asking me if I was sure, she told me I didn't need to get married. I could keep the baby and we could live as one big family. She still looked after Ike's young ones through the day, now Ike was settled in a flat, and living with Alice, they all went home with him at night.

Dad refused to hear anything of the sort, he couldn't bear to think of his daughter as an unmarried Mother and argued with Mam that the wedding was going ahead. I hugged myself, couldn't believe my luck Dad on my side for once. Albeit only to save face, I knew that. After the arguments over which college I would go to, you see he wanted me to go to secretarial college and get an office job. I loved machines and wanted to do mechanics. Along the way I met Tom and fell in love. We truly didn't mean for me to get pregnant, that just kind of happened. I was so glad it did and I told Mam quite firmly that I loved Tom and wanted to be with him.

Once she'd seen my mind was made up and she couldn't alter it, or my Dad's mind, she planned the wedding with great gusto, to make the day perfect and indeed it truly was. I became Mrs Tom Lister, something I only ever dreamed of. Tom is quite a bit older than me you see. He's tall, dark and really good looking. I couldn't believe he would even look at me. Ede Wagstaff, plain as they come and a school girl as well! It wasn't long before I realised we both had feelings for each other and one thing led to another. Well, you know how it is. We tried to be careful, but... I was scared and at the same time, quite excited at becoming a Mum. I knew it would put my mechanical work on hold, but I'd grown really used to kids, caring for Ike's. They seemed to respond well to me. I worried, all the same, what sort of Mother I'd be. Alice said I should stop and enthused I'd be a great mother. She loved Ike's kids but I had a feeling she would like one of her own. It didn't seem to be happening, she confessed to me. I was bemused and couldn't understand what she was saying. Weren't she and Ike sleeping together? Of course, I was too embarrassed to ask. I mean it was my brother we would be talking about. I told Alice her time would come and she should be patient. I felt it was the right thing to say. Alice seemed pacified as she nodded her head in agreement.

Chapter Six

Tom burst in through the front door calling my name one evening in early November, I ran downstairs.

'Tom, whatever is the matter?' I gasped.

'Nothing my love,' he grinned at me before picking me up in one of his bear hugs.

'Tom, put the lass down.' Margaret instructed, as she and the others came into the hall wondering what all the fuss was about.

Tom lowered me to the ground and clasped an arm around me. A huge grin on his face. 'You'll never guess what?' he asked, looking at our puzzled faces. 'No, well, I didn't think so any road, it's Old Man Busby at the garage...'

'Tom,' I broke in, 'he's okay isn't he, nothing has happened?'

'No love, nothing has happened. He is only retiring and moving out of the flat to live with his sister in Scarborough. You know what that means, don't you?' Tom looked round at our faces.

'He'll sell up and you might lose your job?' Sadie spoke what I'm sure had been on all our minds.

'Nowt of sorts lass.' Tom chided, giving her a playful nudge. He turned to me and grabbed hold of both my hands. 'It means my darling Ede that he has offered to rent me the garage and the flat goes with it.

'Oh my God Tom... I can't breathe.' I gasped, tears filled my eyes. Our own place and Tom's own garage. 'Really, honestly, he's going to do that?'

Tom picked me up again and swung me round. My legs bashed Sadie on the way past, she yelled at him to put me down. Tom didn't care, he carried me upstairs and kissed away my tears of joy. 'Just think Ede, our own place. See I told you it wouldn't be long. We'll soon get the flat into shape, before this young man arrives. What do you think?'

I couldn't think, I was bursting with happiness, our own home! This was the best day of my life so far, well excluding my wedding day and er night!

The next few weeks went by so quickly. Mam was pleased too and sorted out lots of crocks and pots for us. Tom's Mam also gave us a load of bedding. I just wept the day Tom took me upstairs to the flat for the first time. It was small and badly needed decorating, but it was ours. Mr Busby had left an old sofa, table and chairs which filled the living room. The bedroom furniture had been moved to his sisters. I was glad we could get new, or rather second hand but new to us, as I told Tom. He shook his head and declared it would be new, had I not heard of the flat pack furniture, it was being produced really inexpensively and you had to put it together yourself.

We searched for hours, I quite liked the new furniture colour black but Tom preferred white. In the end we settled on cream and spent our evenings putting together various bits and pieces of bedroom furniture. Our Sam even bought us a small telly. I was in rapture and after only a few weeks we'd decorated the bedroom and the kitchenette so we were able to move in.

What it also meant was, I could go down and help Tom in the garage, whenever I wanted to and most of the day was spent down there. Tom's reputation for mechanics was growing and so was business. Tom said it helped me being female, as all the ladies on their own felt more comfortable bringing their cars to us. I know I got a few admiring comments when I told the ladies what was wrong with their cars. Oh yes, there were a few who looked down their noses at me and sneered as if to say what do you know? I shrugged them off, however one day...

It wasn't long after we'd moved into the flat. My belly was huge, unable to fit into my overalls, I had to wear smock tops. Tom had gone to get some parts, so I was on my own in the garage. A smart red car pulled up outside and a tall, slim, very elegant woman got out.

'Excuse me, is the mechanic around? My car has developed a noise,' she purred in a posh voice.

'Yes, I'm here, I'll take a look for you, if you'd like to drive it in here.' I offered politely, thinking there might be a tip, as well as good payment for any work done.

'You! You! I want a mechanic!' she spluttered.

'I am a mechanic.' I counteracted.

'You're a...a girl.'

'Glad you noticed, now tell me where you think the noise is coming from and lift the bonnet and I'll get it sorted for you.'

'No! I want a proper mechanic! Besides you...you're pregnant!' she looked down her nose. It was obvious, to me, she was assuming I was single.

Now I'm not sure if it was my hormones but at this point I was getting rather rattled.

'So what if I am pregnant and MARRIED! Do you want your car looking at or not?' I yelled at her, just as Tom pulled up outside.

'What's to do Ede?' he asked, seeing my flustered face.

'Ah, good the mechanic, this chit of a girl tried telling me she was one, but we can get something sorted with my car, now you're here.' The woman slid up to Tom and smiled at him. 'A very handsome mechanic too,' she purred.

I totally lost my rag, picked up the biggest spanner I could find and advanced towards her. 'And my husband, now clear off!'

Tom grabbed my arm holding the spanner and as she took a step back against some tyres, she lost her balance landing on her backside in a tub of old oil.

'Oh my God!' she screamed. 'You will pay for this, my suit, my suit is ruined.' To make matters worse, as she stood up, she tried to brush the thick oil off with her hands. I couldn't help it, I laughed out loud and tears ended up rolling down my face.

She tottered out of the garage to her car muttering that we would pay for this.

'Serves you right bitch.' I called after her.

She turned and stared at me, red in the face with anger. I knew I'd gone a step too far. Tom held onto me from behind.

'Apologise now Ede!' he whispered.

I shook my head.

'You will Ede, now, before she goes.'

I shook my head again defiantly, no way was I going to apologise, she had put me down and then flirted with my husband. Why did he want me to apologise? I hissed the question at him.

'To stop her from suing us,' he hissed back.

I was too late, the woman grabbed a rug from the back seat, placed it on the driver's seat, got in, slammed the door and drove away.

'Oh my God Ede, what have you done?' Tom let go of me and looked defeated. 'Just when we were starting to make good, you spoil it all with your tongue. She was obviously well to do, and could have brought us loads of business. I think she might report you to the police!'

'Tom, don't be daft, why would she do that?'

'Because you threatened her with a spanner and called her a bitch! She's sure to bring the cops, we'll be in court, and end up owing her hundreds.'

'She won't do that, will she Tom?'

'You heard her as clear as I did, she said we wouldn't hear the last of it.'

I sat down and felt afraid, 'I'll apologise, I'll write to her. I will Tom, I promise I will, it's just, she...she was flirting with you and I saw red. I'm so sorry.'

'Do you know her name? Do you know her address?'

I shook my head, I hadn't got far enough to ask her address. I hadn't seen Tom looking so exasperated.

'So what if she was flirting, if it brings us good business then they can flirt all they want and I tell you this girl, I will damn well flirt back if I want to!'

I ran upstairs, how could he speak to me like that! Throwing myself on the bed the tears came hot and fast. How could he, how could he? I asked myself over and over again. I cried myself into a fitful sleep. The woman couldn't possibly prosecute us for an accident, could she, would she?

I soon got my answer, it was late afternoon. I heard two pairs of footsteps on the stairs. Tom called my name and opened the bedroom door. He looked pale and serious.

'Ede love, can you come? There's a policeman here who wants to talk to you.'

I grabbed a hankie from under the pillow and wiped my face.

'It'll be okay love.' Tom said softly, 'Come on, just tell him it was an accident. I saw it remember? I'm so sorry for shouting at you, but say nothing about calling her names or the spanner. I'll back you up.'

'You'd do that Tom?' I choked back more tears as he

pulled me into his arms.

An oldish policeman with a square face sat on the sofa waiting, he stopped tapping his fingers on his knees and rose when I entered the room in front of Tom.

'Mrs Lister?' he asked quietly.

I nodded and started to gabble on, asking if he'd like a cup of tea. He shook his head and asked if we could sit down. He proceeded to tell me the police had a serious complaint reported to them by Mrs Elsie Parker-Smith. She told them that I had threatened her with a spanner, causing her to fall into some oil, then called her names.

'No sir, that ain't right, is it Tom?' I looked at him beseechingly, if push came to shove would he really back me up?

'No, that isn't how I recall officer.' Tom said. Going on, he told the policeman, how he had returned to the garage, to find this lady and me in conversation about the problem with her car. She had taken a step back, toppled over some tyres and landed into the tub of oil. When we tried to help her she got angry and had driven off.

The policeman smiled, 'I guess that's what must have happened. An accident then, are we all agreed?'

Tom and I nodded and spoke in unison, 'Yes, just an accident.'

The policeman stood up, 'Sorry to bother you, but we have to follow a complaint through, not that it's the first complaint from Mrs Parker-Smith!' he rolled his eyes.

Tom and I looked at each other and I swear we both breathed a sigh of relief at the same time.

When the policeman had gone Tom folded his arms round me and made me promise not to be so hot headed and he promised not to speak to me again as he had done. I cuddled into him and our baby kicked wildly making us both jump.

We did, however, hold our breath a little in case this Mrs Parker-Smith took her complaint further. Gradually, as days turned into weeks, we relaxed in the knowledge that she wasn't going to.

Chapter Seven

Alice became a very close friend, even though Ike still felt awkward around Tom, Alice assured me he was accepting our marriage. She said he wasn't very happy about Sam seeing Phyllis. I didn't know if she was joking or not.

A real serious lad was my brother Sam, still is. Mad about gardening and loved his job in the plant nursery. Back then it was just holding its own amongst the encroaching housing estates being built round it. Sam and Phyllis had, kind of, got together at my wedding. Their friendship was growing, though Alice told me, they didn't seem to be, what you might call going steady. I guessed my Dad and Ike might have some influence there, after all Phyllis is a Lister, although totally different to the rest of the family. She got a job in a library, Tom said that would suit her down to the ground as she always had her head in some book or other. Sam was thrilled as she always got him out the new gardening books that came in.

Alice was great for Ike, so down to earth. Ike's kids adored her and I knew it wouldn't be long before they would have one of their own. Alice, as much as she loved Ike's four, longed for a baby. I mentioned it to Ike one day, he looked horrified and declared hadn't they enough with the four. Talking this over with Alice she agreed Ike was right, but I knew she would be drooling over her new niece or nephew, my baby of course. I loved that Alice was becoming the sister I never had.

I told her about the garage incident and how Tom had spoken to me. I couldn't help but chew it over in my mind.

'He told me he could flirt with who he liked Alice.' I said, tears threatening.

Alice turned me to her, placed both her hands on my shoulders and said, 'Ede, that man loves the very bones of you. Trust him. Yes, he may say the odd thing to another woman, if it brings him trade, but believe you me Tom Lister is crazy about you, he'd never look at anyone else I am sure of that, got it!'

I nodded, still unconvinced. I was scared, my body was huge, how could he still fancy me? I was becoming edgy as it was hard to sleep properly. Many nights I got up and sat on the sofa, sometimes from midnight until dawn, when I crept back to bed curling my cold body round Tom's warm one, he often woke turned over and drew me to him. Well, as close as he could get. I could feel his need and willingly gave myself to him, without the baby getting too much in the way. Afterwards we would both fall asleep, more often than not I would wake sometime later to find Tom's side of the bed cold and hear noises of work going on in the garage below. I longed for the day when the baby arrived and I could sleep comfortably, although as Alice said the baby would keep us awake anyway!

I was scared though, far more than I let anyone know. Scared about the birth, part of me just wanted it over with, another part of me just wanted to stay pregnant. I asked Alice about a Caesarean operation, couldn't I have one? Alice laughed and said she didn't think so, she thought it was only for women who couldn't have a normal birth. As the weeks grew ever closer to my due date, I became more and more anxious. At last Tom got it out of me the reason for my moods and anxiety. He told me he would be there, I would be okay and we would be great parents.

I knew for a fact he would not be allowed to be with me at the birth. I knew though, he would make a great Dad. Mam told me I would be a great Mam too, as look how Ike's kids loved me. Yes, they did and I loved them but they weren't babies, what if I hurt it or worse still dropped it? What if I couldn't love it after the pain it would cause giving birth? All these thoughts and more whirled round and round in my head till I was convinced I was going mad. I was feeling very, very scared.

I voiced my fears to Sadie, Tom's sister. She worked on the buses, had no intention of settling down and boyfriends were many. She seemed to get bored with having a steady boyfriend and they never lasted long.

She laughed loudly, when I told her how scared I was. 'What are you asking me that for? I've no bloody idea and never will have, if I have my way!'

Her tone of voice brought tears to my eyes, Sadie came over and put her arms round me.

'Oh God Ede, me and my big gob, I don't know what to say except my Mam always says giving birth is just like needing a big crap. Do you know wor' I mean?'

I couldn't help but laugh at her Mam's description. The whole family were like that, said it as it was, no bones. Well except Phyllis, she was more genteel and I'd never heard her swear. Of course Tom did, but even Tom was careful around me with his language.

Sadie however didn't care what she said. Often she would remind those, pulling her up about her colourful language, that 'Bloody's in the bible, bloody's in the book and if you don't bloody believe me, have a bloody look!'

It made my day to see the shocked look on the people's faces when she said it to them. Many just grunted and turned away, leaving Sadie and I in hysterics.

Her words did little to console me, I just wanted this baby out. 'Why can't I have a caesarean?' I wailed to Tom one night.

'Come on now lass, ye'll be fine, it ain't nowt to be afraid of, your Mam's been through it, what does she say?'

'She said that as soon as it's out, the pain is forgotten, do you think it will be Tom?'

'Well if your Mam said that then I'm sure she's right. I'll be there.'

'You can't be, they won't let men in.'

'I know, but I'll be there, right outside, just imagine me holding your hand, can you do that lass?'

I nodded and choked back my tears. I could do this, I was sure, wasn't I? After all thousands and millions of women give birth every day, if they could then so could I. Tom was so excited about holding his own baby.

'Of course I've held the young ones in the family, but this baby is different, he's ours Ede. We made him, just think of that, he'll be part of us, you and me. You and he will be just grand.'

'It might be a she,' I whispered, secretly hoping it would be. The thought of my own daughter thrilled me and I was also convinced, by that time, my baby would be a girl. How would Tom react if it was? He was so sure it was a boy.

'Yeh, it might be a girl and she'll be as beautiful as her Mam.' Tom whispered back.

It would be okay. That evening I felt safe in his arms, I would give him his own child and no matter how painful it was, I could do this. That evening I felt sure of it.

Chapter Eight

Christmas was approaching and I was busy wrapping little gifts for the family. Tom came in dressed in his underpants and towelling his hair after his nightly bath. He would not sit in our flat, even for a meal, until he had washed the day's grease, oil and sweat off himself. Tom's reputation was growing and the garage was busier than ever. I was in there most days trying to help, even though the baby often got in the way. Many male car owners often scoffed, seeing me trying to bend over a car to look at the engine. Tom would ask me to do the paperwork, for jobs, when he saw me struggling, he would glare at the scoffing customers, making them mutter apologies and go back to their papers, as they sometimes stayed and sat, waiting for a job to be done.

Tom sat down in the chair opposite me. We had been able to replace the old sofa with a three seater settee in fake black leather; it came with a matching chair. I made some bright orange cushions to liven it up a bit and they matched the black and orange seat cushions. We also had a small coffee table which was my work top for wrapping presents. Though I had to sit on the floor, there was no way I could lean over.

'Ede, bout Christmas,' Tom said quietly, I looked up in alarm.

'Tom, what about Christmas?'

'Well, Mam popped in today when you were at the shops.' he began. 'She...she wants us to go there for Christmas day.'

'Oh.' I didn't know what to say, I just imagined it was a foregone conclusion we would spend Christmas at my family home, I'd never been away from them. Well, except for part of the day last year, when I had an argument with my Dad over which college to go to. I had stormed out and gone to see Sadie. Tom had answered the door, wished me Happy Christmas and kissed me. My first ever proper kiss and from Tom too, it was so special. I had fun the rest of that day, they were such a lively happy family and made me part of it. Yes, I could see us with Tom's family enjoying the day.

'Tom, Mam said she hoped we would be there with them, Ike, Alice and the kids. I thought we would be too. What shall we do?'

Tom shook his head and droplets of water sprayed over the wrapping paper.

'Hey you, my presents.' I said, waving my fist at him.

He got up and pulled me to my feet wrapping me in his arms. 'Want my present now.' he said, half carrying me into the bedroom.

What to do about Christmas? I couldn't ask Mam as she was sure we would be spending it there. Sadie would want us there, so it was no good asking her, I turned to Alice.

'What are we going to do Alice?'

'Well, I'm kinda in the same boat my folks are hoping we'd go there. I had to say no that we'd go on Boxing Day. I think the kids would want to be where they know everyone on their first Christmas without their Ma.'

'Has Ike heard owt from her?' I asked cautiously.

'Nope, he has made enquiries to try and find her, so he can get the divorce under way. Seems she has vanished into thin air.'

'Oh Alice, how could she just up and leave her kids like that? I know I'll never leave this one or any others we have.' I said stroking my belly.

'Any others!' Alice squealed. 'So you have got over your

fears?'

I shook my head and told her I had tried to take my mind off things with Christmas. I'd made paper chains for our home and my Mam and Dad's. Decorated a small tree in our sitting room with ginger bread shapes and tinsel. Mam gave us a few baubles to hang on it too. It was looking very festive. Now I was busy buying little gifts and wrapping them in tissue paper, cos it was cheaper than the fancy wrapping paper. The garage was doing well but there were still things we needed to buy for the baby. I was also saving to buy Tom something special, yet had no idea what. I asked Alice.

She shook her head, 'I'm in the same boat there too. No idea what to get Ike. Shall we go shopping on Saturday?' she suggested.

'That's Christmas Eve Alice, what if we can't find anything?' I wailed.

She laughed it off and assured me we would. A day shopping with Alice was something to look forward to. In the meantime, I looked in magazines for ideas. I'd already made Tom a Christmas card, which I designed myself with hearts and holly. I even thought up a soppy verse, telling him how much I loved him. Yes, I was sure I'd find him something special on my shopping trip with Alice.

Saturday came and I felt a little uneasy, yet didn't know why. I fidgeted my way through breakfast with Tom. He eyed me curiously.

'You okay Ede?'

'Yep I am, just thoughts on last minute presents I need to buy. Now get down to work, I've sandwiches to make for your dinner. You are closing at dinner time, aren't you?' I gabbled. Saturday was normally half day closing.

'Yes, I'll close unless there's an emergency. I'll get a bath and lunch then I have to pop out for something.'

Oh…I wonder what that will be.' I giggled. Could it be my present?

'Never you mind Mrs Lister, now get in that kitchen and get me some sarnies made.'

'Yes Sir!' I said, saluting him before giving him a kiss on the cheek.

He grinned and disappeared downstairs, just as Alice came up them.

'Ready for the shops?' she asked. 'Are you okay Ede?' she added.

'Yes, I'm good, just got his Lordship's dinner to make and then we'll get off. Oh, it will be grand to see the big Christmas tree in City Square and the festive shop windows. I've only been round our local shops so far. So a trip into town will be great, it really will.' I enthused, glad it was Alice I was going with.

Alice and I caught the bus into the city centre. I felt mighty uncomfortable as it rattled along. A couple of times Alice put her arm round me to steady me when it lurched to a stop. The bus filled up and the air seemed stifling.

'You sure you're okay Ede?' Alice asked quietly.

I nodded. I could see concern in her face. I turned to take some deep breaths and peered out of the window. Rows of shops began to appear and their bright Christmas lights sparkled on tinsel decorations.

'Our stop.' Alice broke into my thoughts. 'Where shall we go first?'

'Anywhere to get some air, it's stifling in here.' I gasped, waiting for the stream of passengers to get off. As I reached the top step, I felt a sharp pain in my side. 'Ouch!' I yelled.

The conductress took my arm, 'You okay there missus?' she asked in a kindly voice, as she hopped down to help me off the bus.

'Ede what's wrong?' Alice stopped and turned so swiftly, I bounced into her.

'I'm alright honestly, a stitch in my side that's all.' I saw Alice and the conductress glance at each other with doubts in their eyes. 'Come on Alice, let's get our bits and have a cuppa somewhere, I am okay, honestly.' I said as we waited to cross the street, while the bus trundled on its way.

'By, you gave me a fright Ede when I heard you shout, thought you were going into labour or something.'

I laughed and shook my head, assuring Alice, as best I could, that it was too early. Well it was, wasn't it? What had the midwife said? She thought it would be the middle of January at the earliest. I felt okay and eager to see the shops. I linked arms with Alice. 'Come on I am fine! Let's go and get done.'

We wandered along Boar Lane and made our way to Kirkgate Market. The shops looked very festive. The market had a small Salvation Army band and choir singing carols. We stopped to listen and even joined in with Away in a Manger, before heading down the rows of stalls. I bought some fruit and dates. Don't like dates myself but I remembered Tom tucking into them, when we were at his last year. I pulled Alice to a stop at a lovely stall adorned with Christmas decorations of all kinds. A pure white angel with feathered wings drew my attention. She was beautiful, her features so delicate. She would be perfect for our little tree. I asked the price and felt dismayed at the five shillings cost. That would only leave me with ten shillings and I'd yet to get some holly, mistletoe and a special present for Ike. Well, we could do without holly and mistletoe, and I felt sure I could get Ike something, with enough left over for a cup of tea.

'Please can I have that Mister?' I asked quickly, before I changed my mind.

He wrapped it up carefully and handed it to me wishing us both a Merry Christmas.

'Thank you, same to you.' I breathed and placed my treasure in my basket.

'A bit pricey Ede?' Alice looked at me questioningly.

I nodded and told her, I didn't care, the angel was perfect for our tree. 'Now Ike's present.' I unconsciously put a hand to my side, the niggling pain was still there.

'Ede, you still got pain?' Alice whispered, clutching my arm.

'Stitch that's all, too much rushing.' I reassured her, I could feel my face burning as I blushed and I quickly turned away, pretending to look at some watches on a stall. I hurried on knowing I could not afford any of them.

Alice trotted to catch me up. 'Hold up Ede, I realise now why you've got stitch. Slow down and let's go to the market cafe for a cuppa.'

I nodded, I would be glad of a sit down. Concerns about the pain niggled at the back of my mind, that and what present I could get for Ike.

The cafe was busy, market traders queueing for cuppas, shoppers crowded round the red plastic clothed tables. Mugs of steaming tea were being doled out by two middle aged women behind the counter. Under plastic lids, scones and tea cakes and a sponge cake stood.

'Two teas.' Alice asked and pointed to the cake, and two slices of that please.'

'Alice... I can't affor...'

'My treat.' She broke in, grinning at me as she pointed to a table in the middle just being vacated by two shoppers. 'Grab that table Ede.'

I didn't need a further bidding and pushed my way past the queue to the vacant table and sat down. Waiting for Alice to carry the tray of tea and cake over I couldn't resist pulling the angel from my basket and unwrapping it carefully. Holding the delicate ornament gently, I whispered to it. 'My baby if it's a girl will have your name, Angel.' I wrapped her back up before Alice came.

'Oh my gawd, it's so busy in here and hot too.' She gasped, drinking deeply from her mug.

'Like that's going to cool you down, hot tea!' I giggled.

'Yes, my Mam said you can't beat a cup of hot tea if you're hot and bothered and I think she's right. I feel better already.'

Alice did look flushed and ate her cake ravenously.

'I aren't going to take it off you.' I laughed.

'No, I know, it's just I am starving, missed my breakfast, didn't feel like any when I got up. It's nearly dinnertime now too. Guess we should have got a sandwich!'

'What was wrong this morning Alice?'

'Oh nowt really, just felt a bit sick...' her voice trailed off. I could see she was working something out in her mind, suddenly she blurted out, 'Oh my word... Oh my!'

'Oh my what, Alice?'

'Well, I think I might be pregnant! Oh Lord, what will Ike say? We were going to wait, till he'd got his divorce you know. Oh Ede, what will he say?'

I took Alice's hand in mine and tears filled my eyes. It would be wonderful for Alice and Ike's baby to grow up with mine. Ike would be over the moon, try as I might to convince Alice, she was sure Ike's response would be the reverse. Well, he would be thrilled, wouldn't he? How wrong could I be!

DEVOTION
DANCE HALL
DEVOTION
DANCING

Chapter Nine

Christmas morning arrived and I lay in bed with Tom, enjoying a rare lie in. For once the baby had kept still all night and I'd been able to sleep. Usually he or she was kicking around inside me and the movement would keep me awake much of the night, but last night, baby slept. I thought about Alice and wondered when she would tell Ike her news. She had begged me not to let on, as she wanted to be doubly sure and she didn't want anything to spoil their Christmas.

We'd all agreed to have dinner at my Mam and Dad's. I wasn't sure how we would all fit in the tiny kitchen! However, Dad bought a fold up table, it had two drop leaves and they would put it up in the living room, so there would be plenty of room for everyone to get round. I couldn't wait to see us all together! After last year, this Christmas, I hoped, would be a happy time for everyone.

Tom stirred and I reached under my pillow for his gift, it wasn't much just a wallet, with a sports car sticker on the front, I was sure he'd like it.

'Happy Christmas husband,' I said, reaching over to kiss him.

'Happy Christmas wife,' he laughed. 'What's this? I thought we weren't buying each other a present.' He sighed as I pushed the small parcel over to him. He pulled at the ribbon and grinned at me, 'Oh Ede, it's lovely, perfect, thank you.'

Pulling me into his arms I laid my head contentedly on his shoulder. 'I know we weren't, but I wanted to get you something. Yes, I know you said the angel would be our present, she is perfect on top of the tree isn't she?'

Tom nodded, 'Good thing I got you this then.' He produced a clumsily wrapped present from under the bed.

'Oh Ike, I love it.' I said, holding up the satin nightgown, I frowned.

'Yes my love, I know it won't fit now, but I thought afterwards, it would be good, if you know what I mean.'

I nodded, he was so thoughtful, I enjoyed being in his arms and it would be lovely to have something nice to wear after baby was born. I felt so safe and warm.

I looked round our bedroom. The tiny rosebud wallpaper went perfectly with the deep pink curtains Mam gave us. Our bed was a small double with wooden head-board and foot-board. Tom had joked the room was all a bit girly, but he didn't seem to mind or want to change it and I didn't object when he put some pictures of racing cars on the wall. He'd bought me a tiny dressing table complete with mirror. We'd managed to get a small wardrobe too and there was still room for the cot, away from the window.

The cot was piled high with baby clothes, nappies, blankets and toiletries. A small bag sat on top of it, packed with the items I needed for baby at the maternity home. It was all ready to pick up when the time came. I just needed to pack a bag for me, plenty of time for that, I stroked my bump and whispered, 'Not today baby.'

The pains I felt yesterday had eased, but on waking I felt a little uncomfortable, achy more than anything. I pulled away from Tom, needing the loo and I wanted to make breakfast for him.

'Hey where are you going?' he said, grabbing my hand.

'I need the loo.'

He let go and I had to rush to the bathroom. Squeezing myself through the door, I manoeuvred myself onto the toilet. Needless to say, the bathroom was small. A clothes rack stood over the bath. It had Tom's work clothes draped over it to dry. I felt comfortable sitting on the loo and didn't want to move. As I forced myself to get up, a searing pain coursed through my lower body, it was so severe and made me scream.

'Ede! Ede!' Tom rattled the door handle.

Why did I lock the door? I don't know. I tried to get up to open it, but another sharp pain made me cry out again and I sat back down on the loo.

Tom frantically pushed the door and suddenly it flew open as the lock broke away. He went down on his knees and grasped my hands. 'Ede, Ede, is it time?'

'No, not today, please not today, I don't want to have this baby today! Mam's dinner, it's too early!' I gabbled and sobbed at the same time. 'Tom, I'm scared, it's too early.' Another pain came and went, I felt a bit better and stood up. Tom guided me back to the bedroom and pushed my clothes at me. I'd laid them out the night before so he just grabbed the pile. 'Get dressed, I'll get dressed too and see how you feel.'

I nodded, not trusting myself to speak, it was too early for Angel to arrive. Yes, I knew, right at that moment, I would have a girl and Angel would be her name. It was too soon, wasn't it? The pain subsided; we were okay. I assured Tom it would be something called the Braxton Hicks, I'd heard about. I'd get dressed and we'd have a nice breakfast, before going to my Mam and Dad's for a lovely Christmas family dinner. Their presents, along with Ike's, Alice and the kids were wrapped and in a bag by the front door. Angel would have to wait a few more weeks before she put in an appearance. I was going to enjoy Christmas Day with both families, we'd agreed to have tea with Tom's family. It was all planned, but you know what they say about the best laid plans...

I couldn't stomach the breakfast and just nibbled on dry toast. Tom laughed when I told him I wanted to do the full works for him, bacon, egg and the rest.

'Cereal and toast will do fine. If I know your folks 'n mine they will want us to stuff ourselves silly.'

I sat at our small kitchen table, wishing Tom would have at least put on a table cloth over the blue Formica surface. What was wrong with me? I chided myself, was I becoming set in my ways? Mam always had a cloth on the table. I thought it old fashioned when you didn't need one with a Formica top, unless it was a special day like today.

I wriggled about, couldn't get comfortable. Something didn't feel right at all. As I stood up, 'Tom!' I gasped, clutching my swollen stomach.

'Maternity Home.' Tom said, pulling his coat from the hooks on the back of the kitchen door. 'What do you need?'

'I... err... I haven't got any of my stuff ready, it's too soon...' My voice trailed off into sobs.

'The list, where's the list?' Tom urged.

'In the drawer, over there.' I pointed to the kitchen unit and watched as Tom read through and disappeared, to return a few minutes later with my tartan shopping bag full, he grabbed the slippers from my feet and thrust them on the top. His face red with rushing, his eyes full of concern. He pushed my feet into shoes. I let him lead me down the stairs one at a time, stopping nearly on each one to breath as pain wrenched at my body.

He helped me into the van and just as we were about to set off, Sam rode his bike nearly into us, shouting, 'Merry Christmas.'

'Sam.' Tom yelled, winding down the window. He quickly explained what was to do and asked Sam to let everyone know. Stepping on the accelerator we tore off down the road, leaving a bemused Sam staring in our wake.

It seemed to take an eternity to get to the maternity home, once there Tom jumped out. I wanted to cry out, ask him not to leave me, but another pain put paid to that. It took minutes for him to return with an agitated looking nurse and a wheelchair.

I was taken straight to the Delivery Ward. I could hear babies crying and also a couple of females shouting out and swearing. I could only assume, at that moment, they were experiencing my pain. I wanted to swear too and swear I did.

A harassed looking midwife came into the cubicle to examine me, nodding to the other nurse and commenting, 'Not another one!'

'It's too soon,' I told them between the pains, 'too soon.' I tried to rise from the bed, they helped me on to. The nurse pushed me back down and the midwife said, 'Pethidine for this young lady.' I noticed she emphasised young and looked at my hand. 'They get wed younger and younger these days,' she added, bustling out of the cubicle.

The nurse, not much older than me, took my hand. 'Don't mind her,' she whispered. 'Her bark's worse than her bite.' As she smiled encouragingly, I noticed her pale face and the dark rings under her startling green eyes. Funny how you notice the most insignificant things at times of trauma. Well, it felt like trauma to me, regardless of thousands of women giving birth every day throughout the world.

'It's too soon!' I sobbed.

'Nonsense, baby is okay and ready to make an appearance into this world.' The midwife said sharply, as she came back with a dish and syringe in it. 'Onto your side.' She pulled up the gown, they had helped me into earlier, I yelped as a sharp stab in my bum came next. It wasn't long before I felt tired, pains interrupted my desire to sleep, and were coming more frequently.

'Tom, where is Tom?' I slurred.

'I'm outside,' he answered, 'please can't I come in?'

The kindly young nurse looked at the midwife. 'Why aren't husbands allowed in for births nowadays?' she asked quietly.

The midwife, Dorothy, as she told me to call her, nodded. 'Well, it is Christmas, this once won't harm.'

The young nurse, Isobel, drew back the curtain and beckoned Tom in. He rushed to my side and grabbed my hand, murmuring, 'Love you Ede, you'll be okay.'

'I just want to sleep,' I slurred. 'Let me sleep.'

'Nonsense now.' Dorothy said from down between my legs. 'It's time, now I want you to push. You've been to classes, haven't you?'

I nodded, not wanting to disagree, I knew I'd have to push, but I wanted to sleep.

'Right, at the next contraction push with all your might Ede, do you hear me?' Dorothy ordered.

I nodded and when the pain came I pushed, Tom and Isobel urging me along. I cried and screamed and swore. Finally, Angel arrived.

The midwife gave me another injection and I stirred to see Isobel wrapping our baby in a blanket.

'She's okay?' I wept.

'Yes, she is fine and how did you know it would be a girl? We haven't said yet.'

'Ede knows everything.' Tom told her, his eyes wet with tears as he took a peek at our daughter. 'She's beautiful, just like her Mammy.'

I took the bundle from Isobel and gazed down at the little scrap I had just given birth to. I felt choked and oddly enough no longer sleepy. 'Angel.' I said, looking up at Tom.

'Aye, she's that alright,' he nodded. 'Our little Angel.'

'Mm... Well, I suppose it's appropriate seeing as it is Christmas Day.' Dorothy sighed wearily. 'Our fourth baby today too. Now young man, go and tell whoever you need to, we have got some tidying up to do in here.'

'Thank you Dorothy and Isobel, I will.' Tom kissed me firmly on the lips and Angel a little peck on the top of her head. He surprised Isobel and Dorothy by taking them by the shoulders and planting big kisses on both of their cheeks.

'Well, I never...' Dorothy gasped, as crimson blotches appeared on both her cheeks.

'Tom?' I looked up at him, I felt weary but I wanted to see my Mam. Reading my mind Tom nodded and going to the room doorway, he beckoned to someone.

'Mam, oh Mam.' Tears filled my eyes as I saw my Mam enter the cubicle, she took one look at Angel and her own tears fell.

'She's...she's beautiful and just like you were.' Mam said, between gulping back tears. She looked from me to Tom, smiled and said, 'Congratulations you two!'

'Dad? Ike?' I asked hesitantly.

'Maybe later.' Mam said, nodding to Tom. 'I think it's time Ede had a rest don't you? You're welcome to come back for some dinner Tom.'

Tom shook his head, 'Thanks Mrs W. I'd best get to my Mam's and tell them the news.'

'Of course,' Mam replied. 'Lib or Mam would do instead of Mrs W!'

Tom grinned, 'Yes, yes of course, er… Lib.'

I felt drowsy but warm and content, Tom being able to call my Mam by her name was just wonderful. He'd always called her Mrs. W. or your Mam.

Isobel bustled into the room, 'You'll need to rest now Ede, I'll just take this young lady to the nursery.'

I wanted to shout no, but a weariness came over me, I just wanted to sleep, I felt Tom kiss my lips, Mam kiss my forehead and then I fell into a delicious warm and cosy slumber.

The week in the maternity home seemed to drag, I was anxious to take Angel home, she was taking her milk well. I didn't really want to feed her myself, though at first, I did try. However, Tom was thrilled about Angel going on the bottle as he would to feed her himself. He spent every evening with us. Mam came in the afternoons, one day with Sam. Tom's family, even his Dad, came too. I could tell the way Sadie was, she would spoil Angel to bits. Sam, Phyllis and the Lister lads were a bit more reserved, just smiled and nodded. Tom's Dad declared Angel was a fine Lister, and just like her Granny Lister too. I didn't agree, I thought Angel looked like my side of the family more, however I didn't voice my thoughts, I knew Tom's Dad could get funny.

My own Dad and Ike didn't appear, I was deeply hurt by this and I wanted to get home and be able to take Angel to see them. One afternoon Alice came in with the most beautiful teddy bear. My other presents had been more practical, by way of clothes, nappies, even a hamper of baby creams, powder and shampoo from my pal Lucy.

'Oh Alice, he's gorgeous.' I cried, cuddling the soft brown bear to me. 'Angel is going to love him, I'm going to call him Terry Teddy.' I chose this name so I could sing the song about Terry, which was a hit a few years earlier. I loved the song, even though it was sad. 'Alice... Ike?' I looked at my brother's girlfriend and could see the sadness in her eyes.

'Sorry Ede.' Alice said, she knew I was asking why he hadn't been. 'I tried...' she continued. 'You will see him when you get home, I am sure of it.'

I nodded and decided to change the subject. 'Did you all get our Christmas presents?'

'Oh yes, thank you, the kids loved them, we had a nice Christmas. Felt like a real family, the kids, Ike and I, until...' Alice broke off and I could see her eyes fill.

'Until what?' I asked, touching her arm.

'Nothing, it doesn't matter now,' she replied. 'Look, I must go and get back for the kids, see you soon.'

With a swift hug and peck on the cheek she was gone. I felt miserable, Alice was the best thing that could happen to Ike and his kids, had something gone wrong between them? I'd find out what, I was sure of it, when I got home. I'd sort it and make Ike see Alice adored him and the kids. What on earth was he thinking throwing it away, like he seemed to be doing, from what Alice said and her reaction.

Part Three

Chapter Ten

Alice went to answer the door of our flat, we only just heard the knock. The kids were so excited playing with all their new toys.

'Ike, Ike.' Alice called urgently.

I got up from the floor, 'Won't be a minute.' I told the kids.

'Okay Dad,' they replied, more or less in unison, the younger ones copying the older two. I went to the door and couldn't believe my eyes.

I took hold of Lily's arm and hustled her outside, slamming the door behind us. I knew Alice would be shocked by my actions but I couldn't help it. 'What the hell do you want?' I snarled.

'I want to see my kids Ike.' Lily replied tartly.

'Well, you ain't, you left them, abandoned them, to run off with my so called mate!' I was livid and Lily knew it, she pulled away from me.

'Ike, they're my kids and I want to see them.' Lily persisted, breathing heavily.

'And I've told you, you ain't seeing them, now bugger off!'

She half turned away, as if submissively, swinging back to face me, she landed a hefty slap across my face. I raised my hand to hit her back and she laughed.

'Yes, go on, I dare you, please do, I deserve it.'

Something made me hold back and I lowered my raised arm. 'Just what do you want Lily?' Her name seemed to stick in my throat. It had been months and we hadn't heard a whisper from her, now here she was on Boxing Day, turning up demanding to see the kids. They had stopped asking for her long ago, had accepted Alice and loved her to bits as I did. They didn't need Lily, none of us did. I looked her up and down, she hadn't changed, still scrawny and face like death, the heavy black eye makeup made her eyes smaller. Her clothes looked dishevelled, as if she had slept in them. I looked past her, there was no sign of Vic.

'He's not here, if that's what you're wondering.' Lily sneered. 'We...we split up months ago. Look, Ike...' She put out a hand to touch me, I flinched away. 'Ike...I'm sorry I really am sorry, could we try again for the kid's sake? They must be missing me; I know I'm missing them. I want to see them; I want our family back together.' Lily hung her head, she sounded tired, her whole body shook and her breathing was raspy.

'Lily...' I put my arm out to steady her. Oh God, what was I doing? She seemed ill and in a poor state, could I turn her away? I glanced round as the flat door opened, Alice stood in the hall staring out at me, her face white. I loved Alice, didn't I? But...but Lily, well, she is the Mother of my kids.

Alice stepped forward, 'Is she alright?' she asked. 'It's Lily, isn't it? How can we help?'

Oh Alice, wonderful, caring, unselfish Alice, I wanted to shout it from the rooftops, however she was more concerned with Lily.

'She wants to see the kids Alice and I told her she ain't!' I said flatly, aware I was still supporting the scrawny frame of my wife.

'Ike, it is Christmas, I'm sure the kids would love to see their Mam.'

Lily lifted her head and nodded, 'I don't know who you are, but thank you.'

I felt defeated, I couldn't see Lily, out on the street, on her own, I wanted to, very much, I could've tossed her into the gutter right there and then, gone inside to the kids and locked the door behind me.

'Yes, I guess they would Alice,' I replied, leading Lily through the door into the flat. 'Kids, someone here to see you.' I called, as cheerfully as I could, though the next words nearly choked me. 'It's your... Mam.'

Conway screamed and threw himself at Lily, the twins looked bemused, they were too young and had no idea who she was. Frankie hung back and reached out for Alice's hand.

'Frankie, it's me, your Mam, come an' give us a hug,' Lily beckoned him.

Frankie shook his head, 'Don't wanna see you Mam.' He turned and ran off to the kid's bedroom.

Lily sat down in the nearest chair and hung her head. 'Oh Ike, what have I done?' she murmured.

I could see tears filling her eyes, but I didn't feel moved. What was she doing here anyway, after all these months?

'Would you like some tea Lily?' Alice asked.

Lily nodded and tried to extradite herself from Conway's arms.

The twins, Buddy and Shirley, sat on the mat and resumed playing and chattering to each other in their own brand of baby talk, that only they seemed to understand.

'They've grown.' Lily nodded towards them. 'How old are they now?'

'Oh my God Lily, you don't know the age of your own kids! You really are something else.' I raged. I pulled Conway away from her and lifted him up, the little boy looked confused.

'They don't know me...' Lily broke off as Alice came in

with a tray of tea and some Christmas Cake. 'Quite a little family aren't you?' Lily sneered quietly, before grabbing a mug of tea and gulping the hot liquid down. She took some cake and stuffed that in her mouth, it was like she hadn't eaten for weeks.

I looked at her in disgust. Alice sensed my unease, 'It's okay Ike. Lily...' she asked gently. 'When did you last eat? I can make you a sandwich.'

'No thanks, I've just come for my kids.' Lily replied with a cold determination in her voice, she pushed her dirty hair from her face. I could see the bruises on the side of her head. Alice gasped but kept quiet.

'I told you Lily, they are staying with me.'

'Yes, Mam, we are!' Frankie ran back into the room and all the hurt Lily had caused when she left us, burst out from this little boy. 'Alice is my Mam now, not you, we are staying here with Dad, go away!'

'Well, well, got them really trained haven't you! The perfect family!' Lily got to her feet and I sighed as she made for the front door. 'You ain't seen or heard the last of this Ike. I am your Mother Frankie and you will be coming to live with me, whether you like it or not. The courts will always let the kids go with their Mother, you see if they don't, you just bloody well see!' The door slammed behind Lily and she was gone.

'Dad.' Frankie and Conway said in unison. Even Conway was a little upset and I knew it wasn't because Lily had left.

'It's alright lads. Now go and play with Buddy and Shirley.' I said as I ruffled their hair. Frankie took hold of Conway's hand and led him to where the twins were playing, Shirley with a doll and Buddy with a train.

'Ike, come into the kitchen.' Alice urged.

I followed her and sat at the kitchen table, putting my

head in my hands. Alice sat beside me in silence, resting her hand on my arm.

'It's okay Ike, you saw the state of her. There's no way will she get the kids, looking like she does, I bet she ain't even got anywhere to live.' Alice whispered.

'I hope you're right Alice, oh my God, I hope you're right.' I replied, doubts filling my head. Lily was right, I'd heard at most hearings the Mother always got custody. That would be over my dead body, I vowed to myself.

What a Christmas that was, my baby sister Our Ede, giving birth to Lister's bastard! Oh, Alice had begged me to go and see Ede, but not on your life. It had been bad enough seeing her marry a Lister. Seeing my baby sis, after the pain of childbirth, no way. Now Lily coming back like that! I wondered what bombshell was going to land next and how could I stop my bitch of a wife getting custody of the kids. There had to be a way there just had to be!

The rest of the Christmas holiday seemed to fly by, our days filled looking after my four kids, Alice loved it. She was a natural and the kids adored her. We visited both of our folks. My Mam and Dad made the usual big fuss of the kids. They in turn worshipped Granny and Grandad. Mind you, my Mam did look after them a lot, before and after I came home, and when we were working. She didn't mind, but I noticed a few more grey hairs every day and it bothered me. I tried to talk to Dad about it, but he just told me Mam was fine.

I didn't mention Lily's visit, hoping it would be forgotten. Conway however kept asking for his Mam. I heard Frankie telling him straight, she'd gone away again and he hoped for good too. He was too old and wise for a little boy of his age.

The mill closed for two weeks over Christmas and New Year. This, and the annual two weeks in summer were our holidays. It started snowing on New Year's Eve. They said Ede was going home that day. Ede was still a child herself, how was she going to cope with a baby? It was ridiculous and I loathed Tom Lister for getting her pregnant. I know Alice had taken Ede to the clinic and the woman there had suggested Ede get rid of it. This would have been by far the best thing. She could have gone to college and done what she wanted, the full time mechanics course, I would have persuaded Our Dad. He'd been dead set on her becoming a secretary. I knew Ede loved finding out how things worked, she was a natural. I would have helped her realise her dreams. But oh no, she had to go and get herself involved with Tom Lister, just because he worked in a garage. He was still a Lister and a right shower they were. They all looked like gypsies. The lads, always in trouble for stealing, but Harry Lister was a nasty piece of work and frequently in trouble for fighting as well. The girls were no better, Sadie and Joan had a reputation for putting it about, if you know what I mean. You know, blathered in make up and wore skirts more like belts. Now our Sam was infatuated with Phyllis, the youngest girl. She was different from the rest, quiet, shy and mousy. She always wore sensible clothes. But she was still a Lister! I found out at Ede's debacle of a wedding that my Dad and Margaret Lister had been an item till Old Man Lister came and swept her off her feet. Well she'd paid for it, working all hours God sends to keep the family fed, while he lounged about, down the pub, doing nothing. What a family and my own siblings infatuated by two of them! It really sticks in my throat, it really does. I can only hope it doesn't last and it won't. Then Ede will come home crying, with her brat and Sam will... well he'll just go on looking after his plants at the nursery, where he works.

I did think Sam had a girlfriend there, as some days he would come home looking like the cat who'd got the cream. I gather now it had just been an infatuation with a married customer, would you believe?

I told Alice, yet again, I was not going to see Ede. I couldn't stop Alice going, but she knew I didn't like it. I thought of Alice and her mass of curly ginger hair, freckled face and her sweet nature. My heart sank when she came into the room that morning and informed me she was going to Tom and Ede's to make sure everything was sorted for Ede coming home.

'You could come and give us a hand Ike?' she smiled encouragingly. I shook my head and turned to the kids playing with Frankie's train set. He was the image of my Dad. Conway had a look of my old Grandad, as I remember, on my Mam's side. The twins took after their Mother, both of them skinny and dark haired.

Alice can't have been half way down the street, when an urgent knocking came on the door, she must have left her key.

I opened it to find Lily on the doorstep, she was having a coughing fit and bent over double. I noticed her hair was even more lank and greasy, her clothes were really dirty, she looked awful.

'Mammy.' Conway screamed from behind me. He held out his arms to her and as Lily fell to her knees, he shoved past me, wrapping his small body round her. Lily coughed even more, she raised her head and tears fell down her cheeks.

'Help me, Ike...please...'

I stood staring down at my small son clinging to his Mother. Did I have a choice?

I grasped her arm and pulled her to her feet, she fell against my body and I half carried her inside.

'When did you last eat?' I asked quietly. Lily had always been thin but now she seemed emaciated. As I helped her in, I could feel her bones sticking out through her dishevelled clothing. Lily shook her head.

I took her into the kitchen and sat her down at the table. Our table, the one Alice and I sat round for meals with our kids. 'Conway, go and play son.' I ushered my little boy out of the door and closed it behind him, ignoring his whimpering cries for his Mammy.

I set about making Lily some tea and toast. I just needed to keep myself busy while I thought of my next move. I sat opposite watching her slowly devour the food and drink. 'What's going on Lily?'

She took a dirty handkerchief from her pocket and rubbed her eyes and face. She pushed back her lank hair. 'Ike, oh Ike, I...' she broke off as another spate of coughing engulfed her. She put the hankie over her mouth, when she withdrew it, I saw it was blood stained.

I got up and drew a glass of cold water from the tap, pushing it into her hand, she drank deeply and the coughing subsided.

'You need to see a doctor about that.' I said lamely.

Lily nodded and stared at me, I could see remorse in her eyes. 'I'm sorry Ike, I am so sorry,' she took another drink. 'I...made a dreadful mistake, I shouldn't have le-left you.' Tears rolled down her grubby cheeks.

For one brief moment I felt sorry for her. She was, is my children's Mother, what had happened to her? I longed to shout my questions at her. Instead I put my hand out and stroked her hair, lifted her chin and looked into her face. 'Oh Lily.' I snatched my hand away as if I'd been burnt.

What was I doing?

She started coughing again, deep raking coughs. 'Look Lily, I think we'd better get you to hospital.'

'No, no...I'll be okay,' she spluttered, between coughs.

I was just wondering how I could manage, when a voice in the hall shouted. 'Hello Ike...' Sam broke off as he entered the kitchen. 'What the hell!'

'Sam, I'm glad you're here, look she's ill, I'm going to take her to the hospital. Can you see to the kids.' I knew I was babbling.

Sam nodded, and I helped Lily to her feet. Conway and Frankie met us in the hall.

'What is she doing here?' Frankie demanded.

'Mammy.' Conway sobbed.

Sam put his arm round the two small boys, 'It's okay, yer Mam's not well, yer Dad's taking her to the doctor.' He nodded his head towards the door as he led the boys to where the twins were playing. 'Go,' he mouthed. 'We'll be fine won't we kids?'

I put my arm round Lily and half carried her downstairs. I was thankful a phone box was nearby as I needed to call for a taxi, which I hoped wouldn't be long. I ignored her pleas, she cried saying, she didn't want to leave her kids. I swallowed the words I wanted to say, that she should have thought of that months ago. When she left, running off with my so-called mate and where was he now? I knew these questions had to wait, I could see the woman was very ill and needed treatment. I needed time to think about her threat of custody, plus my own feelings towards her. I was angry at what she had done, but she was our kids' Mother. But what about Alice? She was a real Mum to them. Had I just felt sorry for Lily, when I stroked her hair, or did I still have feelings for her? I felt so confused, holding her close to me while we waited for the taxi.

Once at the hospital, I answered their questions as best I could, no I didn't know where she lived and Lily just shook her head. A porter came and helped Lily into a wheelchair, I was told to stay in the waiting area until a doctor had seen her.

'She's your wife?' the receptionist asked coldly, staring at Lily, as she was wheeled away.

'Er, well yes, no, er… ex-wife.' I said, 'She just turned up at my door today, I don't know where she has been, haven't seen or heard from her for months.'

The receptionist nodded and wrote something down on the forms she'd been filling in. I went and sat down, I couldn't just leave her there could I? The kids would be okay with Sam. Alice was busy at Ede's. Alice would understand that I needed to be there.

A small child sat a few seats away, whimpered and curled up to his Mum's arm. She was concentrating on a magazine, ignoring the child. A teenager had his foot on a chair, obviously broken or something. Others sat, looking blank eyed, waiting. That's all I could do, surely someone would come soon and tell me what was happening to Lily. Why was I bothered? I struggled to make sense of my feelings. Why was I sitting there waiting? I could have brought her, left her and gone back to my kids. Well, I could, couldn't I? Maybe I should, I rose from my seat to tell the receptionist I was off, when Alice came rushing in through the door, she flung herself into my arms.

'Ike, oh Ike, are you okay?'

'What? Yes, what are you doing here?'

'Well, I went home, of course, after sorting out at Tom and Ede's, Tom gave me a lift, he was going to come in to say hello. Sam told me what had happened. Tom dropped me off here, he's away now, to pick Ede up.' Alice gabbled.

'Stop.' I said a little too loudly, realising people were looking. 'It's okay Alice, look, can you go home and look after the kids, please.' I looked down at her upturned face, I could see concern and fear in her eyes. 'I'll be home as soon as I can. I need to see if she is okay. She is my kid's Mother after all.' I added lamely.

Alice nodded briefly, tears filled her eyes, she pecked me on the cheek and left. Surely she didn't think. I wasn't sure what she thought, I knew my exchange with her made my mind up to stay at the hospital, till I knew Lily was going to be okay.

'Mr Wagstaff?' A small man, in a white coat, called from a doorway. He was grey haired and lines furrowed his brow.

I went over, 'That's me.'

'Can you come with me please,' he said gently, too gently. He led me into a small artificially lit room, there were no windows, just a few bench type seats. 'Mr Wagstaff, your wife is…'

'Er.. you could say ex-wife.' I broke in.

'Oh, then may I ask who her next of kin is?'

I told him her Father lived in London.

'Ah I see, please can we sit down. London you say, there won't be time, I'm afraid.'

He was scaring me now, time for what, did Lily need an operation, couldn't I give permission. 'Time for what?' I said, voicing my thoughts.

'Time for him to get here, I'm sorry Mr Wagstaff but your wife, er... ex-wife is seriously ill, in fact she's dying,' he paused for a moment. 'Would you like to see her?'

I gulped back the threatening tears. No, not Lily, he couldn't be talking about my Lily! How? Why? I was sure she just had a chest infection or something. 'Why?'

'I just thought you might like to comfort her in her last moments.'

'NO!' I screamed, 'Why is she dying? It's just a cough, only a cough'

'I'm sorry Mr Wagstaff, your wife had an x-ray and she has mass in both her lungs. We think it's most likely to be very advanced lung cancer, we can't treat her, of course, she's left it too late, much too late. I'm so sorry, there is nothing we can do for her, she is very near the end now, would you like to be with her?'

I nodded and he led me out of the room into a stark, white side ward. The curtains on the windows and door were closed. Lily lay among the white sheets, a mask over her face giving her oxygen.

'She can probably hear you Mr Wagstaff, talk to her, let her know at least there is someone here she knows.'

I nodded to the doctor and a grey haired nurse beckoned me to the bed. She had tears in her eyes. 'So young,' she murmured. 'Do you have children?'

I nodded again and whispered, 'Four.'

'Oh my,' the nurse mumbled. She turned to the doctor, who nodded to her and she left the room.

'The buzzer is there Mr Wagstaff, please press it if you need anything. We will be back in a few minutes to see how she is. Is there anyone we can call? Should we call her Father? Do you have a number?'

I shook my head, not daring myself to speak. I sat down where the nurse had been sitting and took Lily's small, thin, pale hand in mine. 'Oh my Lily, my Lily.' I whispered, raising her hand to my lips. I knew, at that moment, I still loved her, loved her deeply and I forgave her for deserting us.

Lily stirred and her eyes flickered open, she pulled the mask from her face 'Ike,' she said, so quietly I only just heard. 'Ike, I couldn't cope, depression...'

'It's okay Lily, hush now, I'm here, you rest and get well.'

Lily shook her head and I knew, she knew. 'Ike, promise me, promise me you won't let the kids forget me.' She closed her eyes, the effort of her words exhausting her.

'Lily of course I won't, but there'll be no need, we can sort something out perhaps, perhaps we can make another go of it. Like you said, just like you said.'

Her eyes flickered open again and they filled with tears. 'It won't happen Ike, you know, don't you? I'm dying, but I need to tell you.' Lily continued and whispered to me words I needed to hear.

I tried to reassure her somehow as cheerfully as I could muster, I said, 'Don't be silly! It's just a chest infection, they'll have you right in no time.'

'I'm so sorry Ike, they've told me, if only...'

Closing her eyes, she fell back to sleep, her chest rattling with the exertion of breathing. I sat watching it, heaving up and down, holding her hand. Tears in my eyes.

'I still love you Lily, don't leave us.' I whispered, before my tears really started to fall.

The door opened, the doctor and nurse came in, they looked at the monitors, put the mask back in place advising me to try and get her to keep it on. It would help with her breathing and her pain. I could only nod and they left the room again.

I sat there, thoughts whirling round and round in my head, what would I tell the kids and her Father? They would all need to know. I didn't even think her Dad was on the phone. How could this be happening? It was just a few days ago she was standing in front of me, telling me she was going to get custody of the kids. I damned her then. But now?

Lily stirred and once more grappled the mask from her

face.

'No Lily, you must keep it on.'

'Ike did you…did you mean it, you…still love me?' Lily spluttered and coughed out the words.

'Yes darling, of course I did, we will get through this, just you see, we'll be a family again.'

'No…Ike I'm going.'

'You're not going anywhere my love.' I said, wiping the tears off my face with the back of my hand.

Lily nodded and gasped, her breathing became shallower and shallower, I tried to get her the mask back on but she pushed it away.

'Ike,' she whispered hoarsely. 'Kiss me.'

I leant over pushing the mask further aside and kissed my dear, sweet Lily's lips once more. She responded and half raised her head to meet me. 'Love you Ike,' she whispered. 'I always have.'

'I love…' I began to say, my words abruptly broken by the sound of an alarm. Lily's head had fallen back on the bed, her eyes were wide open. Doctors and nurses appeared from everywhere. I was ushered back, all I could do was stand and watch, as they tried to revive her. I knew, oh I just knew, they were too late. She had gone, my Lily had gone, gone for good.

Chapter Eleven

The next few days passed in a blur, Alice fussed and fussed until I could stand it no longer. Mam and Dad had taken the kids to theirs.

I told Frankie his Mam had gone. 'Good,' was his reply.

Conway wanted to know if she would be coming back, when I shook my head, he sobbed loudly.

There was to be a post mortem. Lily's death was sudden, despite the x rays, lung cancer was only suspected, it had to be completely verified, they said. We couldn't arrange the funeral till after then, so I decided to go to London. Mam and Dad argued with me and begged me to let the London Police inform Lily's Father of her death. I was adamant and just two days after Lily died, I found myself, on the train, going to London. Alice wanted to come with me, but I said no. I wanted to be away from everyone, Alice especially, how could we go back as we were, after the realisation I still loved Lily? But the kids, they loved Alice. It was such a mess, I needed to be away and sort my head out. London provided just the excuse I needed.

I hastened from leaving the train at Kings Cross, heading towards the flats where I'd met Lily's Dad for the first and only time. It was strange going back, past the pub where Lily had worked, the place I lodged, even the flat we once shared with. I didn't want to think about my so-called best mate, he could rot in hell for taking Lily off me.

It seemed her Dad had moved, a few discreet enquiries led me to a flat on the third floor of another concrete block. Rubbish strewn over the landings and the lift was out of order. I chastised myself for getting so out of breath going up the stairs. I found the number and stood outside what had once been a half glazed door. Pale green paint flaked from the bottom half and a black painted lump of plywood covered the hole where the glass had been. I knocked on the plywood a couple of times and heard a man's voice shout.

'Esme, get the bloody door.'

Slowly the door eased open and a small plump, shapeless woman stood before me, a puzzled look on her face, her greying hair was secured back in a hair band. She wore a filthy wraparound apron over a dirty dress. Ragged slippers donned her feet and she shuffled about on the bare hall floor.

'I'll ask you again, what do you want?'

I wasn't aware that she'd even spoken before then. What could I say? 'May I come in a moment please?'

'Er no, I don't think so mate, what do you want?'

'I'd like to speak to Lily's Dad, is he here?' I asked quietly.

'Who is it Esme? Either get them bloody in or shut the bloody door.' A man called from inside, Lily's Dad.

Esme stood for a moment regarding me solemnly, then beckoned me inside. I closed the door carefully behind me.

'You're him aren't you?' Esme whispered, staring down at her slippers. 'You're Lily's husband aren't you?'

'Yes,' I mumbled, 'I have some bad news.'

'You'd better tell me quick and get out of here, before he...'

'What?' Surely her Dad didn't hold a grudge after all these years? 'I'm sorry, I don't know how to say this, except just to say it... Lily is dead.'

Esme gasped, 'Oh no!' she cried.

'You bastard, I'm going to kill you!' Lily's Dad shouted as he came down the hall, he thrust Esme to one side and she fell heavily onto the floor.

'I said, I'm going to kill you!' He snarled as his punches rained down on my head and arms. 'You come here after all this time, just to tell me she is dead! You bastard! You took her away from me in the first place! I am going to kill you!'

I stumbled back against the front door and grappling behind me I felt for the handle. Esme got up and tried to launch herself between me and him, giving me a chance to get away. But he was too strong for her and pushed her savagely away again. I tried to say sorry, tell him how much I loved Lily, that I didn't know she was ill, how I wanted to come and tell him myself. He didn't hear any of it, he kicked and punched me, I felt I hadn't the strength, or the will, to fight back. Let him kill me, I'd be with Lily then for eternity. These were my last thoughts, as I slumped to the floor and a darkness came over me.

Part Four

Chapter Twelve

'Come on my little family.' Tom beamed at me and Angel, as he helped us into the van. I cradled Angel firmly on my knee. Tom leaned over and kissed us both gently on our heads. Tears filled his eyes and mine fell too.

'She's a perfect Angel, isn't she Tom?'

'Yes, my Ede, she is but can I just say about her name.'

'What about her name?' I felt indignant at his obvious doubt. 'She's an Angel.'

'Yes Ede, she really is but what about when she is older, the teasing.'

'No one would dare tease a Lister.' I laughed, though doubts crossed my mind and I looked down at our precious bundle. She may have arrived early but she was strong and sturdy. She hadn't needed an incubator. Perhaps Tom was right, kids would say she belonged on top of a tree, I could almost hear them. Kids can be so cruel.

'Ede, what about Angela?' Tom said gently. 'I need to register her birth tomorrow you know.'

'Yes I know, and yes Tom, that's perfect, she will be our Angel but to the world she is Angela Elizabeth Lister. Is that okay, about her middle name I mean?'

'Yes Ede, that's perfect too.' Tom grinned and started the van. He seemed to drive home so slowly, I chided him to go quicker, as we needed to be home before her next feed.

I found feeding Angela myself rather hard work and it was agreed with the doctors that she should be bottle fed.

Tom's Mam had always breast fed her babies and I felt a little guilty not wanting to feed Angela like that, or even be able to. Tom said he didn't get a look in with any of his brothers or sisters until they came off the breast. I knew he was going to be a fantastic Dad and I wondered if his Mother knew how he had felt, not being able to bottle feed his siblings.

The flat was so clean, fresh flowers on the table and a little crib for Angela was made up with fresh bedding, topped with a lovely lemon quilt, decorated with tiny rabbits. Apparently, the crib was the one me and my siblings started life in. Made of wood and on rockers, Dad had done it up for us. I wondered if he was glad to do it or if Mam had badgered him into it.

Dad still hadn't properly come to terms with my enforced marriage, he didn't speak much to Tom either. Tom didn't mind, he told me he knew the reputation the Listers had, which wasn't down to him, he assured me. His Dad was idle and this irked Tom greatly, his brothers were always in bother one way or another. When Tom was younger, his Dad coerced him into stealing from the post office. The police knew it was the young lad Tom Lister, but couldn't prove it. They could prove that old man Lister was at the scene and he got sent down for it, as he had been several times since for one thing and another. Tom knew it was no life for him and worked hard to make a good name for himself. But the name Lister always stuck. He vowed to me that he would prove my Dad wrong, that he was a good person and would be the best Husband, Father and Son in Law my Dad could ever want for his daughter. I was thrilled, but knew it would be a long time before my Dad accepted Tom or any of the Lister family properly.

Then of course there's Sam, he was dancing with Phyllis, Tom's youngest sister at our wedding. I knew they had been seeing quite a lot of each other since. I had no idea what my Dad thought of that. Sam was like Phyllis, both the quiet ones of the family. Sam liked gardening and loved his job at the plant nursery. Phyllis enjoyed books; she even got her ideal job in the local library. She looked totally different to the rest of the Lister clan. Tom and his other siblings were well built, with raven black hair and good looks. Phyllis was well, plain, her mousy blonde hair, just...well...it made you wonder, people said. But there was no doubt she was a Lister. I'd seen the same look in her eyes when something didn't suit as I'd seen in Sadie's. Unlike Sadie, Phyllis didn't voice her thoughts.

We'd barely been home half an hour when a knock came on the door downstairs. Tom hurried down and I heard him say, 'Oh no!' A thundering of feet followed him up the stairs and there, crowding round our small sitting room, were the entire Lister family. Even Joan, who had come over from Sheffield. Sadie, Joan and Phyllis cooed over Angela, as did Tom's Mum. His Dad, Billy and Dennis produced a crate of beer. 'To wet the baby's head,' they chorused.

I felt weary and Angela began to whimper fretfully. 'She's ready for her bottle.' I announced.

'Right you lot, out!' Tom yelled. With mutters and groans, along with the crate of beer, they left and peace was re-gained. 'Sorry darling,' Tom said, as he went to the kitchen to make up the bottle. I had to go and supervise of course, to make sure he got the right amount.

It was much later that evening Alice came round, she looked agitated and upset. 'It's Lily,' she said, looking long-ingly down at Angela, who was now fast asleep in her crib.

'Oh no,' I sighed. 'She's back then?' I'd heard, from Alice, about the fiasco of Lily's visit on Boxing Day.

'Yes, she came back, ill, now she...she's dead.' Alice sobbed.

'Good.' I said and wondered why Alice was so upset. I mean Lily had abandoned Ike and the kids. Hadn't been in touch for months, suddenly she was back upsetting Ike and Alice's perfect family life, Ike's kids adored Alice. 'Oops sorry, I mean now she won't bother Ike again.'

'That's just it Ede,' gulped Alice. Between sobs I got it out of her, Ike had gone home from the hospital and was deeply upset. He shrugged off Alice's attempts to console him and just kept crying, saying Lily's name over and over. Sam, not knowing how to cope, took the kids to Mam and Dad's, they hadn't seen their Dad in such a state. 'I don't know what to do Ede.' Alice stared at me with her tear-filled eyes, I felt helpless.

'Look Alice, Ike will have got a shock, but he loves you now and he'll get over this.' I tried to sound sympathetic, inside I felt this was the best thing that could have happened. Heartless I know, but it seemed Lily wanted the kids back. That would send Our Ike over the edge again. So yes, it was the best thing all round.

I looked at Alice and knew something else was on her mind. 'What else Alice?'

She stared at me, tears rolling down her cheeks. 'I...I'm not pregnant Ede.'

I took her in my arms, didn't know what to say. Yet I think we both knew that it was for the best too, well it was, wasn't it?

I was dismayed at the news from Sam that Ike intended going down to London himself, to tell Lily's Father. It seemed the funeral couldn't be held anyway until a post mortem had taken place, Lily dying so suddenly. I'd heard about Lily and her parents. I believed the only reason she married Our Ike, was to get away from her Dad. Her folks hadn't even been at the wedding! I asked Ike on the day and he just told me they weren't invited. Oh, how I feared what would happen when Ike went down there and broke this news to them or rather to him. I knew Lily's Mother had died. There was nothing I could do and I prayed my Dad would go with him. Though it seemed it was something Ike wanted to do on his own and they'd let him go alone!

I was kept busy with our little Angel, she was a happy baby and seemed very content with life around her. I swear she smiled when she saw Tom, but the midwife said it was wind and I should get her some gripe water. While she slept, I turned into quite the proficient housewife and mother. Cleaning, washing and cooking, Phyllis brought me cookery books from the library and Tom bought us a drying cabinet. It had wood rails and heat came up from the bottom and dried the clothes. I longed to be able to dry them outside, but we hadn't anywhere. They always came out of the cabinet stiff and hard, but there was nothing else I could do. I tried to imagine putting dried, stiff towelling nappies on my Angel! I couldn't, and was so glad Tom agreed to the expense of disposable ones.

Alice came back round a couple of days after Ike had left for London.

'How did it go for Ike down there?' I asked.

Alice shook her head and burst into tears, 'He's not back yet,' she sobbed.

'Oh well, I guess he's catching up with mates while he's down there,' I replied as casually as I could, but fear gripped my throat. What if...what if Ike got mixed up with the same lot again and went back on the drugs? After Lily left, that is what happened, when he came home he was very ill. At the time I had no idea drugs were the reason. What if? I voiced my thoughts to Tom later on, after Alice had gone home.

'No Ede, Ike would not go down that road again, he saw what happened before and what was happening to the kids. He wouldn't risk losing them and Alice.'

'That's just it Tom, from what Alice told me, it's as if Ike doesn't want her any more, she can't seem to do right for doing wrong. He could have...well you know.'

'No, I don't know and neither do you, so please stop speculating and getting yourself chewed up over nothing! Can't you see it's upsetting Angela!'

I nodded and stared at the baby in my arms, she was wriggling about and her blue eyes brimmed with tears. I cuddled her into me and she stilled. 'Your Dad's right, Uncle Ike will be home in no time. If he won't come and meet his niece then we will go and see him.' I grinned up at Tom, he nodded back encouragingly.

Little did any of us know that at that precise moment Ike was, struggling to survive, in a London hospital. Lily's Dad had been arrested for Grievous Bodily Harm and the hospital were trying to identify Ike and find out his next of kin. The woman at the flat, Lily's Dad's girlfriend, hadn't a clue, she was in a state of shock. She had managed to get up and push Ike out the door, just before he collapsed. A neighbour had phoned for an ambulance and they called the police. Ike was unconscious and stayed like that for several days, leaving the rest of us, in Leeds, totally unaware of what had happened.

Angela was a real treasure, she fed well on the bottles and Tom loved giving her the evening feeds. I felt really well and my expanded stomach decreased by the day. I gave a twirl one morning as I put on my slacks, I felt really good. The day before Alice had minded Angela while I went to the hairdressers. I decided, now I was a Mum, my long hair had to go. I had an elfin cut, like the one model Twiggy had, I felt so different. Tom wasn't best pleased and grumbled that he loved my long hair. I assured him it would soon grow, but for now it was easier to wash and dry.

One morning the district nurse came and said Angela could go out in her pram, well it wasn't a pram as such, we'd got a carry cot with wheels. I was thrilled and wrapped her up well, donned my overalls and carried her downstairs to the garage.

Angela slept for quite a while and I was able to get to work on the engine of an old Ford Popular. It belonged to Mr Patel, who had the corner shop up the road from us. He was proud of his vintage car. Just lately, he told us, she was misbehaving and he didn't know why. We checked the spark plugs and changed them, but still it ran for several seconds then juddered to a stop. Even Tom scratched his head. We tried a different battery, Tom tightened this and that, with exactly the same outcome.

'Got me beat has this un Our Ede.' He sighed and went to wash his hands. Angela was stirring. 'Dinner time I reckon Ede, then I'll get me thinking cap on.' I knew he would probably spend the afternoon pouring over manuals.

'Would it be okay to take Angel out, do you think?' I asked cautiously, as Tom had muttered doubts about her being in the garage. However, it was an unusually sunny, mild winter's day.

'Well, I suppose, you reckoned the nurse said it was okay?'

I nodded furiously and, after dinner, left Tom with his research. I bundled Angel into her carry cot, along with spare nappies, also bottles made up with milk formula and was out before he had time to change his mind.

It seemed like an age since I'd been home to 1,Congleton Terrace, yes I still referred to it as home, as it was the terraced house I had grown up in. Mam and Dad had lived there all their married life, it was the house Dad grew up in too. Mam had wanted to move to a modern new house on the outskirts of Leeds. Dad refused point blank, he was born there and we all knew it was his wish to die there.

'Ede lass, come in, come in.' Mam called, coming out to help me up the steps with the pram. 'What are you doing out so soon?'

'It's okay Mam, the district nurse said I could.'

'Well, I'd just be coming out of hospital now, when you three were born.' Mam sighed and held out her arms for Angela as I took my baby out of the carry cot.

'My, she's a beauty you know, just like you were.' Mam sighed again and stared at me.

'I know, but I think she has Tom's eyes.'

'Aye well, they could change colour you know Ede.'

I shook my head hoping Angel's eyes would stay the same colour as they were.

'Mam, have you heard owt of Our Ike?'

Mam shook her head and her eyes filled with tears, 'I have to say this to someone Ede,' she sobbed. 'Ike, well I just have this feeling something is not right. You'll realise this when Angela gets older, you get a feeling you know. Oh, it's hard to explain. But it's not like Ike to go off and not contact us or the kids.'

'Where are they?' I asked, realising Mam was home on her own.

'Alice has got a few days off and has them at theirs. Conway still cries for his Mam, and there's the funeral to arrange. I just don't know what to do Ede.'

'What does Dad think about it all, could he go down to London and find Ike?'

'Oh lass, where would he start? We don't know where Lily lived, or who he might stay with, nothing.'

'We can start right now, we'll ring up everyone we can think of and start with the hospitals.'

Mam gasped, 'You don't think?'

'Look Mam, it's to rule out that he hasn't had an accident and seems the logical place to start.'

Mam cuddled our sleeping Angel, I knew I would have to start calling her Angela, Tom did, and the rest of the family did, but she was my little Angel and always would be.

I called directory enquiries for numbers of several hospitals in the area Ike and Lily had lived. When I rang them there was no Ike Wagstaff listed as being there. I was relieved and could see the relief in Mam's face.

'Do you think...we should call the police Mam?' I asked cautiously.

'God, no Ede, your Dad or Ike wouldn't want a fuss like that, no there's no need to involve the police.'

We didn't involve the police, they involved us. A few days later Mam and Dad had a visit from Sergeant Bert Timmings, our local bobby. He broke the news that Ike was indeed in hospital, actually in one of those I'd telephoned. Apparently, at that time, they didn't know who he was. Eventually Lily's Dad had admitted thumping Ike and told the police who he thought Ike was. It hadn't taken long for them to trace him back to Leeds and to Mam and Dad's.

Dad decided, once again, to go straight to London. Bert had warned him that Ike was in a pretty bad way and it had been touch and go for a while, Bert confessed that he might have been bringing tragic news. I didn't know any of this until later on when Our Sam came round to tell us what had happened.

I wanted to go to London with Dad, at the same time I wanted to be with Mam. Sam was still living at home and assured me Mam would want me to put Angela first. 'There's nowt to be done Our Ede.' Sam said matter of fact.

I agreed and knew we would just have to wait, pray and hope. I thought Sam wasn't fully explaining Ike's condition to me, his tone told me it was more serious than just getting a clout off Lily's Dad. But why? It wasn't Ike's fault Lily died, surely he couldn't blame Ike for that? Lily's folks hadn't been at the wedding, maybe they thought Lily could do better, or did her Dad blame Ike for them having to get married, my mind was a whirl. Perhaps Ike would tell us when he came home.

Part Five

Chapter Thirteen

'Ike lad, oh Ike,' Alf Wagstaff sat by my bedside, for how long I had no idea. I stirred as I heard his voice, he instantly called for a nurse.

My head ached tremendously and I felt as if I'd been run over by a steam roller. Where was I? Why? Questions seeped into my fogged mind. What was Dad doing here?

Slowly the memory of Lily dying, going to her Father's and the reception I got from him flooded back. Tears ran down my face as I murmured her name. Lily, my sweet Lily had gone. I drifted back into an abyss.

Next day I woke feeling stronger and aching less. A pretty blonde nurse had hold of my wrist.

'Now then Mr Wagstaff, I do believe you are much better today.'

'What day is this?' I was totally unaware that I had been in hospital for almost a week. 'My kids!' I croaked, when she informed me of this. Focussing my eyes, I could just read her name badge, Freda Black. 'Any relation to Cilla?' I asked.

She shook her head and smiled. 'My, you are feeling better, I get that all the time. Now you must rest Mr Wagstaff, you have a concussion, cracked ribs, a broken arm and bad bruising, It's going to take you a while to be right.' She held up her hand to quieten me. 'As for your kids, your Father tells me they are being well looked after by your Mother and your girlfriend. Now you get yourself back to sleep for a while and then you might feel like something to eat.'

Feeling utterly exhausted I closed my eyes. Alice was looking after the kids, they adored her. But me? I knew I would have to seriously think about that one.

That afternoon, I was sitting up in bed, drinking a cup of tea, when Dad came in for a visit.

'I'm sorry Dad,' I began.

'Look lad, no need to be sorry, you did what you had to do, who knew it would turn out like this? Him blaming you for his daughter's death!'

'Dad, there's more to it than that.'

'Well, that's not what he's saying to the police.'

I opened my mouth to tell him why Lily's Father had been so incensed, it wasn't because she had died, it was because I had taken her away from him! I wanted to tell my Dad how Lily had been abused, somehow I couldn't. Mam and Dad lived a good life and knew little of such things.

'What's happening to him Dad?'

'Well lad, at least he owned up.' Dad went on to explain how the hospital didn't know who I was, until Lily's Dad told the police, when he admitted hitting me. 'He tried to say you fell against the railings outside the flat and that's how your ribs got smashed, your arm, he'd said, broke when he was trying to help you up! It's okay, the police could see from your injuries that it was a load of twaddle.'

'He is up in court in a couple of days, he will go down and you know what? You now have an eye witness to prove him wrong.'

I shook my head, there was no one else there.

Dad grinned, 'You'll never guess, but his girlfriend is going to testify against him.'

I shook my head again in disbelief and then Dad told me

what he knew. 'The girlfriend Esme, I think she's called, she knew Lily and her Mam had lived a terrible life with him. It seems Lily's Mam was overjoyed when you took Lily away. He was very angry and Lily's Mother bore the brunt of his anger. It would seem, from what Esme told the police, she was too scared to leave him. I reckon she just gave up in the end. His girlfriend suffered the same too, though, at first, she thought she could change him. When he brayed you and injured you so badly, she decided enough was enough and made a statement to the police, he's going down lad.'

I lay back against my pillows and closed my eyes trying to take it all in.

Dad touched my shoulder, 'I'll go now lad, come back later, let you rest. But answer me this, why didn't you fight back lad?'

Opening my eyes I stared at Dad in amazement at this question. 'I couldn't Dad, he's an old man and I was telling him his daughter had died.'

'You did know he had abused Lily?'

I nodded, 'Yes, that was the reason she got pregnant, to get away from him.'

Dad frowned and I could tell what he was thinking, he didn't need to ask. It was what I thought myself at the time. Was Frankie mine? I told Dad yes he was, because Lily's Father had an operation, after she got pregnant by him before. 'Frankie is definitely mine, you only have to look at him to see he's a Wagstaff.'

'Aye lad, I just had to make sure, after what I've been told. Well, it beggars belief, that a man, any man could do that with his daughter. It's well...it's?' Dad shuddered. 'I'll let you rest lad, see you tonight. I'll ring your Mam and Alice, tell them you're doing okay.'

I nodded, 'Give Mam my love.' I closed my eyes again.

'And Alice?' Dad asked quietly.

I nodded, and listened to his footsteps retreating down the ward before opening my eyes. Alice filled my mind. I stared round the ward with its pale green walls, flowery green and orange curtains hung across the windows and round each bed. I hoped Alice wouldn't take it into her head to come down. No, she wouldn't leave Mam to look after the kids. I couldn't get any answers, as to what I should do.

'Are you okay Mr Wagstaff?' Freda asked quietly.

I'd been oblivious to her approach, I looked up into her blue eyes and the stray strand of blonde hair escaping from under her starched cap. I nodded and mumbled I was tired. She pulled the curtains round my bed and ordered me to sleep. I only wished I could, I really did. I'd been asleep for a week, wasn't that long enough? Right then I had a lot of thinking to do. The police would be coming for a statement, what was I going to do about Alice, more so what about the kids, what about the kids? I closed my eyes and dozed off, next thing I knew someone was gently shaking my shoulder.

'Mr Wagstaff, Mr Wagstaff, are you well enough to speak to the police? They are here, I can tell them to go if you wish.' Freda spoke quietly, she had a faint trace of a cockney accent.

'I'll see them Freda, by the way the name's Ike. Mr Wagstaff makes me sound ancient.' The fact that my aching body made me feel ancient hadn't anything to do with it. Well, if I see the police at least that's one thing out the way, I thought. 'Show them in love will you.' Freda nodded and departed leaving the curtains, round my bed, closed. It wouldn't have mattered if they'd been open, what I had to say to the police wasn't private. The rest of the men, in the ward, knew what had happened to me anyway, so I would happily give the police my statement. Let them take the lead as I didn't really know what their questioning would entail. Just let me get this one step over and done with, then I could concentrate on my other problem. What to do about Alice?

You see I realised, when Lily was dying, I didn't love Alice, not in the way she deserved to be loved. So was it right to carry on such a relationship? She deserved better than second best. The kids though? They had lost their real Mam, they didn't deserve to lose Alice too, who they looked on as second Mam. So there was the quandary, what should I do about Alice?

DEVOTION
DANCE HALL
DEVOTION
DANCING

Chapter Fourteen

The days passed by in a haze, some days I felt good and desperate to go home. The doctor and Freda assured me I was in no fit state. Other days I seemed to sleep a lot. I must get myself right and get back to Leeds.

The police were satisfied with my statement and Lily's Father was going to plead guilty. I felt relieved, but what about the funeral? Oh my Lily. I questioned Dad next time he came in, but he assured me there was no rush to organise that just yet, it seemed they were still carrying out the autopsy. Lily dying suddenly, as she did, this was necessary to find out why. I was keen to know myself, was it really lung cancer? Perhaps it would also reveal if they could have saved her.

'Ike,' a voice whispered, rousing me from my doze.

Any thoughts of the future seemed to make me so very tired. I didn't recognise the voice and gasped, as I opened my eyes, it was Esme.

'Ike, I'm so sorry,' she whispered, her brow furrowed with concern. 'He will get what he deserves. I am just so very sorry it came to this.' Esme twisted the straps of her handbag and looked down at her hands.

I felt stronger and angry, 'He should have got what he deserved years ago.' I spat.

'You knew?' Esme raised her head in disbelief, 'You knew what he did to Lily?'

'Yes, I knew.' I struggled further up the bed. 'How did you know? Why wasn't he stopped, why?'

'I didn't know till her Mam came to tell me Lily was leaving. Isla and I were friends you see. Isla told me Lily had met you and she was pregnant and you were going to be married. Isla broke down when she told me she was glad Lily would be away from her Father. Then she told me what had happened to Lily. Oh Ike, it's been such a mess, such a time, horrible.'

'How could her Mother not do anything if she knew? She had a bloody abortion!'

It was her turn to look shocked and she gasped, 'When?'

'When Lily was thirteen!' I cried, raising my voice. Other patients and their visitors turned their heads in our direction. I lowered my voice, 'You mean her Mother didn't know?'

Esme's hand flew to her throat, her other hand grappled in her coat pocket for a handkerchief, she wiped the tears from her eyes. 'Oh my God, no, no! It can't be! I remember Isla telling me Lily was ill, he took her to the doctors. Oh poor Lily, and poor Isla.' Esme sobbed loudly into her hankie.

I reached out a hand and touched her arm. 'What could you have done?'

'Something, Isla thought it was happening, but she was scared of him and after Lily left, he was awful to her Ike. He was different after Isla died and I...I thought he really had changed. I soon found out different, I...I'm so sorry.'

Before I had a chance to reply Esme rose from her seat and walked quickly away.

'Ike, you okay?' Freda said, pressing a cup of tea into my hand. 'Who was she, your visitor? She looked familiar.'

I quietly told Freda who she was and she nodded, telling me she thought she recognised her, as she was on the women's ward once when Esme had been admitted.

'Fell from a bus by all accounts, but we all knew.' Freda

whispered so not to be overheard. 'We knew he'd beaten nearly the life out of her. He used to come to visit, looking very sheepish, brought her chocolates and flowers. The caring, loving husband – Ha! Oh we all knew!'

'She's his girlfriend and has just told me she thought he'd changed. Why didn't she report it?' I asked.

'Said she had fallen off the bus and kept to her story. We told her we knew, but she vehemently denied it, so what could we do? The police even came and asked her. We have to report what we think are suspicious injuries you see. She told them the same story. I think they even went to the bus company and they hadn't known of any accident. But you can't do anything...' Freda's voice trailed off and I knew she was feeling very sad for Esme.

I patted her hand and thanked her for the tea, 'He'll get what's coming to him now Freda.'

She turned away and went with tea to the next bed. I took a deep drink of mine, the hot brew calmed me down. Mam always said a good hot cup of tea was the best remedy. She was right, I couldn't do anything about Lily's Mam, but I was relieved, at least Esme was safe and away from him. I forgot to thank her, for had it not been for her pushing me out of the door, I fear I wouldn't have lived.

A few days later the doctor declared I was well enough to travel home, as long as it was by train. 'Can't have you bumping about in a car or on the bus.'

'No worries,' Dad told him. 'I have my return ticket and will get a single for him.'

It was then I realised that somehow, somewhere, I'd lost my wallet, which of course contained my identity and my return train ticket. I tried to explain to Dad but he shook his head, no one had any idea where it had gone. He told me not to worry he'd sort everything out.

The following day, I gingerly got into a taxi to take the short journey from the hospital to Kings Cross Station. The train journey was very uncomfortable, but I dozed on and off. Dad fussed about, worse than Mam would have done, making sure I had my pain relief medication. He even asked the guard for a blanket, of course there weren't any and Dad was told, in no uncertain terms, the train was not a sleeper.

Dad had earlier rung Mam and told her what train we would be getting and what time we would be arriving, for once it was on time. No one was more surprised than Dad and me when Tom Lister greeted us off the train. We both stood staring at him, he announced he had a car waiting and he would be driving us home.

I knew Dad was going to protest but I was, in a way, only too glad to get home, it didn't matter who took us. 'Tom, you only have a van.' I said, putting my hand on Dad's arm to silence his complaint.

'Not today Ike, not today. I've still got the work's van, but...give me your bag and Ike's, Mr Wagstaff.'

Dad opened his mouth but was too stunned, he released the bags and put his arm through mine. We followed Tom outside, to a gleaming, white four door car. 'It's a Ford Cortina,' he announced, proudly. 'Time I got a family car.' Tom grinned happily and held the back door open for us.

I climbed in, grimacing with pain. Dad went round the other side and climbed in the back with me, he muttered something illegible under his breath. When we got to Congleton Terrace, Dad quietly said his thanks. I put my hand out and shook Tom's hand, his grip was warm and firm.

'You're very welcome Ike, Mr Wagstaff, Ede will be so pleased you're home. She's been so worried, in fact we all have.' He nodded to us both, got back in the car and drove away.

'Well of all the nerve!' Dad said grabbing up the bags and marching into the house. Mam flew past him and wrapped her arms round me, seeing my pain she loosened her grip and there were tears in her eyes as she welcomed me home.

There I was, back again at number One, under the care of Mam and Dad. I asked about the children and was secretly quite relieved when I learned I would be staying there, the kids were fine, Alice was looking after them at the flat. She would be along later and Mam told me Ede would too.

I'd time in the hospital to think about my kid sister, for she was still a kid to me, not a married woman with a baby of her own. I could hear Dad moaning about being picked up by a Lister. Mam appeased him all she could, but it didn't stop him. I was directed to a bed in the front room. It was where I spent months, after I came back from London, previously. I shuddered at the state I was in then, although I didn't feel much better now!

Ede arrived later that afternoon, I could hear Mam cooing over Ede's baby. Ede pushed the door open and whispered, 'Ike, are you awake?' I couldn't avoid her forever. I knew that, so I turned over giving an involuntary moan and faced her.

Ede had tears in her eyes, 'Ike, oh Ike, you're okay. Would you like to meet, I mean, would you like to see your niece Angel...I mean Angela?' Ede's face looked strained by the enormity of the question, I couldn't let her down.

'Just for a minute,' I said quietly.

Ede turned and bustled out of the room, returning moments later with the baby in her arms. I could see the proud look on her face as she told the child. 'Angel, this is your Uncle Ike.'

A sweet, heart shaped face turned to stare at me, as if she

understood what her Mother was saying. She was beautiful and just like Ede had been, as I remembered. I knew the agreement over her name. 'Hello, Angela is it?' I reached out a finger and stroked her pink cheek. 'She's like you Ede.'

'Do you think so? I think she has Tom's eyes. She's like both of us and I swear she smiles, Mam says its wind, but I am sure she smiles. She's looking right at you and smiling now.' Ede gabbled.

My eyes went from Ede's excited face to the baby and sure enough Angela seemed to be looking right at me and her rosebud mouth formed a perfect smile.

'I'd best go Ike or Our Mam will be in here dragging me out. You need your rest and Alice will be along with the kids. They can't wait to see you, she's just picking Frankie up from school. Did you know she's put Conway's name down already?'

I nodded, 'Thanks for coming Ede, yes I am tired, but it's been good to meet Angela.'

Ede took the hint and departed. So Alice and the kids were coming. I couldn't wait to see the kids, I'd been away from them again for too long. Alice, well, how would that go, how would I feel? I was mourning my Lily and knew I would be for a long time. It wouldn't be fair on Alice, would it? I knew, or thought I did, that she would say she would wait for me. But did I really want her to? Freda had given me her address, I thought about her kind gentle ways and a warm feeling came over me. My kids loved Alice, perhaps I could learn to love her, couldn't I? For their sake? Again doubts crossed my mind, was it fair? Oh, life just wasn't fair at all, not at all! I lay on my back staring at the ceiling and with the jumbled thoughts going round in my head I must have drifted off to sleep.

It barely seemed a few minutes till children's voices outside my door woke me.

'Hush now, quiet, let me see if your Daddy is awake,' Alice told them. She opened the door and poked her head round.

'I'm awake, let the kids in,' I said.

They didn't need any encouragement, Frankie ran in shouting 'Daddy, Daddy!' Conway came up behind him, followed by Shirley and Buddy tottering along, each with a firm grip on Alice's two hands.

'They're walking!' I gasped and tears filled my eyes, I'd missed their first steps.

'Well not properly, if I let go they'll fall down.' Alice laughed and led them to hold onto the side of the bed. They lifted their faces and grinned at me saying in unison, 'Da, Da.'

I heaved myself up, ignoring the tearing pain in my ribs. I held out my plastered arm and my good arm and folded the kids into them. Burying my face in their hair, breathing in their scent. My kids, 'Our lovely kids,' I whispered.

'Yes, our lovely kids Ike,' Alice said.

I raised my head quickly and before I could stop myself I said, 'Mine and Lily's kids,' I bit my tongue, Alice looked so hurt.

'Yes, of course they are Ike,' she said in a cracked voice, I knew she was close to tears.

'Sorry Alice, I...'

'Yes, I know Ike.'

How could she know? How could she know what I was thinking and what I was feeling?

'Come on kids, your Dad needs to rest and you'll be wanting your tea.' Alice gathered them up and they left, the kids waving a solemn goodbye.

'Oh what am I going to do? Why did you have to leave me

Lily twice? If you'd stayed with me, I could have saved you. I loved you Lily, I still love you.' I cried out in anguish, not realising Mam had taken the kids off and Alice was leaning on the front room door able to hear my every word.

I didn't see Alice or the kids for the next few days. I slept and slept, again I felt guilty, this was the second time I'd come home needing Mam's love and care. The first after Lily left and I got mixed up in drugs. Now the beating her Father had given me. Dad had mentioned on the train how he thought getting mixed up with Lily would do me no good. He didn't exactly say I told you so, but I knew that's what he meant.

Mam insisted, when I enquired, that the kids were fine, Alice had taken more time off work and Our Ede was helping out too.

Ede, my little sis, I'd been so unfair to her. No, I didn't like the arrangement with Tom bleeding Lister! Yes, I thought as much about the Listers as my Dad did, layabouts and bad uns, Dad told us that, more than once. By, he was right too! Tom Lister getting my little sister pregnant and her not even sixteen! Dad wouldn't hear of the police getting involved, I nearly went myself, but Alice insisted I leave well alone. It made me so mad. I didn't want to see them after the wedding and I didn't. The first I saw of Ede was that afternoon, when she came into the front room, my bedroom, at home.

Tom and Ede seemed to be getting on with their life and now had a little one too. I had to admit she was a perfect little Angel. I smiled to myself, I knew all about the name the baby had been given and how they'd changed it to Angela. The baby was so like, I remembered, Our Ede was.

When Our Ede was born I was so mad, because it meant I had to share a bedroom with Our Sam. I'd got used to my own space. I remember when she was about one, she said my name and grinned at me. It felt like she only had eyes for me and I loved being the centre of her tiny world.

Ede had grown up too quickly, she was stubborn and determined to do what she wanted in her life. The involvement and marriage to Tom Lister had proved all that.

I knew I must forget about them and let them get on with it. I thought it would all end in tears. Was my relationship with Alice going that way too? I knew I must tell her how I felt.

After about a week I felt stronger and was taking short walks outdoors. I visited my mate Sid who lived down the road. Gingerly sitting back in his Dad's chair, while his Mother bustled about making tea, we chatted about Leeds, how it was growing, the new pubs and clubs.

Sid also told me about his girlfriend, she lived in Quarry Hill Flats, he was obviously smitten and talked of them living together. I asked why not get married, it seemed wrong to me that you should just live with someone as man and wife and not be married. Yes, I know Lily and I had lived in sin but, at that time, needs must.

Sid revealed that it wouldn't happen, his girlfriend Amala was a Hindu. Sid told me they were planning to move to London and she would never see her family again as they had arranged a marriage for her, with a much older man, in India.

I was shocked by the revelation and how openly Sid spoke about it in front of his Mother. She nodded sadly and told us she longed for the day when couples could marry for love, whatever their religion.

Sid's Mam was an Irish Catholic and his Dad, an Irish Protestant, they had eloped to England to be together, to escape the stigma, and his Mam being told, in no uncertain terms by a Catholic priest, that her soul would be in mortal trouble if she carried on with the relationship. Neither wanted to part, leaving their homeland was the only solution.

It seemed this was the only way Sid and Amala could be together. I'd heard of this before and felt worried for Sid, wouldn't Amala's Father and her Brothers try to find him? He nodded and confessed this scared him greatly, but they planned to change their names.

I could only wish Sid luck, and sadly bade my friend farewell. His secret plans and life were safe with me, I knew he must follow his heart and told him so.

'Like you did Ike,' Sid laughed. 'Look where that got you!'

I nodded and wearily walked back up the alley to number One. Pushing open the gate I smiled when I saw Our Sam's bike propped up under the makeshift shelter I'd erected for my first motorbike. Okay, it was a moped, but I enjoyed going out into the country, the wind whipping through my hair, as I rode along the lanes. I remembered one time coming across a herd of cows in the road, an old sheepdog and an old farmer were trying to drive them along. Suddenly the cows saw me and were curious, they surrounded me, snorting and mooing as they inspected my moped and me. I was terrified, but they soon lost interest and decided to obey the dog's sharp yaps and the farmer's yells. 'Ye alreet lad?' he asked, turning round to look back at me.

I nodded, the only thing was, when I stopped, I put my foot down into the biggest heap of cow muck. My shoe was covered and the thick brown squelch seeped into my sock.

That was in the carefree days before I decided to try and seek my fortune in London. I tried to warn Sid the streets weren't paved with gold and tried to advise him on certain areas to avoid. I knew they would no doubt find out for themselves.

Being in love gets you into no end of bother. Quite when I realised I didn't love Alice. I don't know, but how could I tell her?

Arriving back home I heard her voice reading to the kids in the living room. I watched from the doorway for several minutes. Frankie had his head on her shoulder, his arm round Buddy. Conway sat at the other side, gazing up into Alice's face, his arm round Shirley the other twin. All four were rapt in the story and listened intently to Alice's soft voice.

I sighed and Frankie turned his head and shouted Dad. There was a mad scramble off the sofa as the kids tried to reach me all at once. I put my arms around them, Mam came in and announced tea was ready and the kids tried to pull me towards the kitchen.

'Leave your Dad alone now. He'll eat later, come on, your fish fingers are getting cold.' Mam instructed the four of them, picking Shirley up under one arm and Buddy up under the other.

Alice made to follow them, I half put my hand out to stop her. Mam saw this and told Alice to stay, she'd feed the kids. Hustling them all out, Mam closed the door behind her.

'We need to talk Alice,' I mumbled going towards the sofa. I sat down and patted the seat beside me.

Alice went across and perched on the edge of Dad's chair.

'Alice, I need to...' My voice trailed off as I struggled to find the words.

'Ike, it's okay.' She held up her hands, as if in surrender, seeing my frown she continued. 'I know you don't love me, like you thought you did. I know I can't match whatever you felt for Lily. But Ike, I love you and I am sure we can make it work, can't we?' She finished off, her voice rising in desperation.

'It's not fair to you Alice. You deserve someone to love you as much as you love him. I don't...don't think I am that person.'

'No please, Ike, no!' Alice cried and tears streamed down her face.

For a second I wanted to wrap her in my arms and tell her it would be okay. I felt such a heel, no, such a bastard, hurting this lovely girl as I was doing! For a moment I damned Lily for coming back into my life, raking up old feelings I had buried. 'It's not fair to you,' I said lamely.

Alice came over and knelt down in front of me, taking both my hands, she told me to look at her. 'Ike, can you really say you feel nothing for me? Lily is gone you know, she won't be coming back this time.' Alice spoke sharply, but looking down at our hands, she continued, 'Oh Ike, I'm sorry, I shouldn't have said that about Lily. I do understand, she was your first love. But I'm sure you can learn to love again, love me.' She let go of one of my hands and brushed the tears from her face.

I looked down at the tousled hair, her pretty tear stained face. I reached down and swept the hair back from her eyes. 'Alice, I don't know. It's not fair. Yes, I still love Lily, for how long I don't know.'

'I'll wait Ike, please, I'll wait, for as long as it takes.'

I shook my head, it wasn't right to ask her to do that. She had so much love to give, no, it wasn't right to expect her to wait.

I shook off her hands and stood up. 'I don't know Alice, I really don't know. My mind is all over the place at the moment! So much has happened!'

Alice knew she had a trump card and now she played it. 'What about the kids Ike?' she asked, almost casually. 'I love your kids Ike and they love me.'

I couldn't answer her, I just looked down into her sad face staring up at me. 'Give me time,' I muttered. Walking out of the room I went into the bedroom and closed the door.

How did the girl know I didn't love her? How could she beg me like she did? Didn't she have any pride? What she said about the kids loving her was like a knife sticking in my heart. It was so true, they adored her and she was so wonderful with them all. She coped looking after all four in ways Lily never did, in ways I never could. It was all such a mess. I sat on my bed, put my head in my hands, wishing the last few weeks had never happened.

Part Six

Chapter Fifteen

I hurriedly pushed Angela away from home. Taking my sleeping baby out of her pram, I climbed the stairs to my other home. The one I shared with my husband Tom.

Sensing my anxiety he came and folded his arms round me that late afternoon. He asked urgently, 'Ede lass, whatever's wrong?'

'It's Ike Tom, he...he's such a mess. His face is almost black and when he moves it's obviously painful.'

'Aye lass it will be.' Tom spoke gently and told me of the time he had cracked a rib when he fell off the school roof onto a shed. Took him weeks to be able to breathe properly. 'I went up there to get me football,' he said, answering my unasked question. 'I niver pinched any lead or owt. I told you afore that were me stupid brothers an' me Dad.'

I nodded relieved, I trusted Tom, he was so different from some of his siblings. He had a quiet assured way about him. He cuddled Angela, she woke and gazed up at him. The love they shared was strong and he was going to be a brilliant Dad. Not that my Dad hadn't been like, but he had old fashioned ways. He'd certainly had his eyes opened, to the ways of a different world, when he went down to find Ike the first time. Now this too, what would he make of it all? Even though Dad worked in a mill, I knew Alf Wagstaff had never come across drugs, or anyone hurting someone as Lily's Dad had hurt Our Ike. Yes, some of the lads in the mill had their skirmishes, but my Dad had usually stepped in and calmed things down. If they went any further it was always out of work hours, away from the mill and Dad wouldn't know anything about it.

Seeing Ike had shocked me, not only because of his injuries, he seemed so desperately sad too. Surely, he wasn't grieving over Lily as Mam hinted he was. I thought he would hate her and be glad she was dead. I knew I was, how dare she come back into Ike's life after all this time! Spoiling things between Alice and Ike. Yes, I was glad she was dead!

Tom said I shouldn't say things like that, he said it was wicked to speak ill of the departed. Well, he could think what he liked, I was glad she'd gone. Now Alice and Ike could get on with their own lives.

Alice and I were great friends, she had been such a help when I suspected I was pregnant with Angel, she took me to a clinic and everything, she'd been there for me all the way through. I loved the girl to bits; she was the sister I never had. Yes, I was pals with Tom's sister Sadie, but she was a bit too loud and brash at times. I couldn't talk to her, not like I could to Alice.

Tom despaired of Sadie ever settling down, now she was a clippie on the buses it seemed she had no shortage of male attention. She wore lots of makeup and very short skirts. I didn't have brilliant legs and always wore my skirts just above the knee. Sadie was one of the first women I knew, when the 70s came, to wear hot pants. Yes, she liked to be up with the latest fashions.

Phyllis, Tom's youngest sister, appeared to be in some sort of relationship with Our Sam. When I teased him about it, he said they were just friends. Tom and I weren't daft and both knew whatever they shared would turn into something serious, sooner rather than later. Regardless of this I wasn't close to Phyllis either, she was very quiet and studious.

Joan Lister had married in a hurry, producing a huge baby boy, after which she and her boyfriend moved to Sheffield, he was going into the steel industry. We rarely saw them. So that left Alice, my pal. Lucy had been my school friend and though we saw each other occasionally, she was living in a different world, she was at Wharton Secretarial College. Lucy loved it and, whenever we did meet, she was forever regaling me with her latest achievements in shorthand and typing.

Alice seemed to know about kids, she was great with Ike's and now I had Angel, we had much in common, as our talks revolved around babies. I felt so sad she had lost the baby I knew she longed for. One of their own just her and Ike. It would happen one day and I hoped soon, so my Angel could have a little cousin.

About a week after Ike came home, Alice called round early one morning.

'Hi Al, I didn't expect you so early?' I said, beckoning her into the kitchen, where I was washing up.

'I've just dropped the kids off at yer Mam's. I need to go into work,' she mumbled.

'Bit early, ain't it?' I nodded to the clock, which indicated it was only eight o'clock. I knew Alice didn't start till nine in the mill offices. 'You seen Our Ike this morning?'

Alice shook her head, sat down at the kitchen table and burst into tears.

'Oh Al, whatever is wrong?' I pulled a chair round to sit beside her, putting my arms round her shaking shoulders, I reached for a tea towel. 'Now come on, wipe yer eyes and tell me what's to do.'

Alice took the towel and covered her face for a while, then

she sat back in the chair. 'I'm sorry Ede, Ike's your brother, I shouldn't. I mean I didn't know who else to turn to, who might understand what's going on in his head.'

What on earth could she mean? We sat in silence for a few minutes, while I tossed thoughts round in my head. I was grateful Angel slept. What was wrong? Would Alice tell me? She sat rubbing her eyes with the towel. I broke the silence. 'Well, you know Alice, Our Ike's been through a lot lately, getting thumped like he did, having his ribs broke and everything... Well, I mean he's bound to be upset, isn't he? Then, of course, there's her coming back, unsettling everybody, I am glad the b...is dead. Oops! Tom told me I shouldn't say things like that.'

Alice smiled for a brief second and I knew she shared my view about Lily. 'But that's just it Ede, she came back and now he says he doesn't love me anymore,' Her voice trailed off as the tears fell once more.

'What? That's madness Al, what on earth has given you that notion? Of course he loves you, loves the very bones of you.'

Alice dried her eyes again, slowly she told me what she had overheard and indeed what Ike had told her. I couldn't take it in at first. It was madness, Ike and Alice were made for each other. All this crazy nonsense about him still loving Lily. The woman was dead, he was in shock. He'd soon realise what a mistake he'd made. I told Alice this.

'No Ede, he said I deserve better.'

'We'll see about that, just wait till I see my stupid brother. He doesn't know how lucky he is to have you. Yes, I'll tell him, I'll get Angel ready and go round now.'

Alice raised her hand and stood up. 'It's no good Ede, he was adamant. I must fathom out what to do next, I must get to work now.'

She hurried away out of the kitchen and clattered down the stairs, ignoring my calls for her to come back. 'Your Uncle Ike needs his head examining,' I said, lifting Angel, now stirring, out of her cot. Yes, I was still calling her Angel.

She had Tom's big eyes and stared sleepily up at me, I smoothed down her tousled blonde hair. It would go darker, my Mam said, I hoped not, the blonde suited her. Though it probably would change colour, as Tom was very dark, however my hair was blonde, so maybe she would take after me. I'd seen photos of me, at Angel's age, my hair was so blonde it looked almost white on the black and white pictures.

Tom came upstairs, he'd been out early to see Philip Short's MG. It had refused to start, so the man had rung Tom earlier.

'Needed the battery charging,' Tom explained, holding out his arms for Angel. I placed her carefully in them and turned to make Tom some breakfast. 'Stupid man,' he continued. 'Only uses the car to go to work and back! In winter he can barely do no more than a few miles a day in it, he has the heating on full blast and the radio. What does he expect? Needs a good run out to charge the battery up. No matter, I sold him a new one anyway,' Tom grinned down at Angel.

'Tom Lister, what are you like!' I exclaimed. 'You could sell ice to Eskimos! Did he need a new battery?'

'No, it just needed charging up, but he wouldn't leave it, needed it for work and no he couldn't possibly get a bus!' Tom laughed and it sounded like Angel was laughing too.

Placing tea and toast on the table, I took Angel, er okay, Angela, from him, while he ate, I told him about Alice and what she'd told me. 'I'm going to see Ike, this morning!'

'Look Ede, I don't think you should. Leave well alone, let them sort themselves out, though it sounds to me as if your Ike has already made up his mind. A bloke can't help his feelings. You know that!'

'Yes, but she reckons he's said he doesn't deserve her and she should find someone to love her properly. But Tom, you've seen them! Ike does love her!'

'You can't know that for sure and if he's still in love with Lily, well, it's going to take time, I reckon.'

'She's dead! Gone! He can't love a dead person now, can he?'

'I don't know Ede, but I think for once, you should stay out of it. You said yourself Ike seems to be coming round to the fact you and I are married, with a bairn. You said how he looked at Angela, do you really want to alienate him further?'

I shrugged, knowing Tom was right. 'I could just talk to him a bit.'

'I know you're just talking Ede, it wouldn't end up like that, now would it? You would have to get your two pennyworth in and say your piece. Stay away lass, let them sort themselves out. If I know your Mam, she'll have something to say to him, I'm sure.'

I nodded, yes Mam would set Ike straight, of that I was certain. Tom knew me so well, he knew I would have to say something more than I should. I didn't want to antagonise Ike, he seemed genuinely pleased to see me and Angela, when we went round the other day. Yes, Tom was right I should leave well alone, but Alice was my friend.

I tossed and turned that night, unable to get warm and thought of Ike and Alice. Angel woke, fretful, about three am, she felt hot and I was worried. I walked round the room, cradling her in my arms. She went back to sleep, so I laid her down in the crib and crept back into bed next to Tom. He didn't wake, I was half pleased, he worked hard for us and needed his sleep. However, I was annoyed he'd slept on, I desperately wanted to talk to him. Instead I curled myself round his body in an attempt to regain some warmth in mine. I began to shiver, I felt tears in my eyes. I just could not let Ike and Alice split up, it seemed so stupid! Ike still in love with Lily! She was gone and I would make my brother see sense. I didn't care what Tom thought. I would go round there first thing!

It snowed heavily overnight, I woke to hear scraping outside, as I looked out, I saw Tom clearing a drift from the garage doors. It was still snowing and I watched as, a couple of times, he looked up into the sky and let the gentle flakes fall onto his face. I knew the kitchen would be warmer so I lifted my Angel up out of her crib and carried her through, grabbing my dressing gown on the way. Tom came upstairs, snowflakes scattered in his dark hair. I kissed him on the cheek. 'You'll get your death out there.' I giggled, as he returned the kiss on my lips, nearly crushing a grizzling Angela. She still felt quite hot and I voiced my concerns to Tom.

He took her from me and felt her forehead, 'Mm, might be something and nothing, see if she takes her bottle okay. I must go and make a start on the Austin, he's coming back this dinnertime and I still don't know what's wrong.'

I ran off a list of ideas for him and he laughed, 'My Ede, you are a wonder, yes I have tried all those. Now leave it with me will you, and look after Our Angela.'

I nodded and laid her in the carry cot, while I prepared her bottle. 'Breakfast Tom.'

'No, it's okay, I had something earlier, I must get on. The snow looks like it's piling up again.'

I glanced out of the window and grimaced, knowing I would not be getting out to see Ike that day, unless it cleared. Even then I shouldn't really take Angela out in it as she was.

Thankfully she guzzled down her bottle. I sponged her down, changed her clothes and she settled back to a peaceful sleep, in her carry cot. I loved the pretty dresses Mam had made for her, but that day I put her back into a nightgown, it would be warmer and comfier. The kitchen seemed to be mildly warm, I turned up the electric heater we had, fetched my own clothes and got dressed in the kitchen. I made some toast and ate it quickly, seeing Angela still asleep, I made Tom some and with a mug of tea took them downstairs. It was bitterly cold in the garage, even though Tom had lit the paraffin stove in there. He had his head under the bonnet of a small Austin car. 'Any joy?' My voice made him jump, as he hadn't heard me enter, he banged his head on the bonnet of the car.

'Ede, you gave me a start then, what are you doing creeping up on folk?' he laughed.

'Guilty conscience Tom?' I said and nodded to the food and drink.

'By you're a good un, just what I need. No, I confess, I didn't get owt earlier. But you knew that!'

I nodded as I watched him devour the toast and gulp down the tea.

'Little 'un okay, is she?'

'Yes Tom, she had her bottle and is fast asleep, but I'll get back to her and leave you to your fathoming, tested the alternator?'

'Get back up them stairs you minx, of course I have.'

Tom handed back the plate and mug. Giggling to myself I hurried upstairs, Angela was still asleep. I touched her forehead and she seemed cooler. Something and nothing I thought. Just in case I poured myself a cup of tea and huddled over the heater with a baby book in my hand. My Angel was more important that morning, Ike and Alice would have to wait.

Ike had to wait for several days; the snow seemed relentless. It just seemed to thaw a bit and then at night more would come. Mam came round one afternoon, stamping the snow off her boots as she came up the stairs. I was never more pleased to see her, but felt guilty she had come out in such weather.

'Oh Mam, you shouldn't have come! How are you? How's Ike? How's the kids?'

'Steady on Ede, let me get in and get my coat off. Have you got the kettle on? It's perishing out there.'

'Yes, of course sit down, I'll make you a tea.'

I watched as Mam bent over Angela's carry cot and smiled down at her Granddaughter. 'She's just like you were Ede.'

I laughed and busied myself making tea, anxious to know what was happening with my brother.

At last, once she had drunk her mug of tea and I'd poured her another, did I feel I could ask?

'Well Ede, I felt I had to come despite the weather, just to see if you were okay. Isn't it time Tom got the telephone in? With the business and that.'

'Yes Mam, I think it's next on his list, why we were just talking about it. We are good Mam, Tom has been shopping for us. I thought Angela was a bit poorly, the other day she felt really warm, but she took her bottle and seemed okay. I was going to come round but then it started snowing. How's Ike?'

'Good lass, glad you stayed put, no fit weather to take a bairn out in this. Ike well he's recovering, can move about a bit. The mill is keeping his job open for him. He's looking after the little uns today. Frankie is at school and I have just dropped Conway off at that new nursery on Lambert Street.

We are managing now Alice...' Her voice trailed off and she brushed a tear from her eye. 'I don't know what's got into your brother. Frankie keeps asking where Alice is. We've not seen her since...'

'Oh Mam, I know all about it, she came here. I can't believe it, she is the best thing that could happen to Ike and the kids. Then he goes and tells her he still loves Lily and it's unfair to Alice, that she should find someone who will love her back in the way she deserves.'

Mam just nodded and we sat pondering, drinking our tea. 'I wasn't sure what had happened Ede. Ike just said they had decided to go their separate ways. It's ridiculous. Yes, I know Lily's death, and getting beaten up, has had a very bad effect on Ike. I was half afraid he'd go off the rails again like he did before.' Mam clapped a hand over her mouth. 'I've said too much you don't need to know anything about before.'

'It's okay Mam, I didn't know, but talking it over with Tom, how Ike was before, we kinda guessed. But this about Lily? After the way she treated him! It's just bloody stupid.'

'Language Ede.'

'Sorry Mam, it makes me so mad.'

'Aye me an' all lass.'

'What does Dad say? Could he talk to him?'

'No, he knows nowt about what's gone on. Thinks Ike is just in pain from his injuries.'

'Would Ike talk to someone, I think there's something like bere...omething...counselling.'

'You mean bereavement counselling. Yes, might be worth mentioning.'

'I'm sure it would do him good and he will see Alice is the right person for him and the kids.'

'I just hope you're right, he can't go on moping as he is.

Lily has gone, he's got to get on for the kids sake, if not his own.'

I nodded and went to lift Angela out of her carry cot, as she was stirring. I gave her to Mam to hold, while I made up a bottle. I felt very privileged talking to Mam just now, we'd not had such in depth conversations before. I felt so grown up, in many ways I may only have been sixteen, but I was married with a baby and my own home. Yes, Mam had helped and advised a lot, before it was as if I was her pupil, now I felt like her friend and confidante. I handed her Angela's bottle, but she shook her head.

'I'd best get back and see if Ike is coping with the twins. You stay put and keep warm. I've a thick candlewick bedspread at home, it was your Granny's, would you like it?'

I nodded, remembering the lovely pink bed cover, on Granny and Grandad's bed, it would help keep Tom and I warm. What would he say? Something else pink in our room, I grinned mischievously at the thought.

'I'll get Our Sam to bring it round when he gets back from work. Thankfully he's been going in late and coming home early, so he can get the bus. Didn't want him biking in this.'

I gave Mam a hug and took Angela from her. The baby wriggled in my arms anxious for her bottle but I wanted to see Mam off first. 'Take care Mam, love you.'

She nodded and told me she loved me too. I closed the flat door, after seeing her down the steps. I shivered and was glad to get back to the warmth of the kitchen. It felt bitter out there, Tom would be frozen, I just hoped the paraffin stove he had in the garage took the chill off.

Feeding and changing Angel, er I mean Angela, I had to get used to her full name. Mam hadn't mentioned the Christening, yes I thought we should have her christened. Tom was of the opinion that we should let her choose for herself if she wanted to be christened. I disagreed, I wanted a christening, so I'd talk him round. Get Sadie on side, she was desperate to be a Godmother, she'd even asked me if she could be. Well, what can you say? I nodded but did I want Angela's Godmother to be someone like Sadie? She was, well to put it mildly, not the right sort. I'd already thought about this and decided I would ask Phyllis and Alice, with Our Sam as Godfather.

Sadie Lister had quite a reputation for being footloose and fancy free. She told me she was getting fed up of being a clippie and she longed for an office job, which would pay more. I scolded Tom when he said if Sadie was a bit more genteel, she might stand a chance of getting a decent job. Sadie, he said, needed to be more refined. Yes, I didn't think my sister in law was Godmother material. You never know, one day she might settle down. Tom doubted this very much and we would laugh about it. I would remind him that, at one time, he would have been just the same. At this, Tom would mockingly scold me and retort, he was nothing of the sort! He was waiting for me, I doubted this, however it was ancient history, and I was Tom's wife. I felt I could trust him implicitly. He was my first and, I declared, only love. My life felt complete and Angela made our family circle.

It was another week before I could make the journey round to Number One Congleton Terrace. I pushed open the back door and heaved the pram up the steps into the kitchen, I could hear childish giggles and Ike laughing too.

'Ike, glad you are much better,' I said, as I went into the living room, nodding to the twins, climbing on their Dad.

'Yes, much better, ouch Shirley, not that side.' He pushed the little girl away, for a moment I thought she was going to cry. But instead she grabbed at Buddy's hair making him scream. 'Now behave you two or I'll set Auntie Ede onto you,' Ike grinned. The twins stared at me in horror for a moment, their faces broke into a smile and they flung themselves round my legs.

'Baby, Baby,' gabbled Shirley.

'Hush now, Angela is sleeping and we don't want to wake her. Go and see your dolly Shirley, Buddy, you go and play with your train.'

Ike sat, open mouthed, as the twins toddled off to play with their respective toys.

I sat down in Dad's chair and looked at my brother. He pushed his long hair off his face. The action raising his arm, even though the plaster had gone, made him grimace.

'Still hurting Ike?'

'Aye lass, the doctor said it's going to take a while and also for the ribs to heal. But look, the black eye is going.'

'Ike, I wanted to ask about it.'

Ike held up his hand. 'If that's all you've come for, Alice, is it?No, I don't want to talk about her, it's over.'

'I was going to ask why didn't you fight back Ike?' I said, defensively.

'Oh,' he sat back and looked defeated. 'Well, how could I? He was Lily's Dad, an old man.'

'He can't be that old, look what he did to you!'

'Aye well, I guess it hurt when I took Lily away from him.'

'Ike, from what I've heard, you saved her from him, he was abusing her, and look how she repaid you.'

'Ede, how the hell do you know about that? Lily had her reasons for leaving me, postnatal depression, not that you seem to have that. She couldn't cope, she admitted she was wrong and she really did love me.' His voice trailed off, broken by tears.

I reached over and touched his knee. 'Ike, she's gone now

and you have your life and the kids to think about, Alice too, she loves you and I know you love her.'

He pushed my hand away. 'Alice deserves better, I can't love her, not in the way I love Lily.'

'Loved Lily,' I corrected.

'Love Lily,' Ike snapped. 'What do you know about love anyway? You're just a child.'

'I'm married Ike, with a child of my own. I love Tom and he loves me.' I could feel my temper rising, yet knew I had to keep calm, Ike was at least talking to me and I didn't want to fall out with him.

'Yes, I know you are! Are you really happy Ede?' Ike leant forward and stared into my face.

'Oh Ike I am, I am so happy, Angela is perfect. She'll wake in a moment and want her bottle, would you like to feed her?'

Ike shook his head, broke into laughter and told me he'd done that plenty of times.

'The kids love Alice, don't shut her out Ike, Lily's gone.'

Ike stood up and told the kids it was time for their nap. I knew I'd said too much, but I had to get him to see how wrong he was.

Mam came in, she'd been shopping, she watched as Ike and the twins disappeared into the front room. 'Oh Ede, what now?'

'Nothing Mam, I just told him not to shut Alice out.'

'Well, I've said as much. In fact, I ran into Alice at the shops and I asked her to come round, but she won't, said Ike made it very clear he doesn't want to see her. What's more she's moved out of the flat, gone back to her Mother's!'

I gasped, 'No that can't be right, there's something seriously amiss with my brother's mind. Has he agreed to counselling Mam?'

'No, he won't even hear of it. I'm at my wits end. He'll lose the flat if he doesn't get back to it.'

'How's he paying the rent? With not working?'

'Your Dad.'

'Oh Mam, you told me, before Christmas, Dad was saving up to take the two of you on a nice holiday. To stay in a hotel and everything. Not just days out, like we used to.'

'Well looks like that's out the window now. It's what you do Ede, when you've kids, you help them out no matter what.'

I nodded, knowing Angela would want for nothing. I also knew my Mam was very tired, looking after Ike and his four kids. I told her I would come round later and give her a hand with teas and bedtimes.

'No Ede, Ike is doing some of it. You've Tom and Angela to look after, Sam's a good lad, he also does what he can.'

I felt like the worries of the world were on my shoulders that day. I wanted Ike to see sense about dear Alice. I also wanted Mam to have an easier life, I know I hadn't made it easy for her, going against my Dad and taking up with Tom, however I was happy, despite what Ike thought. I just wanted to make my Mam happy too and get her that much needed holiday.

I tried to talk to Sam, when he'd brought the bed cover round, but Phyllis was with him so it was difficult. He didn't seem worried and told me in no uncertain terms, Ike and Alice had nothing to do with me.

Perhaps so, I would talk to Tom and see if he could fathom something out. There had to be a solution to all this mess somewhere. I was glad Lily was dead. Yes, I've said it before and I'll say it again. I was glad too her Father had been arrested and would stand trial for beating Ike up. I hoped they would lock him up for a very long time. In fact they did, he got five years for Grievous Bodily Harm. His girlfriend Esme, we heard, had moved away, wanting nothing more to do with him. Why Lily's Mother couldn't have taken Lily and done the same, I'll never know. How could anyone stay with a man like that? But he got what he deserved just a pity it wasn't sooner or longer.

Part Seven

Chapter Sixteen

Why did Our Ede have to stick her nose in? I asked myself, ushering the twins into my bedroom. It was the front room of Mam and Dad's terraced house. It was also their best room, only used on special occasions. Now it had a single bed in there for me, so I didn't have to climb the stairs. It wasn't, of course, the first time I'd used their best room as my bedroom. There I was, back again, I knew I'd have to get myself right and back to my flat. I wasn't earning and I was thankful to Dad, for helping out with the rent, so I could keep it. Frankie asked every day when we would be going back home to Alice. The little boy couldn't understand why she had suddenly disappeared. He even asked me if she was dead, like his Mother. There was certainly no love lost between Frankie and his Mother, he could remember her well enough and seemed to know she wasn't the greatest at parenting. She was still my Lily and my heart soared when she told me she had never stopped loving me. I realised, while I was in hospital, I didn't love Alice, not like I loved Lily, it wasn't fair, Alice deserved much better. Someone to love her unconditionally, someone without four kids in tow. I knew she wanted her own child, but four was plenty for me. No, I'd done right, Alice needed to find someone else. What it all had to do with Our Ede, was beyond me. She'd made her own bed with Lister, she should get on with it! I wanted to tell her so too, but I heard Mam coming through the back gate and didn't want a row with Our Ede, not in front of Mam or the twins.

Mam was a Godsend, she coped with the kids, took Frankie to school, Conway to nursery and collected them. She was great with the twins too, now I was up and about I did what I could, I helped with tea and bedtime, but Mam still looked tired. I often told her she needed a holiday. She would smile and nod, saying they might get days out. We never went away to stay anywhere on holiday. The only time, when we were kids, we stayed away from home was when Ede was born. We went to our Granny and Grandad's, they were Mam's folks.

I vaguely remember Dad's Mam and Dad, they died close together, when I was a youngster, just after Our Sam was born I think. This house belonged to them, Dad had been born there and now it was his. Mam wanted to move to a new house, but he wouldn't hear of it, so she made the best of it. The place needed modernising, though we did have a bathroom. The kitchen needed updating badly, the stone sink had seen better days. Mam did, however, have an electric kettle, washer and a fridge. Not so long since all the perishables were kept on a stone slab in the pantry and she had a meat safe in there, this was a cupboard with sides of mesh to keep the flies off.

There was once a range in the living room, which was used to heat the water and Granny cooked in the side oven. Mam only ever used this once when, one Christmas, Dad brought home a turkey and it was too big to go in the gas oven. The range was replaced with a modern tiled fireplace and Dad was warned not to buy such a big bird in future.

The rooms downstairs, except the kitchen, had wood polished floors with rugs which Mam and Granny made from rags. Upstairs and the kitchen were lino, but just last year Dad got a fitted carpet for their bedroom. I was glad my flat had fitted carpets, these were left by the previous occupants. They must have been very wealthy, as not many homes had them in those days.

I decided I would go back to my flat at the weekend. Mam needed a break and I was sure I could cope with four kids, they were growing up fast and it was time the twins learnt how to use a potty. That would save on time and washing, Conway learnt quickly, copying his older brother. Yes, I would manage and at teatime informed Mam and Dad of my decision.

'I can go back to work Dad, in a couple of weeks, just need a sitter for the twins.'

'I'll do that, you've no need to go back to the flat yet or work,' Mam said quickly.

'No Mam, you've done enough, you and Dad. I am forever in your debt yet again. How can I repay you?'

'Just get yourself healed lad,' Dad said softly, 'before you think of work.'

'No,' I was adamant, 'I'm off back to my flat and to work. I think Mrs Grimshaw in Duckworth Street looks after kids, I'll go and see her tomorrow. She might even pick Frankie and Conway up after school.'

'I can do that Ike,' Mam protested. I could see in her face she was anxious and perhaps a bit hurt that she couldn't help.

'Okay Mam, you get Frankie and Conway. I'll go and see my boss, see if I can't start a bit later and finish earlier. As long as I get round the farms, with the shoddy, I'm sure he won't mind.'

Dad agreed this might be the case, I felt relieved I had made the decision to take charge of my life.

'I'm sure Alice would help Ike,' Mam said tentatively. 'The kids love her you know'

'No Mam!' I broke in. 'Alice has to find someone who can give her what she wants, it's over between us. I've told you that already.' I could feel my voice rising and the kids looked at me with distrust in their eyes.

'Okay Ike.' Sam said firmly, 'You've made your point, now can we get on with tea. I'm taking Phyllis to the pictures tonight.'

Tea continued in relative silence, if that's possible with four youngsters. I was glad I'd made a decision, it would be good to get back to my own home. I wouldn't think about Alice, as every time I did I felt consumed with guilt. As for Lily, I felt a big lump in my throat when I thought of her. She was my first love and knowing, in the end, she loved me too, well that was all that mattered. I hoped, in time, the pain of her death would ease and I might move on. The bereft feeling just wouldn't leave me. I fell asleep every night crying, I even woke myself up calling her name. If only things had been different, if only we hadn't been so impulsive and ended up with four kids. My fault I knew, but I thought it was what she wanted. What's done is done and can't be undone. I wouldn't change having the kids for the world, I adored them, they made my life worth living. For a while life hadn't been, after Lily left, until Dad made me see sense. I blamed myself for Lily's departure, with my so-called mate! I knew different now, she hadn't been able to cope with the stresses and strains of being a Mum. She'd suffered deeply from postnatal depression after the twins were born, it was much more serious than I ever realised. I just didn't understand or appreciate the difficulties she'd gone through. I was so glad of those few hours I had with her in hospital, when she explained some of it to me.

'I will always love you my Lily,' I said to myself as I got into bed that night.

I tossed and turned for several hours before sleep finally overcame me. Tomorrow was a new day and I had to think about my future, with my kids.

The move went well, with Mam's help of course she kept repeating I needn't go. It was strange back at the flat without the presence of Alice's effects. She had cleared everything of hers out and had even cleaned the place. The Christmas decorations had been taken down and the kids beds made up with fresh sheets. It was only a two bedroomed flat but with two sets of bunk beds, all the kids slept in one room with Frankie and Conway sleeping on top. They loved it, I feared at first they'd fall out, but the beds had rails round, so they couldn't. There wasn't much room for toys in the bedroom. Alice acquired a bookcase and the kids had a plentiful supply of books in there. Beatrix Potter and Peter Rabbit were a firm favourite with the twins, Frankie and Conway preferred Thomas the Tank Engine stories. Mam had donated most of the books from Ede and Sam's collection.

I thought of Ede as I placed Shirley's dolls on her bed. No denying that bairn of Ede's was a bonny little thing, just like her Mother. I still doubted the marriage and despised Tom Lister for taking advantage of my little sister. One day he would turn like the rest of the Listers and I would knock six bells out of him! I'd bide my time, feeling sure that day would come.

'Ike, you okay?' Mam asked, approaching the kids' room. 'Are you sure about this son? Will you manage?'

'Yes Mam, don't worry, now let's go and get the bairns. I wonder how the twins liked being with Mrs Grimshaw. It was good of her to have them on a weekend.'

Mam nodded and put the rest of their clothes away, she must have been up at the crack of dawn washing everything the kids had on yesterday and last night. There wasn't a speck of washing to be done anywhere. I took my pile of clothes from her and went into my room. It was small and the dark blue walls seemed to close in. It also felt empty, with Alice's belongings gone. I stared down at the double bed with its clean sheets and blankets, the bed I'd shared with her. I thought of the sweet girl who, after Lily, seemed an answer to all our prayers. No, I shouldn't feel guilty, I'd done the right thing, I couldn't let her carry on, she deserved better.

'Ready Ike?' Mam appeared at the bedroom door. Her thick tweed coat buttoned up to the neck, she pulled on thick woollen gloves. 'Let's go and pick those rascals up. You bring the twins back here, I've left the gas fire on in the room, warm the place up. I'll fetch Conway and Frankie from home. No sense dragging the twins round to ours, in this weather.'

I nodded my thanks, she was right of course. It had stopped snowing but was still very cold outside. The twins were rolling round the floor at Mrs Grimshaw's, giggling their heads off, they'd obviously had a good time. Buddy ran to me but Shirley hung back, I could sense she didn't really want to leave. 'Come on Shirley, you can come back next week when Daddy is at work,' I grinned and picked my little girl up.

For a moment she wriggled and held her arms out to Mrs Grimshaw, then changed her mind and flung them round my neck. 'Thanks Mrs Grimshaw, see you on Monday? You're sure they won't be too much for you?'

The woman smiled and I realised she was actually much younger than I first thought. She had two kiddies of her own both in their last year at Primary School. 'I've told you Mr Wagstaff, call me Judy.'

'Only if you call me Ike.'

Mam shook her head, as Buddy pulled her towards the door. 'What you like Ike Wagstaff? Got all the women's heads turning!' she scolded mockingly, once we were outside.

'Don't be daft Mam, she's already got a husband.'

'Look Ike, I don't mind looking after these two, it'll save you some money.'

'Stop Mam, we've been through all this, you have done more than enough and picking the boys up in an afternoon will suit me just fine. I can drop the twins off at Mrs Grimshaw's, then drop the boys off, it will work out well, you'll see. I'll be glad if you'll have a rest now, you look worn out.'

'Aye Ike, it's been a busy time, to see you all settled is my one wish. About Alic...'

I held up my spare hand, as I still held Shirley. 'No Mam, I've done right by her, she deserves much better.'

'If you say so Ike, but she would never agree, not when she found the best...YOU!'

'Oh, gi' o'er, you're biased.'

'Of course I am, I'm also proud of the man you have become Ike,' her voice cracked with the threat of tears.

'Mam stop it, you'll have us both bawling.'

The kids settled well that night, they had beans on toast for tea and seemed happy with that. I knew I'd have to learn to cook more, so they could have a proper meal. The twins could feed themselves and I sat with them, watching as they devoured their food. Afterwards I left them playing in the sitting room while I washed up, then it was time for bath and bed. The twins first, they were almost asleep by the time I got the older two ready. Frankie asked when Alice was coming back, so I took him into the kitchen and explained as best I could. I thought he was going to cry, but instead he shrugged and told me it was okay. I half wondered if a school teacher had talked to him. They knew the situation; Mam had mentioned it to them. She told me it felt only fair to be truthful with them, in case Frankie had any problems. I would mention it to the school again, on Monday morning, just to be sure.

Silence soon reigned over my little flat, I went into the sitting room and tidied the toys away into the blanket box I'd got for that purpose. Sitting down I opened the bottle of beer I'd collected from the kitchen. It felt good, the quietness of the place. At Mam and Dad's even when the kids were in bed, there was always constant chatter of the family or the TV. A space had been left where my TV had been. I'd got it on the tick, but when I couldn't afford the repayments, I'd sent it back. Dad was going to pay, but he'd already settled the bills on the flat, the TV was a luxury we could do without. Besides it felt good to just sit, think and contemplate my future. How it would turn out I'd no idea.

I woke some time later, the room felt stuffy and hot. I rubbed the sleep from my eyes and realised it was almost six in the morning. The kids would be awake soon so no sense in going to bed. Daft I know, but the thought of being in a double bed without Lily just did not appeal. Even though it was the bed I'd shared with Alice.

I stood up and stretched, pulled back the room curtains, I saw snowflakes swirling round. There'd be no going anywhere today. How was I going to occupy four kids in this flat all day on my own? It had seemed so easy with Alice, she always had some game or other up her sleeve. I just had to try and remember what they were.

The morning dragged slowly and I felt I'd be glad when bedtime came. I'd told Mam not to come round, as she had suggested, I'd manage for a couple of days. Had to get myself into a routine, I told her.

The twins seemed fractious and tried snatching toys off Frankie and Conway, of course this brought about screams and yelling. Perhaps Mam was right, I couldn't cope. Well I had to, they were my kids and I had to deal with them. I plucked the fought over toys off the kids and told them firmly all the toys were going away. Frankie took himself off in a sulk and I heard the bedroom door slam. Conway sat gazing up at me, the twins just grabbed other toys and gabbled to each other in their own language.

'Come on Conway, help me with dinner.'

The little lad seemed pacified with that and I decided to let Frankie come out of his sulk on his own. He was so like Our Ede, she too would flounce off, slamming her bedroom door at the slightest upset.

The sun came out in the afternoon and I took the four of them to Roundhay Park, where we fed the ducks. The twins climbed on the slide, in the swing park, my two older boys ran round, kicking the snow up. The snow had melted quite a lot, but there was enough to build a snowman. The small cafe was open so we all had a drink there. Yes, I thought to myself, watching the kids tuck into milk and biscuits, I can do this.

'Got yer 'ands full there mister,' the waitress laughed, as she placed a mug of tea in front of me. 'Sure ye' don't want anything to eat thyself?'

I shook my head and looked up into her round very red face, probably caused by the heat from the kitchen. She had tight brown curls, a couple of which had fallen into her eyes. I suppressed the urge to reach up and push it back. 'No, I'm okay, tea is just grand.'

She nodded and shuffled back behind the cafe counter.

We begged some crusts from her and set about feeding the ducks again, seagulls joined in the throng. The kids were delighted to see these birds swooping and diving down to the lake's surface snatching bread from the ducks.

We all went back to the flat tired and cold, but exhilarated. Yes, it had been a good afternoon. I was sure I could organise places to go at weekends that wouldn't cost the earth. I'd try and save, maybe in summer take them to Scarborough, they would love the beach and the donkeys.

I felt tired myself that evening and realised, as I was back at work tomorrow, I'd need a good night's sleep. Somewhat reluctantly I took myself to bed and was amazed how quickly I fell asleep as soon as my head touched the pillow. I didn't even have time to think about Lily or Alice, sleep overcame me so fast. Must have been all that fresh air, it felt good to drift off into oblivion so quickly.

Monday morning dawned bright and sunny, after dropping the twins and then Conway off. I took Frankie to school, he looked nervously at me when I said I needed to see the headmaster. I assured the lad it was nothing to worry about and he went off to play with some boys about the same age as my little lad. I couldn't help feeling nervous, myself, explaining to the headmaster

'Don't worry Mr Wagstaff,' Mr Barstow said. He looked at me over the top of his half-moon glasses. He was an elderly man, ready for retirement. His blue shirt was crisp and clean, but his grey suit was wrinkled and needed a clean. From what I'd heard he thought the world of his pupils and encouraged them greatly, to me that's all that mattered. Frankie's teacher was an older lady, she wore long skirts with socks and sandals, flowered tops and her long grey hair was always tied back. She was a kindly woman and the way Frankie spoke, he was obviously fond of her.

I left feeling happy all was well there. Now I had to face work! I needed to go into the office to collect my instructions for the day; Alice took one look at me and beckoned her colleague to see me. I was a little taken aback, I'd hoped we could, at least, remain friends. Her actions made me realise this was going to be impossible. I half called her name, she turned her back to me and Frances came to the desk. The older woman looked at me, tutted and handed me a sheet of paper. I was to collect all the shoddy from the yard and the delivery list seemed endless, I didn't care. I had to work out my own route, this was good as I knew they were happy for me to start later, so I could get the kids to school, nursery and babysitter. My life was working out, I thought. Mam had also insisted, when I went to get the boys from her, we could all have a meal there. I soon fell into this routine, the kids did too. It was bedtime, by the time we'd get home, weekdays were fine and we all coped well. Weekends were a bit of a chew, keeping them entertained. Well, roll on summer, I'd find plenty to do then and my holiday fund started building up a bit too. I paid Dad back for the bills he'd paid on the flat. The days turned milder and Roundhay Park became our favourite place.

I hadn't seen Our Ede for weeks, she'd obviously given up about Alice. I didn't see her at Mam and Dad's, well only a couple of times. Angela was turning into the bonniest baby I'd ever seen. She was a happy little soul with rosy cheeks and her eyes sparkled when she smiled. I'd like to say the same about my own daughter, Shirley was the opposite, rarely smiled and had her Mother's looks, sullen, Our Sam said more than once. I gave him a clip round the ear for his cheek and reminded him Shirley was my little girl and his niece.

Our Sam... Well, it looked like he was smitten by the youngest Lister girl, courting strong Dad told me. I couldn't help but notice the grimace in Dad's face and voice as he said it. He obviously did not approve, he wouldn't, another Lister in the family, the thought of Ede and Tom still pained Dad. Despite them being happy together and making a go of things. Tom was busy in the garage and talked of taking on another mechanic. By all accounts, according to Mam, Ede wouldn't hear of it. Mam felt sorry for Angela, it seemed the baby was in her pram, in the garage, most days while Ede helped Tom.

Of course, this arrangement didn't last and I frequently found Angela at Mam's. Frankie and Conway loved her to bits and she would chortle and smile at them. Mam was looking tired and when I mentioned it and suggested Mrs Grimshaw pick the lads up, I got my head bitten off.

'I'm fine lad,' she declared defensively. 'It's what Mothers do, if you can't help your kids out looking after their wee ones, then it's a rum do. Besides, I love all my grandkids.'

'Mam I know and believe me I am sure Ede appreciates it as much as I do. It's great coming here for tea every night. But I think you do too much, you look so tired Mam.'

'I'm fine Ike, really I am and the little uns are a breath of fresh air. Besides I cook tea for Sam and yer Dad, a few extra veggies and meat don't make any more work.'

Mam wouldn't hear of me paying her either. All the same I worried and if I could get Dad on his own then I would mention it. Mam looked so pale and the circles under her eyes showed she wasn't sleeping well. Her usually permed and set hair, hadn't had anything done to it for weeks. Something was going on and I aimed to find out, I guess I had to swallow my pride and pay my little sister a visit. There would be words, I knew that, as I thought Mam shouldn't be looking after a small baby. I bet she was washing for Ede too. I'd ask Sam to babysit on Saturday night and go round. He'd offered ages since and asked if he could bring Phyllis. It seemed they had nowhere to go where they could be on their own. Mam and Dad rarely went out and the Lister household would be busy with two of the lads and Sadie still at home.

Chapter Seventeen

Saturday night came and with it a sharp frost too. I slithered my way round to Ede's, after leaving Sam and Phyllis instructions about the kids if they woke up. I was pretty sure they wouldn't, bedtimes were pretty good, now they got into a routine. All four were sound sleepers too.

I knocked loudly on the door to Tom and Ede's flat. It was round the side of the garage, down the alley that led to the river. I craned my neck to see if any lights were showing upstairs, but all seemed in darkness. I had no way of knowing if anyone was in. I rapped loudly on the door again and it was a few more minutes before I heard footsteps clattering down the stairs, Tom Lister pulled open the door. The light from a dim bulb spilled out and he looked very surprised.

'Ike, er hello. What, I mean, come in.'

'Tom, who is it?' Ede's voice drifted down the stairs.

'You'll never guess,' her husband teased.

With that Ede came hurrying down the stairs and shrieked when she saw me. 'Oh Ike, Ike come in, won't you? What are you doing keeping him on the doorstep Tom? It's perishing out there. Come away in Ike.'

'Ede, Tom,' I mumbled, following Ede up the stairs. This was going to be harder than I imagined. I was still coming to terms seeing them together.

I gasped as I stepped through the top door, into the flat, the place was so clean and fresh. Little feminine touches here and there, something my home now sadly lacked.

'I'll put the kettle on Ike, or would you like a beer? I'm sure Tom has some somewhere.'

'No, tea would be grand, warm me up, as you said it's very cold out there.'

'Ike, is all okay?' Ede paused on her way to the kitchen. 'I mean… Oh it's good to see you, but are the kids alright?'

'Yes, they are fine, there is something I want to talk to you about though,' I reassured her.

'Are you going to make that tea lass. Sit thissen down Ike and tell me about your tribe,' Tom grinned. I sat back in an armchair, found myself relating the kids progress and the little quirks they were developing. I was surprised how interested the man seemed to be and how lovingly he spoke of Angela. Maybe I had the wrong idea about him?

Ede bustled in, with a tray of steaming tea and a cake. 'It's from the shop,' she admitted, 'I am learning to cook and bake, aren't I Tom?'

'Aye,' Tom laughed. 'But as soon as I make enough money we shall be having a proper cook.'

Ede laughed and admonished him gently, with a grin on her face, 'See what I have to put up with Ike.'

I bit my tongue, I nearly retorted it was of her own choosing.

'Now then Ike. What's to do?' she asked, pressing a mug into my hand.

Slowly I voiced my concerns about Mam and asked, had Ede noticed how poorly Mam looked these days.

'See Ede, I told you there's no need to get your Mam to look after Angela. I said it was too much!' Tom broke in.

'But she offered Tom. Ike…' Ede pondered for a moment and tears glistened in her eyes. 'Ike, do you think Mam could be really ill or something?'

'I don't know lass, I really don't, but she doesn't exactly look a picture of health these days, does she?'

Ede agreed and wanted to know what Dad said. I had to

tell her I hadn't spoken to him, as I'd not seen him on his own, but I'd try to go down to the allotment the next day. He usually went there on Sundays, whatever the weather, Ede volunteered straight away to come with me now. She offered to look after the kids, after I insisted I should speak to Dad on my own. Tom said he'd mind Angela, telling me he usually did on Sundays anyway, as Ede always had her head in some car book or other.

I finished my tea and ate the cake Ede passed me and told them I'd better go, as I didn't want to leave Sam and Phyllis on their own with the kids for too long. Tom grinned saying he was sure Our Sam wouldn't mind being on his own with Phyllis. I opened my mouth to say none of our family were like that, as he was obviously thinking! Catching Ede's eye I sensed she knew the type of remark I was about to say, so I closed my mouth, thanked them both for the tea and left. I promised to let them know what I'd made out, after my chat with Dad.

The next morning dawned bright and sunny, just as I hoped, Dad was sure to be at the allotment. Ede came round early and I could see she had not slept well, I mentioned it and she told me Angela was teething. I thought the baby was a bit young to be teething but kept these thoughts to myself.

The kids were thrilled to see Ede and the older boys demanded to know where her baby was. Shirley snuggled up beside Ede on the sofa and Buddy clambered on her knee. Ede looked so relaxed and happy. I half wondered if being a Mother was really all she aspired to, she was so natural with the kids, Angela would have the perfect Mum.

'You going Our Ike?' Ede waved me to the door, I pulled on my duffle coat and boots.

'Won't be long kids,' I called, opening the front door.

'Take your time Dad,' Frankie shouted, 'Auntie Ede will look after us.'

'Yes,' Ede laughed. 'Now get thissen gone.'

Dad was busy digging over a patch of his allotment, he looked up in surprise as I called his name. 'By heck Ike, don't see you down here often. What's to do? Everything's alright isn't it? Where's the kids?'

'Slow down Dad, it's like twenty questions! Ede has the kids for a bit, just thought I'd come down and see how you are.'

Dad looked at me, suspicion written all over his lined face. He hadn't shaved that morning, he never did when coming to the allotment. Always had a bath and shave when he got home, you could set your clock by him. Mam usually had Sunday dinner at one and Dad would be in the house by twelve to give him time to clean up and change. He'd be back downstairs just before one ready for his dinner.

'I'm grand lad or I will be when I get this patch dug over. Just hope we'll get some more late frosts to break it up a bit. I didn't get down earlier on this year what with...well, no worries it'll 'ave to do what it will lad. Now I reckon you want to say summat, so thee better come into t'shed. Mam gave me a flask as usual and there's plenty for two cups.'

I followed him into the garden shed, it was a shabby affair constructed from old doors a number of years ago. I'd heard Dad and his folks would go there if there was a threat of bombing, Dad often told us the Germans were bombing factories, airfields and the like, they weren't bombing open spaces, so he reckoned they were safer there.

He indicated an old, wooden orange box and asked me to sit down. I recognised that box, it had stood in mine and

Sam's bedroom for many years, serving as a bedside cabinet. Mam made us a blue curtain for it, this had covered the front, the crate stood on its end with the division acting like a shelf. I lowered myself down, not really sure if it would hold my weight, but sure enough it did. Dad perched on an old kitchen chair and carefully poured tea into the flask top. He passed it over and took a tin mug from a shelf behind him and poured his tea into it. I looked round, cobwebs hung from the roof. The one shelf in there, held boxes of brown envelopes which contained seeds. Tools, fastened to the walls, were clean and oiled ready for use. Plant pots stacked up in every corner and seed trays between the two seats. I took a swig of tea and a deep breath.

'Dad, I wanted to ask you.'

'I knew it Ike, could see by your face you wanted something, what is it lad? Not behind with the rent are you?'

'No Dad,' I held up my hand. 'Nowt like that, it's about Mam, is she...is she alright?'

'How d'you mean lad?'

'Well, it's just...she looks so tired and pale, Our Ede has noticed it too.'

'I meant to ask you lad, are you and Ede alright now?'

I nodded, 'Yes Dad, we are talking, I must say she is grand with Angela and my tribe adore her. I think, well, yes, I'm sure she will be alright with Lister.'

Dad frowned, so I continued.

'I'm sure he's different from his Father and his brothers. Yes, I know he had a bit of trouble with the police when he was a kid, but he seems to be working hard and he's good at his job by all accounts. Mr Lumb, at the mill, suggested I see about taking the lorry there if I have any problems. Seems like Tom Lister is making a name for himself. He adores Angela and Our Ede come to that. Think we may have got him wrong, takes two to tango Dad you know.'

'Hmph!' Dad snorted and I could see he was still reserving judgement. I just hoped I was right in what I'd just said about my sister and her husband.

'About Mam, we are a bit worried.'

Dad looked down at his muddy wellies, he sighed deeply. 'Aye lad, there's something not right, I can see it. Will she go to the doctor? When hell freezes over! She refuses point blank! I've been suggesting it for a couple of weeks now. I'm at a loss lad, I don't know what it is. She just says she's tired, it has been a busy worrying couple of months you know.'

Guilt consumed me, 'Yes Dad, and I am so sorry.'

'Nay lad, it's not thy fault, you did what you thought was best this time. I'd have done the same, guess none of us bargained for Lily's Dad being so vindictive.'

I felt my eyes fill at the mention of Lily's name, Dad touched my arm. 'Come on lad, now what are we going to do about your Mam?'

'I'll talk to Our Ede, she might be able to get Mam to the doctors.'

'That she might Ike, that one could sell ice to the Eskimos. By the way, I just hope you're right about her and Lister. I have to say that little Angela is a bobby dazzler.'

We left family talk at that and chatted about the allotment, Leeds Rugby and Leeds United. I supported United, while Dad was a rugby man, it had often sparked lengthy debates in the Wagstaff household.

Opening the front door, shrieks of laughter spilled into the hall. Kicking off my boots I hurried into the sitting room to find Ede, crouched on the floor and my four kids bashing her with cushions.

'Give in now Auntie Ede?' Frankie yelled.

Ede nodded.

'You promise not to be the tickle monster anymore!' Frankie insisted.

'Yes, Frankie, yes,' Ede giggled.

'Enough now kids, you'll wear your Auntie out. Come and get a drink and a biscuit.'

They followed me into the kitchen, begging for chocolate ones. Sitting them at the table each with a drink and a bourbon biscuit. I filled the kettle and made two cups of tea. Nodding to Ede to return to the sitting room, as we sat down I relayed what Dad had said about Our Mam.

Tears filled Ede's eyes, 'Oh Ike, what are we going to do?'

'We've got to get her to see a doctor, but how, when she refuses, I don't know.'

We sat in silence for several minutes, chewing over our own thoughts and ideas.

'I know!' Ede cried, jumping up from her seat, she dropped down on the floor in front of me and grabbed my hand. 'I've got it Ike, I'll make her an appointment and tell her it's for me and would she come with me to look after Angela. They'll call her name and I'm sure she won't refuse to go in. I'll go with her and tell the doctor our concerns.'

'And if she does refuse Ede? You know what Our Mam's like.'

'She won't Ike, not if I'm there and there's other folk in the surgery.'

I wasn't convinced but Ede was so sure, I had to agree it might be worth a try.

It appeared Ede had an appointment with the doctor two days later. She asked Mam if she would go with her to look after Angela, while Ede saw the doctor. Mam, of course, agreed and it looked like Ede's plan would work.

However, when they sat in the waiting room and the doctor called Mam's name, she took one look at Ede and walked out. Ede came round that evening to tell me.

'I knew it wouldn't work Ede,' I tried to say soothingly, as she was in quite a state.

'Mam was so angry Ike, I've not seen her like that before. She walked home with me, didn't speak, didn't even ask me in for a cuppa or say ta-ra. She just said bye to Angela. Oh Ike what do we do now?'

'I don't know Our Ede, perhaps we should leave well alone. I'm sure Mam is just tired with all the upset. Look, Easter is coming up, perhaps Dad can take her away for a couple of days.'

'I hope you're right Ike, but I worry it's more than just tiredness.'

'Try not to worry Ede, I'll talk to Dad.'

I did talk to him a couple of days later and asked him about taking Mam on holiday. He frowned, money was tight. I knew he'd helped me out with the money they were saving for a holiday.

'I can give you a bit more over the next few weeks, I'm sure I can Dad. Mam needs a rest and the change will do her good.'

'Okay lad, I'll see what's what and how much we can afford. You're right of course, it's been a tough year for all of us. No, I'm not blaming you Ike, so don't look at me like that.'

'I'm sorry Dad.'

'No need lad, what's done is done.'

It never ceased to amaze me how forgiving and laid back my Father was, but then his own parents had been just the same. I hoped I'd be like that with my kids when they brought their troubles home. Already I shouted at them a bit too much, but they needed it now and again. Frankie was getting very bossy with the little uns, and the twins had started bickering over toys. I heard Fathers at work talking about their kids, when we were together in the canteen, and realised it's all part of growing up. It wasn't like some of the bad problems other kids had, one lad had spat at his teacher. He'd got the cane for it off the headmaster, and a good hiding off his Dad when he got home, the lad was only eight. I'm not sure I agree with smacking, to me it showed violence to kids and I'd never seen that at home. Well, except for the time Dad hit Our Ede, she was being clever and answering him back, it was all over the engineering college. The more I thought about it, the more I realised, it was Our Ede getting her own way! In the Autumn she was going to engineering college one day a week, she'd get her qualifications she told me, come hell or high water. Aye, she'd got it all worked out, but her plan with Mam had failed.

I told Dad and he nodded, told me he'd heard all about it off Mam when he got home from work. 'By she was blazing Ike, said she didn't need a doctor, she just wants peace. But I tell you lad I've never seen Lib like that, so perhaps there is summat up!'

I could see Dad was worried. 'Take her away for a couple of days Dad, she likes Scarborough. I wonder how much it is to stay in that big hotel that overlooks the bay?

'The Grand, you mean? An arm and a leg I would think. But I'll look into it, I know when we've been for day trips, I've seen some nice little bed and breakfast places, on the North side right by Peasholm Park. I think she'd like that.'

'Yes Dad, I'm sure she will,' I conjured up an image of the two of them walking through Peasholm Park, hand in hand. Yes, true they may have been married a long time, but Dad always took Mam's hand whenever they went out. It was very reassuring for us kids to see them. Some kids would be embarrassed, not us, we'd grin at each other and feel secure that our folks thought enough of each other to still do that.

Chapter Eighteen

The weeks passed quickly and we all fell into a routine. In the spring sunshine, even Our Mam looked a bit better. Easter was just around the corner and just as he said, Dad was taking Mam to stay at the Grand Hotel in Scarborough for the weekend. I chipped in to pay a bit towards it, as being Easter it was probably double to what they would normally charge.

The kids settled into a routine of their own, Judy Grimshaw was happy to take the older boys in the school holidays and all four seemed to enjoy going to her house. Judy was mousy, although she looked middle-aged, I guess she was only in her mid to late thirties. She didn't mind being teased by Frankie, when she had her rollers in her hair, secured with a headscarf. Frankie had even called her Hilda one day, Judy laughed when she told me, she said she was quite pleased to be called after the famous Coronation Street character. I hadn't a clue who she was talking about. How Frankie knew anything about it I had no idea, guess it was from the older kids. Mam told me she noticed Frankie always came out of school with some of the older boys, when she picked him up. Mam mentioned a few of their names and I began to worry, their Father's might be some of the lads I knew and disapproved of, when we were young, some of them were always getting into mischief. I just hoped I was bringing Frankie up not to be naughty just to keep up with his peers. In my youth, I was often pressurised, but knew it was wrong. I had a strong enough character, back then, to say no and I did more than once. I felt guilty, I hadn't said no to the drugs, events had left me weak.

I saw Alice now and again at work and she would politely ask after the kids. They had got used to her not being around and stopped asking for her.

They were inundated with chocolate Easter eggs from everyone. Mam and Dad got them two each, not to mention Ede, Sam and folk at work. I got Angela a teddy, well she was only a few months old and too young for chocolate. She seemed to have a big smile on her face every time we saw her. Ede looked radiant too and everyone could see how happy she was.

I mentioned Judy Grimshaw to her one day, when Ede was rabbiting on about going to college after summer. She smiled, nodded and mused how she wished college's had child care places, as there seemed to be more and more older students, with children, wishing to go back to learning. Ede felt sure one day it would come.

At times I felt jealous of Ede's relationship with Lister. It was obvious they thought the world of each other, you only had to look at them to see that. I'd never shared that with anyone. Well, maybe Lily in her last few hours, I sighed deeply thinking of her.

'What's up Dad?' Frankie asked, clambering onto my knee.

'Nothing lad, just a bit tired,' I told him, stroking his dark hair. 'I'll have to take you to the barbers lad, your hair's growing so fast, just like you are.'

We laughed together and he snuggled into my shoulder, it was only for a few moments, then Conway and the twins wanted to be in too, before I knew it, I was on the floor, trying to put my arms around them all. They giggled, I felt a lump in my throat that I couldn't explain, I only felt Lily should be there with us.

Mam and Dad returned from their Easter break, both

with a spring in their step. The weather had been good and Mam raved about the hotel and the food. They'd been on the North Bay Railway to a place called Scalby Mills, right at one end of Scarborough's North Bay. Mam had been thrilled by the concert they had been to, at the Open Air Theatre. But she declared nothing could beat the fish and chips, eating them out of newspaper, as they strolled along by the sea.

I agreed, I remembered the fish and chips we'd always had, before returning home, after a day trip to the coast. Mam usually packed sandwiches for a picnic lunch, which we ate in the car when it was too cold to go on the beach. If it was warm enough then it was sandy sandwiches all round, us three would then try and bury each other in sand, kicking it off wildly when told the tide was coming in. We always had a few pennies to roll in the arcades. Then our fish and chips and the drive home, singing numerous songs.

I was very surprised Dad had agreed to take Mam away, as far as I knew back then he had never stayed away from Number One Congleton Terrace.

Dad caught the sun a bit and his face had a rosy glow. In summer, with working on the allotment, this glow would turn golden brown, his hair looked greyer than I remembered. Mam looked well though and declared they were saving up for a trip to Morecambe, in the summer. Now this was adventurous, as Morecambe, for those who don't know, is on the West Coast. Dad said he didn't know about going that far, until I pointed out it was probably not much further from Leeds than Scarborough, which is on the East Coast. We laughed, in the end that summer, they went to Blackpool.

I began to feel lonely, the company of four young kids didn't make up for the company of another adult. I confided in Our Sam and he said, why didn't I ask Sadie Lister for a date? I stared at him in horror. Sadie had quite a name for herself, I wanted none of that. Besides two of Dad's children being involved with Listers was more than enough.

'Oh you sound just like Dad,' Sam said, when I echoed these thoughts to him. 'Sadie's alright you know, okay she's loud and brash, but underneath all that she has a good heart and can be very kind and gentle.'

'Oh aye and how would you know young Sam, been there have we?'

'Don't be so vulgar Our Ike! You know I am with Phyllis and actually, I'm…'

'Go on, spit it out.'

'Well,' Sam looked down at his hands and mumbled, 'I'm thinking of asking her to marry me.'

I stared at him in horror, my kid brother was thinking of marriage. 'You're too young!'

'I'm older than Our Ede!'

'Aye well, she was much, much too young, we know why that was allowed to happen! Phyllis isn't in the family way is she?'

'God no Ike! What do you take me for?'

I stared at my brother, realising, he and Phyllis hadn't even slept together, in fact I didn't think Our Sam had slept with anyone. He looked so young and naive, what could I say?

'Well young Sam, just make sure of a secure job, with plenty of money cos you'll need it.'

'Oh, we would only be getting engaged, probably a few years before we do get married. By then I am hoping to be made a supervisor and Phyllis could be higher up in her job at the library.'

Sam had obviously thought it all out, but he frowned and wrung his hands together.

'Sounds like a plan, but what's up Sam?'

'What...what will Dad say? You know how he feels about the Listers! He won't be very happy, will he?'

'He knows you're seeing her?'

Sam nodded, 'Well yes, of course, I rather think he's hoping it will fizzle out. He's polite enough to Phyllis, when she comes for tea, but he isn't very friendly. Do you know what I mean?'

I nodded, Dad was never one to show or share his feelings. I was sure he would accept Sam's choice and be okay with it, I said to my doubting brother.

Sam got up to leave shaking his head and mumbling he wasn't sure, wasn't sure at all.

'Sam wait, look lad,' I laid a hand on his shoulder, 'it's your life and like Our Ede has always claimed, you must follow your heart, Phyllis loves you and you love her right?'

Sam nodded.

'Well then, don't let anything or anyone come between that,' I told him.

Sam left smiling and I was glad. Phyllis Lister may be the quiet one but she and Sam would make a good life together. I smiled to myself, me giving out advice to someone else, when I should be giving it to myself! Sadie Lister? Dad would have a fit. Besides Sadie had always seemed one of the lads, I had no feelings in that direction at all. So I hoped Sam would forget that idea.

Little did I know he'd been talking to Ede and the pair of them had come up with the idea of me asking Sadie out. I saw Ede the following day at Mr Patel's shop. Ede had left Angela in the pram outside and Frankie declared he was staying with her to see she was okay. I bustled the other three into the shop and Ede was just leaving.

'Hi Ike, Mam and Dad had a good time, didn't they? Mam

looks so much better.' Ede enthused, I nodded and couldn't get a reply in before she went on. 'Say, Ike, it's time you had a bit of fun in your life. You know Sadie is free at the moment, why not ask her out? Sam and Phyllis would babysit for you.'

'Now look here, you and Sam can forget that notion! I am not going out with Sadie Lister. Not now! Not ever!'

'Why not?' A silky voice crooned, I turned quickly and looked straight into the face of the woman we'd been talking about. I hadn't seen Sadie for a while and she had changed, her hair was long, she had curves in all the right places and she looked good in her bus conductress uniform, she wore the skirt well above her knees, which seemed to emphasise her shapely legs.

I had the grace to turn crimson with embarrassment and muttered I wasn't ready to go out with anyone, I hadn't meant just her. I felt I was digging myself in deeper, so I hustled my three up to the counter, grabbed the bread and milk, I'd gone in for, and left, leaving Ede and Sadie gabbing outside the store, they were laughing. Was it at me? I had no idea. I just knew I wanted to be away double quick.

'Hold up Ike,' Ede shouted, as she ran up behind me, Angela giggling at the speed of her pram. 'Look I'm sorry, I know you still think about...' Her voice trailed off as I glared at her, nodding to the kids. They didn't need reminding about their Mother. 'Sorry,' she mumbled, looking round at my four solemnly and then giving them all a hug and a sweetie from her pocket.

The kids were delighted and hugged Ede back warmly. I realised, when she produced a bag of penny sweets bought from the shop, she was still a bairn, she always loved those penny goodies. I used to buy her a packet of them when I was at home from my pocket money or my pay. Mam used to say I spoiled her. Guess I did, well I only had one kid sister as she was then and still is now.

'Ike think about Sadie, it's time she settled down and she does like you,' Ede persisted.

'Look Ede, no offence but don't you think two Listers in our family is enough? Sadie will never settle down, you and I both know that, besides I am capable of finding my own friends. But right now these scallywags are more than enough for me to think about! Right?'

Ede nodded and mumbled something about Tom's dinner and said goodbye to us all.

'Can we go to the park Dad, please?' Frankie said, his mouth full of goodness knows what.

'Don't speak with your mouth full Frankie. We'll see after dinner, it may have dried up by then.'

Frankie seemed placated with that and took Conway's hand in one of his and Buddy's in the other. I held tight onto Shirley's small mitt, she was a tyke and often struggled away from me wanting to toddle on her own. We slowly made our way back to the flat and I was glad to have five minutes peace while I prepared lunch.

Sadie Lister had changed, gone was the heavy make up she always wore. Her hair was long and she was bonny, I recalled her huge brown eyes laughing at me. Frankie soon brought me out of these thoughts. 'Dad, Buddy has pooed and Gawd it don't half stink!'

I bundled him out of the kitchen, chastising him lightly about his language whilst laughing to myself. Frankie sounded so grown up and his accent was a right mix of Yorkshire and East End of London. I took the offending Buddy into the bathroom and decided the best course of action was to remove his nappy and give him a bath. It wasn't long before the others traipsed in and started undressing themselves to join Buddy, well Shirley wanted to get in as she was. Soon we were all laughing and splashing water all over. It was times like this I loved being with the kids, their shining faces wreathed in smiles, as they splashed one another and me. Lily hadn't, very often, had moments like this, even if she wasn't working, she always left me to bathe them, I loved it. Lily had missed, and would miss, so much. Ede was right, it was time I forgot Lily and moved on with my life. I'd had to be both parents to the kids for so long and needed to continue. The boys were fine, but Shirley, she would need a Mother at some point, I forgot momentarily that boys need Mothers too. Look how much I had relied on mine. Thank goodness the holiday had perked her up. She looked more like her old self, thinner, but had colour back in her cheeks and didn't look as tired. We three knew Mam was the lynch-pin of our family and quite what we would do without her didn't even bear thinking about.

Losing Lily, well that was something totally different. The feelings still raged through me. Anger at her leaving me and the kids in the first place and I still felt angry at her leaving our lives permanently even now. Yet I loved Lily, despite everything, I always had and part of me always would. I was devastated when she came back and wanted the kids, I hated her then, but something inside me ignited the flame I once felt and I thought I could persuade her to come back to us. I was just glad I could spend the last few moments with her and I warmed at the realisation she actually loved me. I guess now it was the kids themselves she hadn't been able to cope with, she was young and having four so quickly, I think it suffocated her. I could partly understand, but then look at them splashing in the bath, how could any Mother leave her babies like she did? Love, surely, conquered all other feelings. Well, that's what I believed.

My thoughts turned to Our Ede and I wondered, she was so young to be married with a baby, I hoped she wouldn't feel the same and she would have a life, before any other babies came along. Yet Ede loved kids, she was great with my four. She seemed to glow when she was around Angela. I thought of Tom Lister, how could he have been so stupid, to get my sister pregnant. I thought of Dad and how he seemed to accept it and allow Ede to marry at just turned sixteen. I knew Ede still had designs on training to be a mechanic. I guess she had thought about it all. I knew Alice had taken her to the clinic and an abortion had been suggested. Perhaps that would have been best for her and perhaps for Lily. No, that wasn't worth any thought! As my Granny would have said, 'We'd made our beds, we must lie on them.' All the same I hoped things would be different for my kids, Ede and Angela too. Tom Lister had stepped up to the mark and he appeared to idolise both of them. One day I might find someone else, but for now my four needed drying and feeding. A mammoth task in itself with all four together. Frankie got out first and he's a good lad, he helped dry the others, maybe not properly but enough to keep them occupied, while I got each of them finished off and dressed. Yes, Frankie was growing up and seemed older than his few years. Would he always be there to help? I hoped so, but I knew I wouldn't expect him to or take him for granted, of that I was very set in my mind.

DEVOTION
DANCE HALL
DEVOTION
DANCING

Chapter Nineteen

The days led into weeks and months, time rolled by. The kids were growing fast and the flat was filled with childish chatter, giggles, rows and tears. Somehow, I coped. Mam helped out on Saturdays, babysitting, while Frankie and I did the shopping. Judy Grimshaw was amazing and took the kids more than I, actually, paid her for. The kids loved being with her during the school holidays. I was enjoying my driving job taking waste out to the farms.

The days were warming up nicely and the world was seeing many changes. There was even talk of sending men to the moon. Leeds, itself, was growing, with new shopping centres and the like. Thankfully, the market hall remained untouched and I loved spending time there, wandering about with Frankie, picking up the odd item of clothing, or a toy, for the kids. Money was tight and most of the clothes, the kids wore, Mam picked up for me at jumble sales. I remember she got Our Ede some lovely designer baby dresses for Angela. Ede was thrilled and Angela was the best dressed baby in the area. Ede wanted to enter her in a bonny baby competition, but she told me Tom wouldn't hear of it. I agreed with him on that, I even admired him for standing firm.

One sunny afternoon in late June, I was driving the lorry out Wetherby way. My arm hung out of the driver's window as usual, I hummed the latest pop tunes to myself. Suddenly a female on a bike pulled, out of a lane, straight in front of me. I cursed as I stamped on the brake, simultaneously yelling at her, 'What the hell do you think you are doing?' The sound of my angry voice must have startled her, the bike wobbled ahead of me and fell over, depositing it's rider onto the grass verge.

I jerked the hand brake on, jumped down out of the cab and ran to her aid. I was still angry. Grabbing her arm, I pulled her up and yelled, 'Why can't you look where you are going?'

'I... my...' the girl burst into tears, a look of sheer terror on her face. 'My brakes wouldn't work,' she sobbed.

I felt such a heel, 'Oh my, I'm sorry, I shouldn't have yelled. Are you okay?'

She sniffed loudly and rubbed her eyes on the sleeve of her blue shirt, the colour matched her eyes. I pulled out my hankie, glad it was clean, and held it out to her. She took it and blew her nose loudly, folding it over she wiped her eyes. For a moment I thought she was going to give it back to me. 'It's okay, keep it,' I said quickly.

She muttered her thanks and turned to pick up her bike. She wore trousers tucked into wellingtons. Her auburn hair was a mass of tousled waves. She was slim and about my height, I guessed she was about twenty. She made to get on the bike, I reached out and put my hand on the handle bars. She blinked rapidly and stared at me, fear flashing in those remarkable blue eyes. 'It's okay,' I reassured her, 'I just...I mean, you can't ride that bike with no brakes. Mind if I take a look?'

'I... Oh no... I mean... Yes, thanks,' she stammered.

'Good, now let's see what's amiss,' I said, lifting the bike and turning it upside down. It was clear the brakes were well and truly ceased up on one wheel and the brake pad on the other was none existent. I tried my best to free the jammed brake, but my efforts were in vain. I turned and smiled at her, then confessed I couldn't fix it. I turned the bike right way up. She returned the smile a little hesitantly and muttered her thanks, taking the handlebars of the bike, she made to walk off.

'Where are you going?' I gabbled, 'I mean, how far?'

She stopped and turned, smiling more confidently this time. 'Oh, about a couple of miles, my Mam rang the farm… where I work, she's not well, so I need to get home in a hurry and I grabbed this old bike out of the barn.'

'Well, you're not going anywhere with that. I'll put it on the back of the truck. You hop in and give me directions, I'll soon have you to your Mam's.'

'I can't...put you to any bother...but thanks.' She released her grip on the bike and this time her smile reached those lovely blue eyes.

I hauled the bike into the back of the lorry. Thankfully it was empty as I was on my way back to the factory. I explained my job to her and told her my name.

'I'm Eleanor, well most folk call me Ellie, which I like. Can you turn left here please?'

'Okay Ellie, is this where you live?' We were driving towards the small village of West Kirkby, about a dozen or so houses, most of them painted white and they gleamed brightly in the warm sunshine. One of them still had a thatched roof and looked very idyllic, it even had roses round the door. For some reason I was delighted when Ellie asked me to stop outside it, as this was where she lived with her Mum. She jumped down and went towards the gate, seemingly forgetting about the bike.

'It's okay, you go and see your Mam, I'll get the bike, or would you like me to take it back to the farm?'

She shook her auburn curls, she would get the farmer to come by and pick it up, she told me before hurrying into the house. I got the bike out of the back of the lorry. No harm in having another look at it. I remembered I had an oil can somewhere. Locating it, I turned the bike upside down and began oiling and coaxing the brake into working once more. I couldn't do anything about the worn pad on the other side, but I figured she had one good brake.

I looked up as the cottage door opened, Ellie grinned at me, relief in her face. 'Mam's okay, she had a bit of a fall, but nothing broken just shook her up and she panicked.'

'You're sure she's okay? I mean does she need to get an x-ray? I could take her?'

'No she's fine, nothing swollen just a sprain, luckily the neighbour heard her cry out and the doctor has just been. He checked her over and it's fine, but he did ask if she could get me to stay at home for a bit, as she needs to rest, I know Mr Gill at the farm won't mind, sorry I'm gabbling on. Thanks, by the way, for the lift.'

'Good, I'm glad your Mam's okay and the pleasure was mine giving you a lift. How do you normally get to work?' I asked impulsively.

Ellie's face was flushed pink, 'I walk,' she mumbled.

'Look, I could take this bike and get it properly fixed up for you, might take a day or two, but I'll be back round here then. I could bring it for you, at least you'd have a bike to go to work on.' I held my breath, I hoped she would say yes, I knew I wanted to see her again. 'That is if the farmer will let you have it.'

'I'm sure Mr Gill will, it's really kind of you, but are you sure?'

'Of course I am, wouldn't have offered otherwise.' I slung the bike back onto the lorry, climbing into the cab, I added, 'See you in a few days and again I'm glad your Mam's okay, bye for now.'

I whistled, as I drove off, glancing in the rear view mirror

I saw Ellie, standing by the gate, looking my way and waving. I stuck my arm out of the window and waved back. The day was very much brighter as I thought of Ellie, with her auburn hair and blue eyes.

The kid's misbehaviour could not dispel my mood, I put the bike in Mam and Dad's backyard. Sam was home so I asked him if he'd babysit, Sam of course jumped at the chance, 'As long as Phyll can come too,' he asked, shyly.

I nodded, knowing once again, this was a chance for my brother to do his courting. The kids played me up no end and despite my promise to have them all in bed and asleep before Sam and Phyll came, I knew this wasn't going to happen. Frankie was determined to stay up, Conway had just settled when Frankie shouted his Uncle was here.

Phyllis got dragged into the sitting room. Frankie plonked himself down on the sofa next to her with the Thomas the Tank Engine book, Sam and Phyllis had got him for Christmas — how he loved that book. He sat, gazing up into Phyllis's angelic face, completely rapt in the story she read in her soft voice.

Phyllis Lister was so different to the rest of her family. She was dainty, I guess you'd say, with an angelic face, gentle ways and soft voice. Her older siblings were large, loud and brash. I could never understand how or why she was so different. Oh, I had my suspicions that perhaps she wasn't old man Lister's daughter, I kept these to myself. These thoughts had been raised by Alice, who often commented on it. Whatever, Our Sam was completely smitten with the girl and although I didn't approve of the Listers, there was nowt really I could do about my sibling's feelings towards them.

Tom, I begrudgingly had to admit, seemed to be turning

out okay for Our Ede. He worked hard and looked after Ede and Angela. Ede even told me they could afford disposable nappies, I was in awe of this. How easy it would have been when mine were in nappies, instead I managed the towelling ones, steeping them in a bucket to get the stains out. Washing took forever and drying them was a nightmare! Lucky Ede, being able to just wrap them up and put them in the bin! Lily and I couldn't afford such luxuries, especially, when Frankie was a baby, they seemed hugely expensive. The twins were still in nappies and towelling ones, at that, for the same reason, my pay did not run to such luxuries. Judy Grimshaw was training the twins to use the potty; it wasn't going down too well. But we'd get there, as I did with Frankie and Conway, so we would with the twins and life would be much easier.

'Got a date then Ike?' Sam grinned at me.

'No, I'm going back to fix that bike,' I retorted, rather too sharply.

'Oh aye and whose bike is that? Cos it's a female's,' Sam scoffed back.

'Aye, it's for a pal that's all.'

'You need Our Ede then Ike.'

'Well yes, she might be useful, I'll call for her on my way. Now ten minutes Frankie and then bed.'

The little lad nodded and looked up at his Uncle Sam, 'No good giving me that mournful look,' Sam smiled. 'You heard your Dad, ten minutes and then bed. I don't want any trouble off my big brother.' He winked at Frankie and I knew the little lad would play his Uncle up, he'd probably go to bed when he heard me opening the front door. Sam and Phyllis would always tell me he'd gone earlier, but I knew, Frankie could wrap them round his little finger.

Whistling a merry tune, which I realised was an old music hall song, I made my way to Mam and Dad's. I wasn't going to call for Ede, I didn't need her, I could sort the bike out myself.

I let Mam know I was in the yard and set to before it got too dark to see, though Dad had put an outside light up, so I knew I'd be able to see with that if need be. Mam was curious as to the owner of the bike, I maintained it was just for a friend. Well, at least that's what I hoped Ellie would become. For a moment I hoped more, then reality struck home, she lived out in the country and I had no transport of my own. The motorbike had been sold to buy a car and the car had been sold as I couldn't afford it on my wages alone. The only transport I had was the factory truck and that had to be left at the factory every night and at the weekend. I knew I would also have to tell Ellie about my four kids, she wouldn't want to know then, I was sure of that.

I managed to get the bike sorted by the weekend, I'd stripped the brakes down, with new pads and a new inner tube, the bike was sound. I'd even been able to give it a coat of paint. Ede came round to check my work over and told me Tom would lend me his van, when I explained my friend lived in the country. I was hesitant, I didn't really want to be beholden to Tom Lister, but I wanted to see Ellie. So I accepted and on Sunday morning, Mam had the kids, I set off for Ellie's.

She opened the door and gasped a surprised hello. I went to the van and lifted out the bike.

'That's not Mr Gill's bike, is it?' she laughed.

I nodded and explained the work I'd done.

'How much do I owe you? I can't let you do all that and give you nothing!' She cocked her head on one side and grinned.

'Call it compensation for knocking you off it in the first place.' I held my hand up to stop her protest. 'A cuppa would go down a treat though,' I added cheekily.

'Of course where are my manners, come in and meet Mam.' Ellie held the door open for me, I propped the bike against the fence and went into the cottage.

Ellie's Mam greeted me warmly and reached for her purse when Ellie explained about the bike, I shook my head and retorted that a cuppa would be fine. Ellie disappeared into the kitchen and at first it was a little awkward talking to her Mother, soon conversation flowed about the weather, village life, and how her ankle was doing. Ellie returned with a tray of tea and delicious looking slices of cake. Realising I hadn't had breakfast I accepted a piece and congratulated Ellie, when her Mam told me it was Ellie's own baking. I glanced up at the clock as I drained my cup, time I was off back home. My Mam had been looking after the kids long enough. She may look well but I knew she tired easily, this was still a concern for me and Dad, I didn't think Sam or Ede noticed.

Ellie came to the door and put her hand on my arm, 'Thank you,' she breathed, reaching up to give me the lightest kiss on my cheek. It startled me and I drew away sharply, her smiling face turned to horror. 'I'm so sorry,' she said.

'Please don't be, it was, a surprise that's all. A nice one though,' I said stepping back to face her. 'I didn't mean to... Well, you know, I was surprised. I...I'd like to kiss you properly.' My voice trailed away and I studied her face as she absorbed my words.

'Go on then,' she said, so quietly I wondered if I'd heard.

'Look Ellie, I'm sorry...but there's so much about me you don't know. I can't...'

Her blue eyes stared at me. 'I would like to get to know

you Ike.'

'I can't, I just can't.' I turned abruptly and walked down the path. Opening and closing the gate, I let my hand linger on it. 'See you around, take care on the roads on yer bike.' I knew I was gabbling, but I needed to be on my way, yet I needed to stay.

'Thanks Ike, goodbye.'

'Oh hell,' I cried and shot back through the gate, in seconds she was in my arms and I kissed her. 'I have to go now, but I will see you again,' I promised and made towards the gate again.

'When Ike, when?'

I looked at the name of the cottage on the gate. I decided I would write to her to tell her about my Lily and our kids. Yes, that's what I'd do. 'Soon,' I told her and blew her a kiss before climbing into the van and heading back towards Leeds.

I went over and over in my mind the moment our lips touched. It felt right and good. She returned my kiss with longing. Perhaps we could work something out. I would write to her that night. I'd tell her all and after that, I could do no more, it had to be up to her. I doubted she would ever want to be mixed up with someone who had a ready made family. There was no way in this world that would happen and was it fair to her? I knew I would write to explain and pray she liked me enough to reply at least. The words formulated in my mind as I drove along. I'd never been one for expressing myself verbally, in a letter I might be able to. I could only try and hope and pray. I wanted to see Ellie again, so very much. Time would tell, wouldn't it?

Sam opened the back door of Number One Congleton Terrace. 'You sound happy,' he grinned.

I hadn't realised I was whistling, I grinned back at my younger brother, at last he was joining the sixties, he was letting his hair grow longer. I noticed he had a pair of jeans on too. What on earth was happening? As if I didn't know! Phyllis Lister! That's what was happening, she was changing my little brother. He usually wore green trousers for work and had a best pair for going out. He rarely wore tee shirts, always a shirt of some description, but blow me now, not only were his jeans black, he had a red tee shirt on too! I let out a slow whistle of amazement. 'Looking good our kid,' I said, as he pushed past me. 'Mam, what on earth has got into Our Sam? He looks bang up to date.'

Mam laughed and my two boys flung themselves round the table to give me a hug.

'By, you look cheery yourself Ike and I don't think it's seeing Our Sam in his jeans. He got them on his way home from work, went to that big store that's opened. You know the one that sells everything and you help yourself. I worry it will put the corner shops out of business, but I shall still go to them, the greengrocers and the butchers. Can't be doing with these new fangled ideas. Food shops selling clothes, whatever next, I wonder!'

I laughed and reached for the lad's coats, 'Come on lads, we'll leave your Granny to her wondering.'

Mam was right of course whatever next? The corner shop at the end of Elland Street had gone self-service. The kids liked to go to our corner shop and watch two ounces of sweets being weighed out by Mr Patel, he always put one extra in after he had finished weighing them. With self-service, little touches like that would be well and truly flung out of the window. All in the name of progress, but what about customer care and service.

My mind turned to Ellie, she was a beauty and no mistake. I'd write that letter tonight and see what response I got, if any, to her knowing I was a widower with four children, widower, the word choked me, I still thought about Lily. I know I should hate her but I'd forgiven her, I guess when you love someone, like I loved Lily, you can forgive them anything. She was the Mother of my four kids and I wasn't going to let them forget her. Frankie was adamant, he did not want to hear anything about her, the twins were too young. Conway, however listened, he still called for his Mammy when he had a bad dream. It tore my heart out. The kids had adored Alice, but I couldn't think of her, only as a friend and she deserved much more than that. Ellie however, well, we'd just have to see.

That night, after the kids were sleeping, I took out paper and pen and wrote. It took several sheets of paper, most were screwed up and thrown away. But at last I thought I'd made it clear that I liked her and hoped to see her again, however she must know about my children, also about Lily, as she was their Mother, and I would always tell them about her. I told her about my drug taking, Dad bringing me home, Alice, Lily's death, I left nothing out. If I'd learned one thing it was to be truthful and upfront about things. I left it to Ellie, I told her I would understand, she would probably not want to see me again, not want to be involved. I asked her if she would drop me a line, just to let me know how she felt, what she thought. I probably went on much more than I needed to but I just hoped I made myself clear. It was ten o'clock by the time I finished, what I hoped would be a satisfactory copy, I put it in an envelope, licked a stamp to go on the corner and left it propped up by my work bag to post the next day.

Two weeks passed, surely she had got my letter by now?

Well, I guess I had my answer, Ellie wasn't interested, she hadn't even bothered to write back, there was no more to be said, that was the end of that! Part of me still kept on hoping.

It was Sunday, no post today. The sun broke through dark clouds as I pulled back my bedroom curtains. The flat was silent and though it was eight o'clock, it appeared the kids were still asleep. I sat on the bed, pulled my socks on and a pair of jeans. Going through to the bathroom, I heard the first sounds of stirrings, soon the kids would all be awake, chattering away twenty to the dozen. Just for now though I would have a few minutes to wash, shave and hopefully get breakfast on the table before they came paddling through.

In the mornings, Frankie would wash and dress himself, he also helped Conway, which left me with the twins, Buddy was always slow at eating so I could sort Shirley out, while he was finishing breakfast. I hoped it wouldn't be too long before they didn't need nappies through the night. Judy had got them to use a potty through the day, night times were proving more difficult.

At last they were sorted and playing with cars, including Shirley, her dolls cast aside. Having three brothers, I knew she was turning into the tom boy Our Ede had been and still was come to that.

Ede was intent on getting her full mechanic qualifications, she had surprised all of us by how homely she made the flat, also how good she was with Angela. I knew Tom and her were devoted, however Ede's love of engines and how things work had never left her.

I washed the dishes, thinking where we might go that day, when there was a gentle knocking on the door. I assumed it was Our Ede, with a towel in my hands I went to open the door.

'Hello Ede,' The words dried in my throat, it wasn't Ede on my doorstep but Ellie! I was speechless, Frankie and Conway came rushing into the hall.

'Who is it?' Frankie asked, as he ground to a halt and stared at Ellie. Conway stopped too and both boys crowded up shyly behind me.

'Hello all of you, well aren't I going to get asked in?' Ellie laughed as Conway rushed forward and took her hand, he pulled her in through the open door, past me and Frankie. I was still too surprised to speak. Ellie was here, in my home, how did that happen?

'Who is she Dad?' Frankie broke into my thoughts. 'What does she want? What is she doing here?'

He sounded anxious and angry too, if you can feel both at the same time?

'It's Ellie,' I said, adding, 'she's a friend, come on let's make her welcome.'

Ellie breezed into our lives, just as she did my flat, that Sunday morning. The kids adored her and when I took them out to meet her Mum, it was a treat for us all. The only place we had ever been made more welcome was at my Mam and Dad's and Ede's, of course, though Tom was still a little wary of me.

Ede laughed when I mentioned this, she told me Tom was still waiting for me to knock seven bells out of him for getting her 'up the spout' as she put it. I told her there was no way I would do that, not now. Yes, I felt like it at the time when we all found out, but seeing my sister so happy and content with her life was all that mattered really. Losing Lily had brought that home to me. I knew I had to break Alice's heart, as I couldn't love her as she loved me, Lily had been too prominent in my mind. Yes, I hurt and still do when I think of how she died. But part of me left the past behind and I was looking forward to the future.

I still felt lonely at night, could Ellie fill that gap? I thought so, she was so vibrant and full of fun. Always making up stories for the kids about animals on the farm where she worked. Her Mum knitted and soon little cardigans, hats, gloves and scarves came along.

I saw Ellie most weekends, visiting through the week was difficult. I had no transport, only the work truck and I could hardly take four kids in that. Luckily my workmate Davy had a small van with seats in the back and he would lend me that every other Sunday and on the alternate Sunday, Ellie would come to visit me.

Our relationship grew, but beyond a kiss and a cuddle that was the only intimacy we shared. Ellie was waiting, she told me and I respected her. I had to be content and hide my lustful feelings, it didn't stop me thinking of her, as I lay in bed on my own. I was prepared to wait and see what unfolded. It was early days, I'd rushed headlong into two relationships with Lily and Alice, this time I was happy to take it slow. My kids needed me and I needed to be there for them, yes, no matter how long it took, I would wait.

Part Eight

Chapter Twenty

'Ede, what's the matter?' Tom stared at my tear stained face. 'Angela is okay, isn't she?' He pulled the blanket from our baby's face and gasped, he saw she was covered in a bright red rash. 'What on earth Ede? She's burning up, get this blanket off her!'

'I... Yes… Okay Tom,' I mumbled, my heart in my mouth, my baby, what was wrong with her. 'I thought, if she's ill, I must keep her warm and then this rash appeared.'

'Give me two minutes to lock up and we'll take her to Casualty.'

'Oh! T...Tom it's serious, isn't it? Can't we just go to see a doctor?'

'I don't know Ede, we might not get in. No, we'll go to Casualty.

The drive to Saint James Hospital seemed to take forever, our Angel lay in my arms, murmuring softly, her face was red, however the rash seemed to be fading.

A nurse rushed us into a cubicle and soon a doctor came. He examined Angel all over, 'Now then Mr and er…Mrs Lister, it would appear Angela has a slight infection of some kind and I suspect the rash is, or rather was, a heat rash. You said you had her wrapped in a blanket? She could have become too warm and that caused the rash. Look it's almost gone.'

I stared down at my Angel laid on the bed, clad in just a nappy. The rash had covered her body too as I found out when I undressed her, but he was right it was fading and she was gurgling happily. 'The infection?' I asked.

'Nothing to worry about, just give her plenty of fluids, water if you can. I'm going to give her a tiny injection to clear anything up. She'll be fine Mrs Lister.'

I nodded, not daring myself to speak. Would she be fine? An injection, that would really hurt her, I couldn't bear it. I nodded to Tom and he took my place by Angel's bedside. I had to leave, even as I made my escape I heard Angel scream. How could I not be there to comfort her? It was only a tiny scratch, they told me. I turned on my heel and hurried back to the cubicle. Tom was redressing Angela and she was smiling up at him as she always did. The love they had for each other almost made me jealous.

It wasn't long before we piled into the car, to head back home. 'Sorry Tom,' I muttered, very aware I'd taken him away from work.

'Don't be daft, you and our little Angela here, come first and always will.'

I felt relieved, I always knew, from the time we got together, that Tom Lister always meant what he said. Yes, as I keep saying, Angela was a surprise for us both but we loved her and she completed our lives. I often had her in the pram while I helped Tom with mechanical stuff. I was learning fast and couldn't wait to go on day release to college to get a proper qualification. Night school was alright but no time to learn proper stuff.

Our flat was looking great, I'd learned to sew and was making Angela's dresses, also curtains and cushion covers. Mam knitted cardigans, hats and bootees for Angela and Our Ike passed down the clothes Shirley had grown out of. Tom worked hard and was never short of work. Life was good and I was so pleased Our Sam and Phyllis were going steady, perhaps there would be wedding bells soon?

Our Ike bothered me; I was so upset when he split up with Alice. I was sad as I knew I wouldn't see my good friend very much, if at all. Many of my so-called school friends had turned their backs when they found out I, as they put it, had to get married. It was nothing like that, Tom and I wanted to be together. When I suspected I might be pregnant, Alice was wonderful. She was my sister; I did not want to lose her. Then Lily not only turned up but died and Our Ike went into mourning. Though quite why, after the way Lily treated him, deserting him and the kids like that, well I couldn't fathom! He finished with Alice, I went several times to comfort her, but in the end, she said she didn't want to see me any more, because I reminded her of Ike. Wow that really hurt, for a time I felt I had no friends. Lucy, my childhood pal, was always talking about Wharton College Secretarial College, she nearly drove me mad. I had Sadie, she was a good pal, but somehow I didn't regard her as a sister.

Recently Sadie tried to persuade me to go on a Saturday night out with her. She asked Tom and he insisted I went, I didn't enjoy myself one bit. Sadie was only too keen to see which lads we could pick up. I reminded her I was married to her brother. Sadie sneered and said it was only a bit of fun, nothing heavy and she felt sure Tom wouldn't mind. But I did and I told her so! Leaving her in the pub, I decided to get a taxi home.

I was waiting at the taxi rank when a lad lurched into me, he was obviously drunk.

'Well, what 'ave we got 'ere?' he breathed into my face. The smell of alcohol made me reel. I took a step back and he grabbed my arm. 'Now, come on, my beauty that ain't no way to take a compliment.'

I was scared, even though he was far gone from the booze, his grip on my arm was tight. He grabbed me round the waist with his other arm and his mouth came down on mine, I twisted my face away.

'I... I'm married…' I spluttered, gasping for air as his face covered mine again. I tried to push him away and screamed, 'Leave me alone!'

'Where's hubby then? Dooon't seee himmm,' he slurred.

'He'll be here any minute, to pick me up, so please get off me now!' My voice rose as fear gripped me, I closed my eyes and he pulled me closer to him.

All of a sudden, I felt his arms let go of me, I opened my eyes and it was as if he was being lifted into the air by someone. 'You lay off my girl, you drunken bastard or I'll get the law on you!' Sadie stood there grinning as the drunk lurched away, muttering something about lesbians everywhere. 'I'll give him lesbians!' Sadie laughed, taking my arm she guided me towards an approaching taxi. Aware that the drunk stopped and had turned to look back, she kissed me full on the mouth. I switched from shaking with fright to shaking with laughter as we both fell into the taxi.

'Mindst you he weren't bad looking, I could have... Well you know.'

'Sadie, what are you like? I was going home, I didn't want to spoil your night.'

'You daft cow, as if I'd let you out on the streets on your own, my coat had fallen down behind the bench or I'd have been right behind you.'

'I'm glad you came when you did,' I shuddered at the thought of what might have happened if she hadn't come along and rescued me.

'Well, I can imagine our Tom's reaction if I hadn't! I'd be in the hospital!'

'No, Tom wouldn't hit a woman.'

'No, reckon he wouldn't, he's got even softer since you came along, now had it been my dear brother Harry, well...' Sadie's voice trailed off and I wondered.

In late Spring, Harry married Tracy Fletcher, in a rushed and secret registry office wedding. Tracy was pregnant, but a few weeks after the wedding, she had fallen downstairs and lost the baby. She always seemed cowed when she was with Harry and quite nervous about speaking to anyone. After what Sadie had just said, I wondered if Harry was hitting her. Perhaps he had reason to, he'd be mad she'd lost the baby, I spoke these thoughts to Sadie.

'Well, let's leave it Ede, I have my own ideas about that.'

'What do you mean?' I shuddered again, surely Sadie didn't mean Tracy's fall downstairs wasn't the accident she and Harry claimed.

'No, didn't mean nowt,' Sadie said, 'Take no notice of me, just jealous, you and Tom are settled, Harry and Tracy and even our Phyllis!' she laughed.

I knew she was trying to reassure me, but sparks of doubt settled in my mind. I'd ask Tom to find out more, if Harry was being mean to his wife, Tom must stop it.

Later that night, Tom looked at me in amazement, 'Don't be so bleeding daft Ede!'

'Okay Tom, but there's no need to swear, it's just a thought,' I retorted.

'Now look lass, I will not hear any more, as if any of them would resort to hitting a woman, Harry might be some things, but never that, no way, never that!'

I knew Tom was referring to Harry's criminal activities, which were rarely spoken about, all the same I couldn't help wondering about Tracy, I remembered her from school, it was there I started hanging round Sadie's group, Tracy had been in the group too and good friends with Sadie. Tracy was confident, pretty and lively, totally the opposite of what she was now. I half wondered if Tom suspected something too, the way he denied it so vehemently. There was more to this than met the eye.

'Are you sure about it Tom?' I asked him why he'd been so angry about Harry.

Leading me into our bedroom, he asked me to sit down and told me the whole story. I almost held my breath and shuddered as Tom revealed how his Dad frequently hit his Mam.

'But she seems okay, no bruises.'

He held up his hand and revealed his Dad was the cute one, only hurting where it wouldn't show, though one time his Mam had ended up in hospital with cracked ribs. It was then he and his brothers vowed to each other they would never ever raise a hand to a woman. 'That's how I'm so sure Harry would never hit Tracy!' he concluded. Tom knelt on the floor in front of me, both my hands in his. He raised his head to look at me and I could see his eyes were damp with tears.

'Oh Tom, your poor Mam. Could you not stop him?'

'We begged Our Mam to let us give him one, but she made us swear not to, as he would only take it out on her afterwards. The bastard would've done too! So hard as it was, we had to keep our promise. She told us, after being in hospital, he'd sworn not to touch her again. I can't tell if this was true. Odd times I suspected he'd hit her but she denied it and claimed, if she grimaced, it was the bad time of the month, that sort of thing. I don't know Ede 'onest I don't. But I do know Harry would never hit Tracy.'

He frowned, as if he was struggling to believe his own words. He knew I wasn't going to let the matter lie. If Harry was a wife beater, I'd get Tom to sort him out, just a pity he hadn't sorted his Dad out. Would it make matters worse for Tracy? I just didn't know what to think or do, I just knew I had to find out to be sure. Our Ike knew Tracy, he'd gone out with her, it hadn't developed into anything as Ike went to London, I'd ask him anyway.

I went round to Ike's next day; I knew he'd be in on a wet Sunday. I knocked on the flat door, shaking the rain off my brolly. I'd dropped Angela off at Mam's, asking if she would look after her for an hour or two, as Tom had work to do in the garage.

Tom didn't normally work Sundays but with his reputation growing he had a constant stream of customers. He was talking of getting extra training so he could do MOT certificates. They became law in 1960, every car had to have one, but very few garages were authorised to test a vehicle for them. This would bring in even more business, of that I had no doubt. Was our small garage big enough? Tom assured me, with all the extra work he was doing, we could soon afford our own place and he would have me as his assistant. I felt torn, wanting to help Tom, but also wanting to be there for Angela. Tom had suggested a babysitter, but I didn't want to miss Angela's first steps, her first words, I wanted to witness those and knew if she was with someone else they would see all that.

Mam was only too glad to help that day and didn't even ask where I was going.

Conway opened the flat door, inside I could hear childish laughter and then Our Ike laughing and, what sounded like, a female giggle. I caught my breath wishing silently he'd made it up with Alice.

'Hello Ede,' Ike grinned. I stood in the doorway observing the scene before me. Ike was on the floor with the kids and this woman, they were in a tangle of arms and legs, playing the new game of Twister. Frankie was amongst the tangle and the twins sat by laughing. 'Want to join us Ede?' Ike laughed.

'No, it's okay, I'll come back later, didn't know you had company,' I added pointedly.

Ike disentangled himself, much to loud groans from the kids. He took the woman's hand and heaved her to her feet. Ellie smiled and held out her hand as Ike introduced me.

'Hello, I've heard so much about you and not only from Ike, also from these two ragamuffins,' Ellie smiled.

Frankie and Conway laughed and said together, 'We're not 'agamuffins.'

'Hello,' I muttered. Ike frowned and glared, reminding me to mind my manners. 'I hope it was all good,' I added quickly and grinned.

'Oh yes,' Ellie said. 'Most definitely the best, if you weren't Ike's sister I'd consider you competition.' Ike and Ellie laughed together.

I looked from Ike back to Ellie, they seemed very at ease with each other. Who was she? Where was she from?

'Look kids, you carry on and no cheating Conway. Us grown ups will go and make your Auntie Ede a cup of tea and she can be introduced properly to Ellie.'

I followed them into the kitchen and Ike told me how he'd nearly killed Ellie. She said killed was a bit strong, he'd only knocked her off her bike, it was her fault anyway she added, cos the bike had no brakes. 'It has now,' said Ike and they laughed sharing a private joke. 'Now Our lass, what brings you round here on a wet Sunday morning?'

'Oh nothing much really, I...it'll keep,' I said.

Ike looked at me quizzically, sensing I needed to talk, Ellie told us she would go into the room to check kids hadn't tied themselves in knots, 'For it surely sounds like it,' she added.

'So that's who the bike belongs to,' I said.

Ike nodded, 'Okay Ede, what gives? There's something on your mind,' he said, pressing the tea into my hand, he sat down beside me at the kitchen table.

Gradually, trying to ignore the peals of laughter from the room, I told Ike what Tom said about his Mam and Dad and my suspicions about Harry.

'You knew Tracy Fletcher Ike, have you seen her with Harry since they got married? Ike, is she the same as she was before? Do you know what I mean? Cos she has changed!'

'Now look Ede, yon Harry is a nasty piece of work, but I don't think he'd stoop so low. I tell you this if Tom Lister so much as raises a hand to you, then I'll swing for him!'

I told Ike of the promise Tom and his brothers had made, how I didn't think Harry kept that promise, also Sadie had hinted Tracy's fall down the stairs was no accident.

Ike nodded, 'I can see the way it looks, but I'd stay out of it lass. As I say Harry Lister is a nasty piece, I've seen him in a fight, but causing a miscarriage? Well no, he wouldn't do that I'm sure.'

'How sure Ike? How sure are you?' I pressed.

Ike put an arm round my shoulders and told me again to stay out of it. He added I had to tell him straight away if Tom raised so much as a finger to me.

'Yes Ike, look I'll go, let you get back to your...er...girl-friend? Thanks for the tea and the chat, yes I will trust what Tom says and don't worry about me.'

Ike showed me to the door, passed me my brolly and gave me a hug. I could tell, the way he kind of blushed, this Ellie really was his girlfriend, though why had he never mentioned her before? Was this her first visit to the flat? I doubted it, she seemed so relaxed there and the kids seemed very at ease with her too.

I felt sad it hadn't been Alice, but maybe, just maybe, this woman might bring Ike happiness, I really hoped so. He'd been sad for too long, far too long. I hurried towards home, then changed my mind. Thoughts of Tom's brother eating away at me. Tom was wrong, I felt sure of it. I made my way, from the tower block where Ike lived, to Cavendish Street. A grand name I'll grant you that, but it was anything other than grand I can tell you. Some lads, of about sixteen, were kicking a tin can around in amongst all the rubbish. A tall youth, stopped kicking the can and stared at me.

'Well, what 'ave we 'ere lads?' he drawled, wiping a dew drop off the end of his nose with his hand. 'How's about a kiss then gorgeous?'

I glanced him up and down taking in his shabby, dirty clothes and worn shoes, he pushed his dirty hand through his long greasy hair, I stared at his acne covered face, his wide mouth grinned at me showing nicotine stained teeth.

'A kiss,' I snarled at him. 'Wouldn't touch ye' wi' a barge pole.'

The other lads fell about laughing, but his grin turned to a scowl and he advanced menacingly towards me. For a moment I was afraid, until one lad grabbed his arm.

'Leave it Rodders, she's Harry Lister's sister in law.'

Dew drop pushed past me with a bigger scowl on his face and the gang hurried after him. So Harry had a name for himself round here; that was very interesting. I felt relieved but still worried about how Tracy would be. I knocked on their door, number seventeen. The lace curtains at the window had seen better days and the brown front door could do with a lick of paint.

'Oh Ede,' Tracy said, as she pulled open the door, 'Come on in.'

I stepped into the hall, paper was peeling off the wall and the brown lino was worn and dirty. Tracy led me through to the kitchen. She hurriedly swept away a pile of papers from a chair and indicated to me to sit down. I looked round at pots spilling out of the sink, the grease covered cooker and walls. It took me all my time not to shudder.

'I just wanted to come to say sorry about the baby and to ask if you are okay?'

Tracy winced and I knew I'd hit a raw nerve. Tracy sat across the table from me, gone was the pretty, confident girl, who'd been at school, now she looked dishevelled, clothes hung on her thin body and badly needed washing. As I waited, the aroma of the house filled my nostrils, sweat, urine and worse. I held my breath forcing myself not to gag. How could anyone live like this? But they did, most of Cavendish Street and the next two or three streets were like this. Slums, destined to be erased and replaced with tower blocks of flats. The residents of the streets would be rehoused there, but how long would it be before the tower blocks became like this? If people didn't care for their homes now, what difference would it make moving them into a new flat? Well, that's what I thought. The powers that be declared it would make all the difference, these folks would be given a new shiny home, of course they would look after it.

Still that wasn't why I was there. I studied Tracy, looking for obvious bruising, but there were none. 'Harry…' I began.

'He's not here Ede,' Tracy broke in. ' Did you wanna see him like? He won't be long, just gone to fetch something.'

'No, no, it's you I came to see Tracy. I was so sorry to hear about your accident.' I took a deep breath, 'How did it happen?'

Tracy raised her head and stared at me. 'What...what d'you mean how? I fell downstairs, it was, perhaps, better I lost it like, this is no place, no home for a bairn.'

'Oh Tracy how can you say that? It was your baby; you would love it regardless of where you live. I mean how did you fall downstairs?'

'Look I fell alright, no I wouldn't love it, cos it might have been a boy and grow up just like him... And if it was a girl how could I have kept her safe?' Tracy coloured, 'Look Ede, thanks for coming but you'd better go now before Harry gets back, 'e don't like me 'aving friends round.'

'What do you mean keep her safe? Besides, I'm not friends, I'm family,' I said, seeing the worried look on her face, I rose to my feet.

'Look Ede, just go, I don't wanna talk about it right.'

'Okay, but if ever and I mean ever I can help you in any way, that goes for Tom too. Well just ask us!'

I left, I didn't want to be there when Harry returned, he was a bit over familiar with me and I didn't like that. It was bad enough the lad in the street trying it on, but my own brother in law! There was nothing I could put a finger on, when he hugged me at our wedding, it was a little too long, when he kissed me as we left the reception, he licked his lips before and after. It all felt a bit too creepy. I didn't say owt to Tom like. He and his brothers were very close and I was not sure I would be believed in any case.

I hurried back home, glad my Tom was normal. There was definitely something not right with Harry. If he had hit Tracy, making her fall downstairs, well I was at a loss what to do, Ike said I had to keep out of it.

Tom bounded upstairs as he always did at the end of his working day.

'How's my two princesses?' he grinned, shedding his overalls and scrubbing his hands in the sink. He turned and hoisted me off my feet in a bear hug. 'What you been up to all day? I know it's Sunday and sorry I had to work but Mr Swiers needs his car for business tomorrow.'

'Nothing much, now put me down if you want some tea,' I laughed.

'You were out quite a while in the pouring rain too.' He indicated my damp hair and nodded towards Angela.

'We've just been to Mam's and Angela is okay, she was well protected from the rain, even if I wasn't.'

'Look, you're just as important to me as that little un and you remember that.'

I put my arms round his neck so he couldn't see my tears, his words meant everything to me. I would talk to him later about Harry. From Tracy's reaction there was something wrong, something very wrong.

Angela settled quickly that night and as Tom and I sat, with a cuppa on the sofa, I cuddled up to him and he automatically slipped his arm around my shoulders and kissed my hair.

'I do love you Ede,' he whispered, his voice barely audible.

'I know, there's something Tom.' I took a deep breath knowing he wouldn't want to hear what I had to say. 'Harry...' my voice trailed off, 'I...I went to see Tracy today.'

'How is she?' Tom sighed, 'You might have upset her taking the bairn.'

'I didn't take Angel because of that reason. But Tracy was scared in case Harry found me there, she said he didn't like friends round. I told her though Tom, I wasn't a friend but family. Tom something ain't right.'

Tom sighed and turned to look at me, 'Did she tell you

how it happened?'

'Well, she said she fell downstairs, but I don't believe her Tom, I think if she did fall then Harry pushed her!'

'Don't be so bloody daft,' Tom's voice rose and I could see he was upset. 'I've said before my brother maybe some things, but to do that, Ede, there's no way he'd do that, no way at all.'

I knew from the stern look on his face he didn't want to discuss it any more and I was right.

'I'm tired lass, let's away to bed.' Tom rose from beside me, he gathered up our cups and headed to the kitchen. I sat listening as he ran water into the cups and then went into the bathroom, a short time later he called, 'You coming lass.'

'I'll be there in a minute, I'll just tidy up.' I needed to gather my thoughts about Tracy and Harry. I came to realise, without Tom's help, I was quite powerless, unless Tracy told me and Tom the truth. Tom would carry on seeing his brother as quite harmless, but deep down I knew, whatever oath they had made, Harry had broken it.

The weeks went by and Angela kept me busy, it was lovely to feel the warm sun on my face. The garage business was growing fast as the country became wealthier and more people could afford cars. Mam had Angela two days a week so I could help Tom out. I couldn't wait to start college, night school only covered the basics of car maintenance. Mam seemed quite happy to carry on looking after our bairn, in turn Angela loved her Granny. Mam was also feeling and looking a lot better these days. Ike and I had heaped her with a lot of worries, but now things were settling down, Mam could see we were both happy and in turn I think it made her happy too.

Ellie saw Ike as often as they could get together, which

was, usually, only on a weekend. Ike had even taken his four to meet Ellie's Mam. I bet that was a shock but it turned out she had welcomed them with open arms.

Sam and Phyllis were going steady, though, despite my earlier thoughts, it would be a long time before we heard wedding bells in that direction.

Surprisingly enough, Sadie seemed to have been having more than just a few dates with a bus driver. Ian Bailey lived on Cavendish Street, the better end Sadie said. I grimaced, was there a better end? However, I was surprised, yes there was. Sadie and Ian invited Tom and I round for a meal one night. Ian's Mother was away and Sadie had moved in for a few days. It was heart-warming to see her part of a couple. Ian's home was as pristine outside as it was in. Sadie confessed to me later she was terrified of making a mess. The meal was great and we didn't out stay our welcome, anyone with eyes could see the lovebirds wanted to be alone. Sam and Phyll were babysitting and said we had no need to rush back.

'Let's call and see Harry and Tracy.' I suggested and without giving Tom a chance to reply, I headed down the street, 'It's daft not to, when we are here.'

Tracy opened the door and gawped at us. I heard Harry shout angrily, if it was somebody selling something she had to send them away. Glancing at Tom, I could see him pale at the tone of Harry's voice.

'Well, aren't you going to invite us in?' Tom asked loudly.

'Ye...yeh, c-come in,' Tracy replied nervously, standing back allowing us to pass.

Harry was sprawled on the sofa, a can of beer in his hand and several empty ones at his feet. He sat up as we entered the room, 'Well big brother, what brings you to this dive?'

Tom explained and I could see his eyes roaming round

the room taking in its shabby condition. 'Sit down, oy you, get yr brother and sister in law a drink,' he growled at Tracy. She bustled off into the kitchen and returned with another can and asked what I'd like. I could sense Tom bristling at the way Harry had spoken.

'Tea please,' I said adding, 'Would you like a hand?'

'Yon's quite able to mek a cuppa, now sit thissens down.'

I moved a pile of clothes from a chair and sat down, Tom sat by Harry and took the can. 'Harry, that's no way to speak to your lass.' He said it so quietly I only just heard him.

Harry threw back his head and roared with laughter. 'No way, my God Tom, have you seen this place? She hardly ever cleans up and the whole place needs painting.'

'You could do that,' I said, a little too harshly. Tom gave me a swift look, which told me to leave it to him.

'Aye ye could Harry, thee's not working and I'm sure a man of your means could get some paint from somewhere,' he gave Harry a knowing wink.

'Aye 'appen I could, but why bother, we'll be given our marching orders soon, they're going to flatten these ya know. Oy where's this lass's tea.'

Tracy came in and passed me a mug of tea, I could see her hands shaking. I sat and sipped it. She perched on the arm of the sofa, next to her husband, refusing to take Tom's seat when he offered it. Harry suddenly slapped Tracy's leg hard, which made her visibly flinch. 'More beer!' he demanded, grinning as Tracy hurried off.

'That was a bit too harsh Harry,' Tom said.

'What you talking about? Them needs a slap now and agin keep 'em in order,' Harry's voice slurred.

Tom paled at what he had just heard, he stood up quickly and pulled Harry up off the sofa with both hands.

'What the...' Harry blustered.

'Remember our oath? You must never hit a woman! You have, haven't you? How long? How long have you been slapping that lass Harry? How long?' Tom's voice was close to tears.

'I... I...' Harry faltered, sobering up quickly, he pulled himself upright and stared back at Tom. 'Who the hell do you think you are? Coming in here, all high and mighty, telling me what I should and shouldn't do to my own wife. Clear off Tom, before I slap you one as well and take that bimbo slut with you.'

I gasped as Tom raised his fist and punched Harry hard in the face, the blow knocked him senseless and he fell back on the sofa. 'Come on Ede, we're leaving.'

Tracy appeared in the doorway with two cans of beer in her hands. 'Oh my God Tom what have you done? H-h-have you k-k-killed him?' she stammered.

'No, but if he ever lifts a hand to you again, I will!' Tom said vehemently, I had never seen him so incensed.

'Tracy, why don't you get some things and come home with us?' I asked, I could see she was trembling from head to foot.

'I c-c-can't, h-h-he'll be angry.'

'Aye with me lass, not you. Ede's right you come with us, give him chance to cool down.' Tom put his arm around her thin frame and hugged Tracy to him.

She relaxed in his embrace and nodded meekly.

Back home, after a vague explanation to Sam and Phyll, I took Tracy into the bathroom and ran her a bath, 'Now you get yourself in there and I'll bring you a nice cup of cocoa.' Tracy nodded and started to pull up her dress, realising I was still in the room, she stopped and turned, pulling it down again. However, not before I had seen the bruises on her legs. I walked towards her and pulled the dress up and over her head gently, trying not to gasp too much as I saw bruising on her arms and deep bruising on her body, these were so black they showed through her thin white under slip. I folded her in my arms, 'Oh Tracy, Tom must see these. Harry, he... He did push you down the stairs, didn't he?'

I could feel Tracy nodding her head and her wet tears, as she buried her head into my shoulder.

'Tom, Tom!' I called, 'Come here!'

Tom appeared in the doorway and without Tracy raising her head I turned her towards him so he could see the bruising. 'She didn't fall downstairs either. You get your bath Tracy,' I said a little too quickly, I saw the anger in Tom's face and knew I had to go to him.

Tom was putting his coat on as I reached him, I grabbed his arm. 'I'm going to kill him, that poor lass, that poor bairn!' His voice was a mix of anger and tears.

'Leave it Tom, she's here now, she's safe. He will probably be unconscious, the force of that thump. Let the law deal with it, we'll take Tracy to them in the morning and get him arrested.'

Tom shook his head, 'Won't lass, they'll not get involved, they'll say it's domestic.'

I couldn't believe what I was hearing, Harry's treatment of Tracy was criminal and he needed to be treated as one. 'Tom please don't go.'

Tom looked down at me and suddenly I was in his arms, he was muttering into my hair that he'd never hurt me, how he was so ashamed of his brother, the oath they had made, how sorry he was. I felt him relax and knew he wasn't going to sort Harry out that night. 'I'll get the others; we'll go and talk to him tomorrow.'

I smiled and hugged him back, the shock of the night's events, seeing Tracy's bruises, I just needed Tom there, with me, that night. I felt so safe in his arms and Tracy was safe too.

The three of us sat for a long time drinking our cocoa and discussing what to do next. Tracy looked so thin, in my satin dressing gown, her hair combed back was still damp, she looked about thirteen. But she was safe, I kept telling her, and at long last she seemed to relax.

None of us realised that Harry had not remained unconscious for long, he had in fact heard us begging Tracy to leave with us and as we sat in our flat safe and warm, he was planning his revenge.

Chapter Twenty-one

Angela whimpered in the night and as I stirred, I thought I could smell something. 'Tom, Tom, what is that?' I shook him hard. Surely Tracy wasn't smoking in our flat, she knew we didn't like it. Yes, it was definitely smoke. 'Tom, Tom are you awake? I can smell smoke!'

Tom sat bolt upright at my words, 'Oh my God, so can I Ede. Get Angela wrapped in a blanket, I'll go and see.'

'Tracy might be smoking.'

'Yes love, you could be right, though we did ask her not to.'

I picked Angela up and followed Tom, wrapping our baby in her blanket as I went.

Tracy lay on the couch fast asleep. We could hear a crackle of flames and the smell of burning rubber.

'Oh my God, the garage is on fire.' Tom cried and shook Tracy so hard she nearly fell off the sofa.

'What?' she muttered.

'Out now, both of you, Ede, go to the phone box and ring the fire engine, I'll go and see if I can dowse it. There's a fire extinguisher, just inside the garage door. Now go you two, and Ede look after our bairn.'

'Tom, no, don't go in there, wait for the fire engine, please.' I cried, grabbing his arm.

He shook me off and pushed us both down the stairs and through the door. 'Get away all of you, phone box now!'

I didn't need telling twice, hugging Angela to me I ran, luckily the phone box was about fifty yards up the road. I made the call, then hurried back to find Tracy staring into the smoke coming from the open door of the garage.

'Tom, Tom, where are you?' I had half a mind to let Tracy hold Angela, go in and find him, however Tracy was shaking so hard I didn't trust her not to drop Angela. 'Tom!' I yelled again, fear gripping my throat. 'Tom, listen they are coming, please come out and leave them to it. Tom, Tom...' My voice subsided into sobs.

Neighbours surrounded me, having been woken by the commotion. Several of them yelled Tom's name.

'Are you sure he's in there lass?' Mr Clayton, from across the road, asked as he grabbed my arm, I could only nod. 'Right well, we'd best get him out and sharp, come on lads.'

I watched in horror as four of them threw back the garage door wider and entered the smoke filled garage. I could hear Mr Clayton calling Tom, and I began to pray. It seemed hours yet was only probably a minute or two before the four of them stumbled out, coughing and carrying Tom between them.

'Oh Tom, you stupid bugger, are you okay? Is he okay Mr Clayton? I mean he's not de...dead.'

They laid Tom on the ground and I knelt beside him, still holding Angela, who had miraculously fallen asleep, oblivious to the state her Dad was in.

'Tom!' I cried, I couldn't help it, tears rolled down my cheeks.

Suddenly he stirred, opened his eyes and sat up. 'What are you crying for lass?'

'Oh Tom, I thought you were dead.'

Tom grinned at me, 'Can't get rid of me so easy, but at least I got the fire out, and I don't think there's much damage.' He flicked his eyes towards the doors and made to get up. Suddenly a bout of coughing engulfed him and he stayed sitting on the ground, hunched forward, his chest heaving.

'Now then lad.' Mr Clayton squatted down beside us. 'You stay put, you inhaled a lot of smoke in there, so t'ambulance blokes will want to check ye out.' He placed a hand on Tom's shoulder to restrain him.

As if by command, an ambulance careered round the corner, followed closely by a fire engine. The two ambulance men carefully lifted Tom into the back of the ambulance and put a mask over his mouth.

'It's alright lass, we're just giving him some oxygen, it will help clear his airways.' The younger of the two men informed me. He glanced down at the baby, 'You his sister then?'

'No!' I retorted sharply, 'I'm his wife!'

'Oh, well, he'll need to go to hospital, probably overnight. Is there someone we can call for you?'

'It's okay,' Mr Clayton appeared at our side again. 'Ede, I've called yer Dad he'll be along directly.'

'Thank you Mr Clayton.' Tracy, what shall I do about Tracy?' I'd forgotten all about her. I turned, Tracy was staring at the garage, trembling from head to foot.

'It's okay lass, I'll take her to ours, it's your sister in law ain't it?' Mr Clayton smiled. He was a good looking man despite his advanced years and grey hair.

I smiled back and nodded my thanks, adding, 'If Harry, her husband comes, well don't let him see her.'

Mr Clayton nodded, turned and taking Tracy by the arm led her towards his house. The firemen declared the garage was safe, Tom had indeed got the fire out. They were going to return the next morning to try and find the cause of it. Possibly, an electrical fault they said. I sighed, at least our home was safe, or if it was the electrics, was it?

'Ede, Ede, oh my God are you alright?' Dad called, hurrying down the street, Mam following in his wake. 'What the hell happened?'

All I could do was shrug and bury myself in his welcoming arms sobbing. Angela stirred and started to cry. 'I must go with Tom,' I said. 'Will they let me?'

The younger ambulance man nodded, and then asked if someone could look after the bairn.

Mam pulled Angela gently out of my arms, reluctantly I let her go, torn between wanting to go with my darling Tom and stay with my baby. Angela stopped crying as Mam cuddled her.

'Look lass you get into the ambulance. We will see all is okay here and Mam will take Angela home,' Dad said, pushing me gently towards the waiting vehicle.

I nodded and was glad Sam appeared, I knew all would be okay with the three of them there. I just had to make sure my Tom was okay. Climbing in, I was guided to a seat opposite him. Tom seemed drowsy, underneath his soot covered face he looked deathly pale. I prayed over and over in my head, I couldn't lose him, not now, not ever. I reached out and took hold of his hand, he didn't stir. I glanced anxiously at the ambulance man as we pulled away. His eyes were glued to a flickering screen at Tom's head, it made a beeping sound. Tom's heart? I hoped so as the bleeping was slow but regular. Tom had to be alright. I squeezed his hand tighter and grinned with relief as I felt him squeeze it back.

At the hospital I was allowed to stay for a couple of hours and then they rang my Dad to ask if he would come and fetch me. He assured me all was safe at home and the garage. He and Sam had checked everything out and locked up. Angela was at home, fast asleep with Mam, so Dad was taking me back to their house.

I was dead on my feet by the time we got there and was

relieved to be ushered into my old bed, after first peeping at my little Angel, she was asleep in a makeshift cot, in Mam and Dad's room. Mam ushered me away as I went to lift the cot to take it into my room. 'No lass, you've had a nasty shock, you need to rest. We'll look after the bairn,' Dad told me firmly and I was too tired to argue.

I went home the next morning, leaving Angela with Mam. Shortly after I arrived three firemen came to check on things. I stood by the garage door as they went in and poked about. Nothing much seemed damaged, Tom would be glad about that, it was all very black and sooty.

'Well, now we have it,' The older one of the three said, walking towards me, rubbing his hand over his chin. 'It wasn't an electrical fault. This looks like a job for the police miss.'

'What...What did you say?' I stared up at him, all kinds of thoughts tumbling through my mind.

'The police, I think this was a deliberate fire.'

I thought I was going to fall down, I felt my knees buckle and grabbed the door for support. He went on to explain the rear window was broken from the outside, bits of burnt cloth were found underneath it. Unfortunately, one bit had found its way into old sump oil, which Tom kept in a tin bowl. That was the cause of all the smoke, but it also contained the fire. He told me how Tom had put a metal cover over the bowl, dousing the flames.

'Who would do such a thing?' I gasped.

'That'll be up to the police, they have been radioed for and will be along directly. We'll wait till they come. Are you okay Miss? Is there anyone I can get for you?'

I shook my head, I was too choked to speak, all I could think was how and why anyone would want to harm us? What would Tom say? I turned away and headed to Mr

Clayton's. I had to see if Tracy was okay. Tracy... I wondered, wicked thoughts filled my head. Harry! No surely he wouldn't or would he? I would confront Tracy, she would know if he could be capable of such an act. I dismissed the very idea, as surely he wouldn't put his own wife, brother and niece at risk. The very idea a Lister would stoop so low was unthinkable. But then Harry wasn't just any old Lister, I had seen evidence of how nasty he could be.

Tracy sat in the Clayton's sitting room, a man's dressing gown wrapped round her body. She held a mug of tea, sipping it gently, glad of the warmth. I stood at the door and observed her for a few moments before I spoke.

'Tracy, how are you?' I asked, trying to keep my voice calm.

She looked up at me with tear filled eyes.

'Tracy it's okay, we are all okay and Tom will be fine.' My voice shook and I fell to my knees taking hold of both her hands, trying not to spill her tea. 'Tracy the fireman said it wasn't an accident, they've sent for the police.'

'Oh no,' Tracy cried. She carefully put the mug on the small table by her side. 'I...I... Oh NO!' she stammered.

I placed my arms round her and could feel her body shaking. 'Tracy, would H...' I was unsure of what to say, so I came straight out with it. 'Would Harry have done it?'

At first Tracy shook her head, but I pressed her further by asking her the same question, after what seemed like an age, she nodded.

'Why? Oh my God Tracy! Why?' I could feel tears burning my eyes and my throat.

'He... He has always threatened to kill me...if I left him, or even if I told anyone about my injuries,' she blurted out.

I dropped her hands and scrambled to my feet, I was too

shocked to speak. That Harry would try and kill his wife, his brother, his niece, was just unbelievable. I turned and walked out of the house, I had to tell the police, tell Tom too, but that could wait, let the police deal with Harry Lister. I knew if Tom got hold of him, first he would kill him. I wasn't having that. I wanted Tom by my side, but he lay in hospital for at least another couple of days, they'd said. I knew he was anxious to get home but I told him firmly to stay put and I would keep him updated. His coughing from the smoke was quite severe.

I walked back across the road just as a police car arrived. 'Can I speak with you?' I asked quietly.

One of the officers nodded, took my arm and helped me into the car. 'The fire crew tell me it's arson, is that what you want to talk about?' he asked gently.

I nodded and stumbled over my words, I gradually told him what had gone on between Harry and Tracy Lister and how she ended up with us the previous night. I also relayed what she had just told me.

The policeman looked very solemn, and muttered he wouldn't put anything past the Listers. He wanted to talk to Tracy and I told him where to find her, would she tell him what she told me? For some reason I doubted it, misplaced loyalty to her other half, or fear of the reprisals? I scrambled out of the car and followed him into the Claytons. Surely with me there she couldn't deny it? But she did, very vehemently too, said I had a grudge against Harry. That I'd found her ill and as Harry was away down South on business, she had let me bring her to ours to look after her. The policeman glanced from Tracy to me. I was trying hard to control my anger.

'I'll just go and see if the fire crew or my colleague has turned anything up,' he said calmly, as he left.

I heard the front door close and turned on Tracy, I felt like hitting her myself, but instead I let my voice do it. I called her all the bad names I could think of. Mr Clayton came into the room and put his arms round me, I think he thought I was going to use physical violence on her. He asked what was going on? Through the tears and anger I told him what Tracy had told me and what she had told the police. I couldn't hold it in any more. 'Why Tracy? Why?' I sobbed turning my face into Mr Clayton's shoulder.

He stroked my hair, 'Hush now Ede, it's alright, Tom's alright and so are you three ladies, well you two and that bonny bairn. If Tracy misled you then I'm sure she is sorry. Aren't you Tracy?'

I glanced round at her and saw her head nodding furiously, she also looked red in the face. I could not understand why she was covering for that pig of a husband. If she had just told the police the truth, he would be arrested and locked up. She could even get him prosecuted for physical injury, I felt sure of that. I could see she wasn't going to move, so I shrugged myself out of Mr Clayton's Fatherly embrace, asked him if Tracy could stay there and left. The only course now was to see if the police had any further leads and if they would check Harry Lister was away down South. He wasn't, but it was her word and probably his, when and if they caught up with him, against mine and Tom's. I had no alternative other than tell Tom what she'd said. Could I get him to promise to let the police deal with it? Get him not to take the law into his own hands. That I doubted very much, very much indeed!

After checking in with Mam and eating the beans on toast she forced in front of me for dinner, I made my way to St James's Hospital, or Jimmy's as we knew it. Mam said it had almost doubled in size after the introduction of the National Health Service in 1948 and now it was being redeveloped further.

I made my way to Tom's ward, feeling reluctant to tell him about the arson. I felt relief course through my body as I saw him sitting up in bed looking none the worse for the smoke inhalation. I practically ran up the ward and into his arms. I buried my head in his chest and wept, knowing my tears were drenching the hospital pyjamas he wore. He said nothing, just held me tightly and stroked my hair. Eventually I pulled away and he gently wiped the tears from my eyes. 'Come now lass, we're all okay. I'll get those electrics sorted when I'm out of here. I feel fine, but they are insisting I stay another day or two. Are you and Angela alright, you'll stay at your Mam's?'

I nodded, unable to find my voice. I knew I would have to tell him, in case the police came. 'Tom, I love you and I was so frightened, Angel and I can't live without you.'

He pulled me to him and kissed me on the lips, 'Silly, you won't have to, I'm going to be alright and be with you and Angel, as you insist on calling her, always.'

It was then I told Tom what the firemen and the police said. He lay back on his pillows looking stunned. I continued before he had a chance to speak. 'I think it was Harry.' Going on, I told him what Tracy had told me and what she told the police. I could see Tom clenching his fists, he made to get up, I pushed him back. 'No, Tom the police will deal with it. Please.'

'I'll kill the bastard,' he growled quietly. 'I'm going to discharge myself Ede and find the twat!'

'Tom, no, please, you must get well. The police are going to check it out, they promised. I don't want you doing anything, that will... Well take you away.' I started to cry again.

Tom pulled me into his arms,   'Oh my Ede, I'm so sorry, of course I'll leave it to the police. I'll stay put till they tell me I can come home. Now stop your bawling and tell me how our baby is with her Granny, being spoiled rotten no doubt.'

I nodded and looked Tom straight in the eyes, his voice betrayed him, I wanted to believe he would let the police see to things, but I could tell by his tone he didn't mean any of the words he'd just said. I could see the anger in his eyes and knew he would be out for revenge and I felt powerless to stop him.

Chapter Twenty-two

Mam helped me tidy up the garage a bit. Mr Clayton told me Tracy had gone back home. I was so furious with Harry and partly with Tracy, I felt she deserved all she got! Uncharitable I know and I would be consumed with guilt if anything happened to her. Mr Clayton told me she was very vague, and she'd said it was for the best that she went home. I couldn't help but agree, who knew what Harry would do next if she were to stay?

I declined Mam's offer to stay with her for another night. I knew I wouldn't sleep, I just wanted to be there, to make sure Harry didn't come back. Mam took Angela with her; I wanted my baby out of harm's way. Mam said she would look after her.

I slept fitfully that night and the next, the bed was strange and cold without Tom. At last the morning came and I could bring Tom home. We'd get a taxi back, I didn't care what it would cost, more than we could realistically afford, but needs must.

Tom was dressed when I arrived at Jimmy's, I was glad I'd already taken something in for him and the smoky clothes he'd worn the other night, were washed at home and hanging up in the bathroom. I hugged him and enjoyed the smell of him, he'd had a bath that morning and was all set to go. He struggled to put on the coat I'd brought, breaking out in a fit of coughing. A nurse hurried down the ward.

'Mr Lister, we have said you have to be careful for the next few weeks. You inhaled a lot of smoke and, as we have said, it will take a while to get right.'

'I'm only putting my bloody coat on!' Tom snapped.

I reached out my hand and placed it on his arm. 'Tom please, she is right, you have to take care, she is only doing her job.' Tears stung my eyes at the tone of Tom's voice and the way he spoke to the nurse.

'Come on Ede,' he sighed, 'let's get out of here.' Putting his arm through mine he marched up the ward, the march became a slow walk as coughing took over once more.

'Oh Tom,' my tears fell. Tom had turned quite pale, should he be going home? With his arm still through mine we made it to the entrance, where we were able to get into the taxi I'd ordered.

'Nearly gave you up,' the taxi driver grinned. 'Where to?' he asked turning to Tom,

'My God man, you look awful, are you sure you're fit to leave this place?'

Tom mumbled our address and told him to get in and drive. The journey home was in silence. I was relieved to get there, I can tell you. Sitting in the taxi beside Tom I could feel his tension. Never mind, I said to myself, he'll be okay once he sees there's no harm done to the garage.

Sure enough it was the first place Tom wanted to see. He nodded at the car standing waiting for new brakes to be fitted.

'I can do that Tom,' I told him firmly, 'Well, I might need a bit of guidance. I rang Mr Brownlow and he doesn't need the car till next week. Come on, upstairs, I'll make us a cuppa. Bet the tea was crap in the hospital,' I grinned encouragingly.

Tom stared at me blankly, eventually nodding. We made our way slowly upstairs, coughing halted Tom's progress several times. I was so scared, but knew our doctor was dropping by later to see how he was. I'd ask him if Tom was really going to be okay.

The rest of the day Tom sat, staring blankly around, even when Mam brought Angela home, he remained stone faced, I shrugged when I saw Mam out.

'It will take time for him to get over this Ede,' she said gently. 'Look, I can take Angela for a bit longer, if you'd like me to.'

I shook my head. 'I can manage Mam, I just want Tom to be back to his normal, happy self, but since I told him about Harry, something in him changed.'

The doctor came later that afternoon, he listened carefully to Tom's chest. 'Yes, still quite a wheeze in there, didn't they prescribe anything?'

Tom shook his head, 'It's just smoke doc.'

'I know,' the doctor said earnestly. 'You must get plenty of rest, do not smoke or let others smoke round you, avoid things that irritate your lungs. I'm sure they have told you all this at the hospital. However, I will do you a prescription for something to ease that cough and an inhaler. Can you get it Ede? They are still free, but I don't think that will always be the case.'

'Oh, thank you doctor, yes I can get the medicine, that's not a problem, what about Tom working?' I glanced at Tom, he was staring blankly at me again.

The doctor turned to Tom, 'No work, until you can go up AND down those stairs without coughing! Is that clear?'

Tom nodded vaguely, I could tell by his face he wasn't going to take any notice.

I followed the doctor downstairs to see him out. 'Doctor, Tom... Well... He doesn't seem himself, if you know what I mean.'

'Yes, I think I do,' the doctor smiled. 'Your Tom has had a shock as well as damage to his lungs, it will take time. Sometimes smoke inhalation can cause change in mood. I'll be back in a day or two, I will keep my eye on him and get him the necessary treatment should he need it. But with you and Angela around him, I'm sure he'll be back to his old self and on the road to complete recovery in no time.'

I thanked the doctor, hoped and prayed to myself he was right. Going back upstairs I found Tom laid on our bed, his eyes closed.

'Tom, I'll go and get your medicine,' I whispered, 'I'll take Angela with me so she won't disturb you.'

Tom gave a slight nod, his eyes remained closed. I left the room, quietly closing the door. Angela was asleep in her pushchair, so I carefully bumped her down the stairs, amazed when she didn't wake. I let myself out and locked the door behind me and hurried to the chemists on York Road. It was quite a hike but I ran pushing Angela along. She woke up and chuckled to herself as the wheels hit every bump in the pavements.

I was quite out of breath when I got back. I felt uneasy, the flat door was partly open, I was sure I'd locked it behind me. Glancing round the front, I saw the garage firmly locked, I half wondered if Tom was starting on Mr Brownlow's car. I went upstairs carrying Angela, leaving the pushchair in the small hallway. It was always a struggle to get by it, but the best place for it really. I'd only helped Mam upstairs with it earlier when they arrived, as Angela had been asleep.

'Tom, are you awake? I've got your medicine.' Pushing open the bedroom door I found an empty bed. I went to the bathroom, empty; kitchen, empty. 'Tom where are you?' I asked the silence. I didn't need an answer, I knew where he had gone. Hurrying back downstairs I got Angela into her pushchair, she started to grizzle. 'It's okay my Angel, your Granny will give you your tea.'

'Ede, what on earth?' Mam was surprised to see me as I

heaved the pushchair up the steps into the kitchen, thankfully Angela had gone to sleep.

'Is Tom alright?' Mam asked, drying her hands and coming round the table to me.

I nodded, not daring myself to speak, I felt choked with tears, fear and anger. Finally, I managed to splutter out my request. 'Can you see to Angela? I... I have to find Tom.'

'What do you mean find him Ede?' Mam put her hands on my shoulders.

'He's not at the flat. I went for the medicine the doctor gave him... When I got back he'd gone!'

'Has he started work again? Surely he's not well enough?'

'No Mam, I... I think he's gone...after Harry.'

'Harry, why?'

'Look Mam, just take care of Angela please, I must stop him, I really must go now.'

I shrugged Mam's hands from my shoulders and fled down the back steps, before she could stop me. I ran down the alley and blindly made my way to Cavendish Street, only slowing to wipe the endless tears from my eyes.

I found Tom bent double at the door of Harry and Tracy's house. His hand raised, he hammered on the door. Flakes of paint drifted down over him, as it peeled off the rattling door. I ran up to him and threw my arms round him, pulling him back from the door.

'Tom stop, let's go home.' I released my hold, as he groaned, I was hurting him in some way. 'Tom please, look there's no one in, let's go home!' I begged.

Tom put a hand on the house wall for support, coughing badly, he slowly lifted his head and looked at me. I could see the anger in his eyes. Tom was there to sort Harry out! I knew all the pleading in the world wouldn't stop him.

The door inched open and Tracy peeped out, 'Oh Tom, Ede, you scared me half to death, I thought... Well, never mind what I thought. If you're coming to get me back to yours then no, it ain't worth the risk! I'm staying put, it's safer! Any road Harry ain't here. Lord knows where he is, but I reckon he's scarpered after what he's done.' Tracy hung her head, I could tell from her voice she was so ashamed of her husband.

'Look, there's no use defending him Trace,' Tom said defiantly. His coughing had abated, but he was breathing heavily. Get him out here, I want to see him... NOW!'

'I told you he ain't here.'

'Look Tracy, Ede is desperate to get me home, but I need to sort this out with that so-called husband of yours. Why the hell did you stay with him? After what he did to you?'

'He...he's my husband.'

'He's a bloody coward, that's what he is, raising his hand to a woman!'

'He...never.'

'Oh, come on Tracy, we know the truth you know, and don't forget he tried to kill you, huh, what is it twice now? Pushing you down the stairs and then the fire...' Tom broke off as he started to cough again.

Tracy stood firmly in the doorway, 'I told you Tom Lister he ain't here!' She shut the door sharply, before Tom had chance to put his foot in it to stop her.

'Come now, leave it Tom, let's go home.' I pulled him away and we slowly made our way back to my Mam's, Tom coughing most of the way, he wasn't right and I felt he should still be in hospital. We reached home to find Our Angela laughing at her Uncle Sam, he was crouched down in front of the pushchair pulling faces at her.

'You wanna be careful Our Sam, your face'll stay like

that,' I laughed, trying to lighten Tom's mood.

'Oh my, Tom!' Mam cried, as she came downstairs. 'I could hear you coughing as you came down the street, shouldn't you still be in hospital?'

Tom shook his head and lowered himself into Dad's armchair. We called it Dad's chair, as it was where he always sat. I used to feel so grown up, sitting in it when he was out.

'You'll all stay here for the next few days, you need looking after Tom. Oh I aren't saying Our Ede won't do that, but she's enough on looking after this little cherub.' Mam tickled Angela under her chin; our bairn looked up adoringly at her.

Tom was about to protest, but Mam was right and I told him so too. Reminding him I could sort things out at the garage.

The next few days flew by; I scrubbed and cleaned the garage and the flat. Sadie came to help me on her day off and we enjoyed listening to her transistor radio as we worked. The flat was sparkling, the garage not so, but it looked better and at least we'd got rid of the smoky stench.

Mr Clayton came over and helped us move the heavier stuff round. I hadn't known he'd worked as a mechanic in the war and I was glad of his help to finish the brakes on Mr Brownlow's car. He also helped when Miss Hildreth brought her car in for a repair, it kept stalling. I was so thrilled she brought it to us, Miss Hildreth was a teacher at my old school. I felt a bit awkward at first, but she was lovely. Mr Clayton and I soon sorted the problem. Miss Hildreth paid in cash, with a little something extra for Angela, she told me.

Tom was impressed when I told him. He was itching to get back home, so after three days, and an okay from the doctor, we left Mam and Dad's. They both seemed quite sorry to see us go, told us how they missed us, Ike and his kids too. I was just glad to, hopefully, get back to normal.

Sadie came round to tell us Harry had definitely done a disappearing act, Tracy was packing up the house and moving back to her folks. I was relieved, as it meant she could get on with her life and we could get on with ours. I knew Harry's actions had rattled all of us. I was prepared to let it go, we were safe and Tom was getting over the smoke inhalation. He was still furious with Harry and I knew if their paths crossed, Harry would certainly come off worse.

Tom's anger was something new to me and I did not wish to see it again. He had never shown the slightest hint of anger towards me or our bairn, not even when the police came when that flirty piece came to the garage and I threatened her with the spanner. I thought Tom would be furious, he was a little annoyed, but he laughed it off and later said he was proud of me in a way. Well, I wasn't having that woman flirting with my Tom, and insulting my experience in car mechanics!

We still laugh about the incident, all these years later. Tom suffered no after effects from smoke, I was glad life was returning to normal. Whatever normal is!

Part Nine

Chapter Twenty-three

'Damn the Lister's,' I thought as Mam brought me up to speed on the events at Tom's garage.

'Now then Ike, don't you be getting involved, it took Our Ede all her time to persuade Tom to let it drop, it seems yon Harry has disappeared and Tracy is going back home to her folks. Ede said they think the fire was an electrical fault.'

I nodded thoughtfully, I knew Harry Lister was handy with his fists and we all suspected Tracy's miscarriage wasn't an accident. Good job he'd scarpered! Now the garage was unsafe! I was angry and Mam knew it.

'You've your kids to think of and your new young lady, how is she by the way?'

I stared at my Mam, she stood at the kitchen table, pouring out two cups of tea. Looking round the place, I couldn't help but marvel at the changes. A new fridge freezer was in place, as well as an automatic washer. She followed my gaze, 'Takes forever though, I could have the whole lot done in my twin tub, the length of time it takes to do one load in that.'

I laughed with her and agreed; glad I had a twin tub to wash the kids' clothes. I soon had them done, it was drying that was the problem, well until Mam got me a drying cabinet, it had rails in it to hang the clothes and soon got them dry. Trouble was, I was forever feeding the electric meter as it seemed to use loads of electricity when it was on.

'Ellie's fine Mam thank you, she's a good friend.'

'Oh, is that what they call them now, a friend?' Dad laughed, as he came through the back door, obviously hearing my comment.

'Now Dad, don't be casting aspersions, she is just a friend,' I retorted perhaps a little too quickly. Mam and Dad glanced at each other knowingly.

'Well the kids seem to adore her,' Mam smiled. 'It's Ellie this, Ellie that. Especially after you took them all down to see her and the farm she works on. I thought Conway was going to burst telling me all about the animals he'd seen and Frankie was thrilled to bits having a ride on a tractor.'

'Yes Mam, they did enjoy themselves. Ellie says Conway will make a grand farmer.' I rubbed a hand over my head.

'What? What is it lad?' Dad asked, he'd taken off his coat and hung it on the back door, Mam poured him some tea.

I looked at them both, wanting to relay my fears and not wanting to face them once they had been said.

Dad nodded encouragingly and we all sat down at the table.

'I, well… I don't know,' I began hesitantly.

'Don't know what Ike?' Mam prompted.

'It's just… You're right, the kids are becoming fond of her, but I'm not sure if it's right what if... I mean, what if we split up, it was bad enough after Li...ly and A..Alice.' I stammered out my fears.

'Now look lad,' Dad leaned forward, reaching across the table, he put his hand on my arm. 'Life is full of what ifs, I'm sure you don't need me to tell you that. But we can't let it rule our lives. This Ellie, is she anything like Lily?'

I shook my head and Dad continued.

'Well, how do you feel about her?'

'I like her a lot.'

'How does she feel about you?'

'Well, she has said she loves the kids and she has indicated she loves me. But what about Alice?'

'What about Alice?' Dad exclaimed, sitting back in his chair a frown on his face. 'You needed to sow a few wild oats, while you were young, and Alice filled a gap.'

'Alf, really!' Mam admonished. 'Ike, would not use someone like that, as well you know!'

'Well, Alice is water under t'bridge lad. You say this lass loves you all? Did you ever get that off Lily? No, I don't think you ever did. You've got to stop thinking about the past and feeling guilty too about Alice. Love needs to be both ways tha knows,' Dad grinned at Mam, winked, then continued, 'Now, focus on the future, your's and the kids happiness. So stop these stupid doubts lad and go with it. What do you young uns say these days? Go with the flow?' Dad laughed loudly, Mam joined in and I too was grinning by his use of that expression.

Go with the flow, yes I did like Ellie a lot and in more ways than I ever felt for Alice. Ellie brought warmth and laughter into our lives. Even her Mam adored the kids, I didn't think she'd approve of her daughter having a widower for a boyfriend and one with four kids at that. The kids loved going to the countryside for a visit. I knew I had to expel my doubts and fears, but you know what they say, once bitten twice shy. Could I forget Lily? How she had hurt us all by leaving the first time and leaving again the second! I'd given my heart and soul to her and I realised she just used me to escape her abusive Dad. But she did say, before she died, that she had loved me, she just didn't like being tied down.

Then there was Alice, I truly believed I was in love with her. She was sweet and obliging, but in a cloying sort of way, I knew she loved me and I thought a lot about her, the time we were together. When Lily came back I realised what being in love really meant. Splitting up with Alice had been hard for the kids, but I knew it was for the best. I needed to get over my grieving for Lily, I knew I couldn't do that with Alice around. Was I ready for another relationship?

Ellie was so different to anyone I'd ever gone out with. She was funny and independent, had a mind of her own, yet she was gentle and homely. She made us some cushion covers, with farm animals on, for my old sofa and some new curtains. I offered to pay but she wouldn't take a penny. 'Labour of Love for me and the kids,' she told me quite adamantly.

Yes, Ellie was completely different to Lily and I began to think of a future with her, us all together, as a family, in a large country house. Well, the latter would never happen, I'd never afford that on my wage. Would Ellie want to move to the city and live in a flat? I doubted that very much. So I decided to take my Dad's advice, he had also added Herbert Asquith's famous phrase which, I think, was probably about the threatening advent of World War One. 'Wait and See.'

One day, a few weeks later, Ellie and I were in Roundhay Park. I lay back on the rug, we'd placed on grass by the swing park and sand pit. The kids were happy playing there and I was too.

'Did you know this park has been here since 1872?' Ellie said, turning to look at me.

I shook my head; Ellie was always coming up with snippets of information.

'Mmh,' she continued. 'It's one of the largest parks in Europe and covers 700 hundred acres. Imagine that Ike, once someone would own all this.'

I propped myself up on one elbow and studied her face.

She looked wistful as if she were imagining living and working on a place as big. My heart lurched; I could never provide that for her in a month of Sundays. Perhaps I should break up with her now, before either of us got in deeper than we were at that moment.

A sudden scream from the sand pit had me on my feet, all thoughts of breaking up forgotten, Shirley stood there howling and pointing at Buddy. I guessed her twin brother had hit her or something. They often seemed to be at each other these days. There's me thinking twins were rock solid and looked out for each other. Not my two, they were always falling out over a book or toy. Buddy sat there, swinging the spade about, grinning at his twin. Shirley had huge tears rolling down her cheeks and she was engulfed in heartbroken sobs. I picked her up and checked her over, no damage done. I felt guilty not keeping my eye on them, I'd been focussing on Ellie.

Ellie was by my side stroking Shirley's hair. 'Hush now sweetheart, it's okay, look Buddy is sorry, aren't you Buddy, what happened?'

At the tone of Ellie's voice Buddy looked suitably ashamed. Frankie piped up he'd seen Buddy hit Shirley with the spade. I admonished my young son for his behaviour and once Shirley stopped crying put her down, she toddled off to play next to Buddy as if nothing had happened.

'Kids eh!' I grinned at Ellie, 'One minute fighting and falling out, the next you wouldn't think anything had occurred. My fault, I should keep a better eye on them. Dunno what I'm doing wrong with those two, at the moment they are always falling out...'

'It's kids Ike, and don't put yourself down, you are a wonderful Dad to all of them, they are lovely kids. I wish...'

'What do you wish for, Ellie?' I whispered, my heart in

my mouth, as I waited for her reply.

'I wish...' Ellie looked down at her feet, but I could tell by her voice she was close to tears. 'I wish I could have kids Ike. There I've said it! I've wanted to tell you for a long time, I can't have any of my own. I'm sorry, I see how you love them and I guess if we were to get together, well, you'd want more?'

I pulled her to me and it was my turn to stroke her hair. 'Oh Ellie, it doesn't matter a ha'penny to me, ain't I got enough kids for us both? But Ellie, I can't give you much. I can tell you belong to the land and I can't, could never afford anywhere in the country.'

Ellie put her hand over my mouth. 'Hush you daft man, yes a place in the country would be great for me and your kids, but if it's not to be then as long as we're together, that's all that matters. As long as you're okay about not having any more that is.'

'Oh, my darling Ellie!' I felt too choked to speak, did she mean it? Could she see a future for us? I realised I would have to look into things and see if I could get us somewhere in the country. After all I could drive, so I could easily work in Leeds, I just needed a better paid job.

I took my family and Ellie home, and my heart was singing. I sat, in the sitting room, with the kids, smiling to myself as I heard Ellie humming a little song to herself, in the kitchen, as she made our tea.

'Dad, what's Ellie doing?' Frankie asked, throwing himself onto the sofa beside me.

'She's humming lad and making our tea,' I replied, ruffling his hair.

'Is she?' Frankie starred up into my face, 'Is she going to be our new Mum?'

The question took me totally by surprise, I bent over and

whispered in his ear, 'I hope so lad I really do, would you like her to be?'

Frankie frowned and I guessed he was thinking about Alice. Suddenly he threw his arms round me and nodded enthusiastically. I felt the warm glow inside me grow warmer and warmer.

'Well, I'll just have to work on it Frankie lad, I really will, but for now keep it a'tween us eh?'

The little boy seemed happy with my answer and nodded as he slid down onto the floor, to resume playing with his toy cars and Conway. I sat back and smiled, life couldn't get much better than this, could it?

One afternoon, several weeks later, Mr Lumb beckoned to me, 'Ike lad, away in the office wilt tha?' Bernie Lumb was the manager of the scrap waste department, broad as his tongue and bald too, his eyes were what you'd describe as beady, yet he always managed a smile. He was kindly too and genuinely upset, when Alice left her job in his office, just after we split up.

'Naw then Ike lad, I've summat to ask thee.'

'Ask away Mr Lumb.' My heart in my mouth wondering what his request might be.

'Well lad, I've bin thinking a while now abaat retirement.'

'But you're not old enough Mr Lumb,' I said shaking my head.

'I knaws I ain't, but ya see it's like this Ike, me old Auntie, in Bridlington, well ya sees she's only up and popped her clogs! Died right sudden like and as I'm well her only kin, she's only gone and left me t'lot, money, hoose, everythin' I tell thee lad I'm fair gobsmacked.' He sat back in his seat and wiped a pudgy hand over his perspiring brow.

'So ya sees Ike, I ain't one to look a gift horse in the mouth,

I'm gonna hang up me overall and move to Brid.'

'Right Mr Lumb, like you say too good an opportunity to miss. Thanks for confiding in me, but what was it you wanted to ask me?' I felt a bit blown away by this intimate revelation from my superior.

'Well Ike, ya sees I've bin asked to suggest a replacement like fer me job and I thawt of thee. You'd fit t'bill proper like.'

I opened and shut my mouth in total surprise at his suggestion. I knew it'd be a bit more money, just what I needed. Mr Lumb told me what the salary would be and I was stunned, it was double what I was on and some more.

'I've also another suggestion Ike, I knows ye are in a flat with thy bairns well I'd like to offer ya ma hoose, reasonable rent like. I wanna keep it ya sees in case living by the sea don't suit me.' Before I could reply, he carried on. 'It has three bedrooms, a big sitting room and a parlour plus out back there's a kitchen of sorts and I also 'ad a bathroom put in, trouble is it were me old Ma's and I ain't done much decorating since she passed, it's a bit of a way out, in the village o' West Kirkby. A fair way to travel like, but ye'll allus 'ave use of t'van, as I do, and it's a grand drive.'

I felt I was dreaming, a job offer with more money, a proper house and in Ellie's village to boot. What more could I wish for? I stood up in my seat, leaned over the desk and grabbed a surprised Mr Lumb by the hand, pumping it up and down, I thanked him profusely. 'I could kiss thee Mr. Lumb, thank ye so much!'

'I...er I'd rather you didn't kiss me Ike!'

I shook my head, feeling my face go red in embarrassment.

Mr Lumb grinned and explained to me the time scale of his departure, it wasn't going to be for a month or two, giving me plenty of time to learn the ropes. Not that there would be much to learn, liaising with farmers who wanted the shoddy and arranging transport of it out to the farms. My post would need a replacement of course Mr Lumb concluded. I scratched my head thoughtfully, I was sure I'd find someone to take my place. Of course it meant I wouldn't get out to see Ellie. But as I might be moving near her, well I could see her every night and may be, well... Perhaps... She might move in with me and the kids. I'd forgotten the kids, it would mean Frankie would have to move school, Conway too. It would be too far for Mam to go and collect them and also who would look after the twins? Maybe I shouldn't have agreed so readily. Mr Lumb saw my frown.

'Look lad, there's a lot to think aboot, like I sez I ain't going nowhere for a good few weeks. Tek thissen off 'ome and think aboot it wilt thee? Let me knaw in a day or two. But before thee decides, come an' look at t'house.'

I nodded and stumbled out of his office, my mind whirling. Whatever the options were, I had to sort out the kids, try and make it work somehow. It was too good an opportunity to miss. It would mean there might be some future for Ellie and me and that was all I wished for right then. I couldn't wait to see her, today was Monday, the run with shoddy, out her way, wasn't till Thursday. I'd just have to bide my time till then. Meanwhile I'd talk to Mam, see what she thought of it all, Dad too.

I put on my coat, my day was over and I rushed out from the mill as fast as I could, over to Mam and Dad's house.

I flung open the back door, Our Ede was seated at the table, her face as white as a sheet. My own news would have to wait, I could see something was wrong, really wrong, it was written all over her face and my Mam's too.

'Someone died?' I said, trying to lighten the atmosphere.

Ede turned her head away and I could tell she was crying.

'What's wrong Ede?' I went over and put my arms gently round her shoulders.

'It...it's Tom,' she sobbed.

'What's Lister done now? Upsetting thee like this, I'll have him!' I cried as my mouth ran away with me.

'Hush now Ike, it's nothing of the sort,' Mam admonished.

'What then lass? What's happened? What's he done?' I asked gently, squeezing Ede closer. I hated seeing her upset like this and if I could prevent whatever Lister was doing or had done, then I would. I refrained from saying I knew it would all end in tears but that's what it looked like. Ede sobbed in my arms, her thin shoulders shook. I looked at Mam for an explanation.

'Tom, has gone to find Harry,' Mam said quietly. 'Tom heard he was back in Leeds!'

'Well, I can't say I blame him, after what that bloke did to Tracy.'

'It's not just that Ike, they believe it was Harry who set the fire.'

'What!' I let go of Ede and faced my Mam, they'd told me it was an electrical fault, now they were saying it was deliberate!

Mam nodded slowly. 'Tom's been in a rage about it since he was told, he even went to their house just after he got out of hospital. It seems Harry had done a runner, Tom is determined to find Harry and give him what for.'

'Is this true Ede?' I asked my little sister.

'Yes Ike,' she sobbed. 'I tried, but I couldn't stop him. Harry will kill him, especially as Tom isn't fully fit, he's still suffering, he's not himself, he's not strong. Oh Ike, I don't know what to do. I'm so scared,' Ede's voice broke off as sobs engulfed her.

'Where was he going to start looking Ede?' I asked earnestly.

'I dunno Ike, he wouldn't say!' Ede sobbed out. 'Tracy gave the house up, she went back home, I think.'

'I will go and look for him and, hopefully, find him before he finds who he is looking for. You and Angela stay here, Mam will look after you.' I felt confused, trying to take in what I'd been told. I yanked open the back door, there was one place I was going to start and that was with that stupid bitch Tracy. She should have left Harry long ago, instead of dragging Our Ede into this and nearly getting them all killed! I had to admit to myself, one of the Listers, was a violent human being! How did I know Tom Lister wasn't like his brother? Perhaps Harry would kill Tom and then all my worries would be allayed. Except one thing, my little sister loved the bones of Tom Lister, his death would destroy her. I knew that, so I had to forget my concerns, go, and find Ede's husband before the worst happened.

'No, I'm coming too Ike. I want to find Tom,' Ede wailed, her face white with stress. I didn't want her anywhere near trouble, I looked at Mam.

'Nay lass, Ike's right, you stay here, teks a man to deal with something like this. You'll be no good to Tom getting all upset. 'Sides I need help looking after this brood.' She nodded at my four, crowded round Angela's pram making faces at the bairn, who was wreathed in smiles.

'Mam's right Ede, she needs help wi' bairns. Please stay, I promise you I'll find him and bring him home.'

I scarpered out the door before she could argue and hurried down the yard. Rain started to fall and I pulled the collar of my jacket up, wishing I had something on my head.

In Leeds, when it rains, it rains, comes down in stair rods as we say and that day was no exception. It had been a grand few weeks, why just the other day we'd had that lovely picnic. Certainly making up for it now.

I made my way to the Lister's and hammered on the door. Glad it was Sadie who answered it. Her face lit up, 'Well, hello brother in law, what can I do for you?'

'Your Tom ain't here is he? Is Harry here? Do you know where he might be?' I barked my questions at her.

Sadie stepped back in surprise, raised both hands in surrender. 'Whoa Ike! What's this about Tom and Harry? What you on about?'

I quickly filled her in with the details, explaining we had to find Tom, before he did something to Harry he'd regret later, or worse Harry did something to him. 'Ede says he's not well, still coughing from the fire.'

'Oh my gawd Ike, I still can't believe Harry would do such a thing!' Sadie clenched her fists. 'I could swing for the devil messen! But no Tom ain't here and we ain't seen hide nor hair of Harry for days. I gather Tracy has cleared off back to her Mam's, perhaps Harry is there? Cos that daft cow is stupid enough to take him back.' Sadie grabbed her coat and pulled the door closed, announcing she was coming with me. I knew from the look on her face it was no use arguing and I was glad, she obviously knew where Tracy lived as I didn't.

I had to run to catch up with her and it seemed we were going so fast we dodged the raindrops, if that's possible! We turned this way and that till we were in a back street off the Halifax Road. Houses here hugged the pavements, there was no room for even a car down the street we were going to, Sadie said. She stopped outside a tired looking terrace house and knocked on the door. The dirty lace curtains fluttered at the single downstairs window, someone was in, but they didn't answer the door. Sadie knocked again. I put my head to the door and was sure I could hear movement.

'Come on Tracy, we know you're there, open this door!' Sadie yelled hammering on the door once again.

The door creaked open an inch and an elderly lady peeped out, 'She ain't here, what do you want her for? She's done with you Listers,' she croaked, holding the door only a few inches open, we could both see the filth on her clothes and smell the stench emanating from the house.

'Look, sorry about yelling, but we need to find Our Tom and Our Harry. Harry lit the fire at the garage, could have killed them all!' Sadie told her.

'The door creaked open a bit further. 'Aye, Tracy said it was that bastard, she should never have wed him. I knew he was a wrong un and it would end in tears.'

'Where is Tracy? We have to find Tom, he's not well, and he is very angry,' I said over Sadie's shoulder.

'Our Tracy has been gone a few days now, said she was going to stay with a mate up Langton Road. But tha knows, I've a feeling the stupid bitch is back wi' him.'

'What number?' I asked earnestly.

The old woman's face grimaced, she shrugged her shoulders and shut the door.

'Come on Ike,' Sadie said, grabbing my arm, 'Langton Road it is.'

I followed her up the street and we weaved our way round the streets, ignoring how wet we were getting, finally we reached Langton Road. A couple of lads were splashing about in puddles, Sadie grabbed one and gave him a detailed description of Harry, Tracy and Tom and asked if he knew what number they were at. The lad pointed down the street to a green door, Sadie let him go and nodded.

'Sadie, how do you know Tom will be here, how would he find out?'

'Look Ike it don't take a genius to realise Tracy's Mother had relayed this to someone else, now stop gabbing and come on.'

Tom had found them alright, we could hear his raised voice as we approached the house, we could also hear Tracy screaming.

'Sadie there's a phone box up yonder, go and phone the cops, I'll go in the house.'

Sadie needed no second telling, she was off up the street like a whippet. I barged in the house, thankful the door wasn't locked.

'I wouldn't do that Harry if I were you!' I snarled. Harry was just about to thump Tom. He looked up in surprise and dropped his raised fist.

'Bugger off Wagstaff, this is a family matter, ain't nowt to do wi' you.'

I hurried to shield Tom who was bent double, coughing madly. 'In case you forgot we are, unfortunately, family. Now you and Tracy can please yourselves what you do, but I am taking Tom home.' I put my arm round Tom and pulled him towards the door.

'I...wanna...kill him,' he gasped. 'He tried to kill my family!'

'I know Tom, Our Ede's out of her mind, now let's get you home. As for you Tracy Lister, get yourself back to your Mother's, if you've any sense.'

Harry took a step towards me but Tracy grabbed his arm and held on. 'No Harry, that's enough.'

'Oh my gawd Tom, look at you.' Sadie shrieked, coming through the front door.

'An' you can bugger off as well Our Sadie, ain't nowt to

do with you,' Harry growled, Tracy was still holding him back.

Sadie took a step towards him, her eyes flashed in anger. I grabbed her hand, 'Leave it lass. They'll tek care of him,' I nodded to the police car pulling up outside. Two tall, burly coppers leapt out, pushed past the three of us and grabbed Harry.

'Ah, Mr Lister, we've been looking for you, now care to join us at the station for a chat.' The older of the two spoke almost convivially, until Harry refused. 'Look lad, I ain't asking you now, I'm telling you!'

Harry stood firm, refusing to budge, but the two of them got one either side and dragged him out. The older cop saying they were arresting him for the attempted murder of three people and a baby.

'No, he didn't have owt to do wi' it!' Tracy yelled at them, 'You was wi' me, weren't you Harry?'

'Mrs Lister, are you trying to pervert the course of justice?' The younger cop asked innocently. Then he reminded her, she was one of the three people in the flat, when Harry set the fire.

Tracy had the good grace to drop her head in shame. I couldn't believe why on earth she was protecting him and said, 'Tracy after all he's done to you…'

'He's my husband,' she sobbed, as the police ushered Harry into the back of the police car.

'I still wanna kill him,' Tom mumbled, leaning heavily on me and Sadie.

'Let the police deal with him Tom, he'll get what he deserves, prison most like and he won't be treated kindly in there once his inmates find out there was a bairn's life he'd put at risk. Now come on home with you.'

Sadie and I practically carried Tom back to my Mam's

house. Ede fell over him sobbing and checking him all over for signs of hurt. Sadie told her I had stopped Harry and Ede poured out her thanks.

Mam ordered us all upstairs, Tom to get changed and into bed. Sadie and I to get our wet things off, I had to borrow some of Sam's gear and Sadie borrowed a dress of Mam's. Everyone was so happy that the police had caught up with Harry and Mam said she was glad her family were in one piece. The kids crowded round and Frankie announced I was a hero.

I decided not to share my news about West Kirkby and my promotion. It would upset Mam, at the thought of us moving away, and everyone was in such a great mood, I couldn't spoil that. Besides, I decided I wanted to tell Ellie first, get her reaction. Mr Lumb said I wasn't obliged to take the house, if I felt Ellie wasn't keen, then I would know how the land lay with her. Mr Lumb added he hoped I would take on his job though, yes, I would certainly, no doubt about that at all. Even the extra pay would help me care for my family. The older two were growing out of their clothes at an alarming rate.

Yes, I would speak to Ellie at the weekend. Mr Lumb seemed in no rush to get a decision off me, until the following week anyway.

Subsequently Harry was charged with arson and attempted murder. We felt sure he would go down, he did too and for much longer than any of us expected. I assumed the judge was making an example, Harry got life imprisonment.

I was at the court case, so was Tracy, the stupid cow broke down in tears when she heard the sentence, crying out that she'd wait for him. I shook my head in disbelief.

In the meantime, I had to hold my breath till the weekend,

as I missed seeing Ellie on Thursday. Saturday I borrowed Tom's van and made my way out to West Kirkby, Mam and Sam were looking after the kids. I didn't want them to hear what I had to say to Ellie.

As I pulled up outside Ellie's house, I smiled as I noticed the roses, round the door, were still in full bloom. I looked up and down the street. I forgot to ask Mr Lumb exactly which house in West Kirkby he lived in. No matter Ellie might know, if she didn't then her Mam would.

'Ike, this is a surprise, I thought we were seeing each other tomorrow,' beamed Ellie, as she pulled open the door. 'Is everything okay? The kids?'

I pulled her into my arms and nodded furiously, not daring myself to speak. Ellie held me tightly, burying her face in my chest.

'Ellie, I have some amazing news. I've been offered a promotion at work.'

'Why Ike, that's wonderful, isn't it?'

'Well yes, but I've also been offered a bigger place to rent.'

'Oh, is it near work?'

'Not exactly.'

'So you can't take the promotion then Ike?'

'Yes, yes I can, but tell me first where does Mr Lumb live?'

'Mr Lumb? Oh yes, of course, he works in a mill in town, do you know him? Why do you need to know where he lives?'

'I just do, yes I know him, he's at the same mill where I work!'

'I'd no idea, of course you must have business with him. I'll show you, it's down here.'

Ellie pulled my arm to follow her down the street, I was bursting to tell her but I'd decided to wait until we were outside Mr Lumb's. We walked past the row of cottages and turned into a lane between two larger houses. At the back of these houses there was a duck pond, at the other side of the pond stood a square house with ivy clinging to its walls, the red brick looked old, as did the door and the windows, still it looked solid enough and quite large.

'Used to be the old vicarage, till they built a new one,' Ellie said, glancing to a new build on the other side of the pond. Down a lane to the left of the new house stood the church, it's tall spire reaching the sky. What a perfect place for a wedding, I thought. I quickly shook myself out of that reverie, did I want to be married again?

'Look, I'll leave you now, so you can see Mr Lumb, poor chap, his Mother died you know and he lives there alone. No family that I know of, but listen to me waffling on, you go see him and call in for a cuppa 'afore you go.' Ellie reached up and kissed my cheek, turning to leave.

'I don't need to see him, well not today at any rate,' I said, pulling Ellie back and putting an arm around her shoulders. 'I wanted to see where the house I've been offered is,' I laughed at her surprised face and explained Mr Lumb was moving and all about him offering me his job and his house to rent.

'What? Ike, oh Ike, you mean you'd move here, here to West Kirkby?' Ellie grinned for ear to ear.

'Yes,' I said, 'Me and the kids and...and you too of course.'

'I already live here.'

'I know that, I think what I'm trying to say Ellie is, would you live in that old house with me? Well, not straight away, Mr Lumb said I'd probably need to decorate it and such, but we could do it together perhaps, as you like it. But could you see yourself living there with us?' I held my breath waiting for her answer, not daring to look at her face.

It seemed an age before she spoke, 'Yes Ike, yes, oh yes!'

she screamed.

I kissed her and my tears mingled with hers. I'd never felt so happy. So complete, yes I knew Ellie would want marriage. 'Ellie, in time there will be a ring on your finger.'

'If that's a proposal Isaac Wagstaff then yes, and before you say more, I know you're cautious with what happened to you and Lily and I'll wait. In the meantime I'll be by your side and helping you make a home for us and our family.'

Our family, she'd said! Oh how my heart soared. It is all a person wants to hear, when they are on their own with a family, someone accepting your family as theirs. I already knew that the kids loved Ellie to bits and she loved them.

Ellie began to tell me how terrific the village school was, adding it also had a nursery Conway and the twins could go to. She even said she was sure she could work her hours to fit in with picking them all up from there, if she couldn't her Mam, she was sure, would love to.

'All she's wanted was grandkids, she was as devastated as me, when I found out I couldn't have any. She already thinks a lot about your four.'

'Oh Ellie, thank you my dear, darling girl. I love you so very much.'

'And I love you Ike.'

Chapter Twenty-four

It took Tom several weeks to feel well, Ede fussed over him like a Mother hen, I almost envied that, I thought of Ellie and knew she would be just the same if I was ill.

Tom, Ede and Angela, stayed at Mam and Dad's all that time. Ede popped down to the garage and seemed to be carrying on doing odd mechanical jobs on her own. I knew she was good, but not that good. Tom had obviously taught her well and she'd know even more, now she was at college.

Ede may have got married at sixteen, but she had her life sorted, knew what she wanted and just got on with it. I'd no doubt she and Tom would grow old together, he idolised her and she loved him. I was wary that he might turn out like Harry, but when I saw how angry Tom was, at Harry's treatment of Tracy and starting the fire, well Tom's actions spoke volumes to me. Ede told me of the pact the Lister brothers had made, Billy and Dennis had been as equally mad at Harry, for breaking the promise, not to mention the fire. If the police hadn't got to Harry, then I was sure the brothers would have given him his comeuppance!

Not long after Tom, Ede and Angela moved back into the flat, another garage about four streets away came up for sale. I knew Tom was anxious to expand the business and do MOTs etc. So I wasn't surprised to hear they had secured a loan to buy it. Tom would work there and Ede would be at Grange Road. It all seemed to be working out for them.

We all cheered at Harry's sentence, he deserved it! We cheered even louder at our Sam's news, he'd only gone and asked Phyllis to marry him. Who would have thought that of my little brother? Dad had a grumble about another Lister being in the family, out of Sam's earshot of course. Mam had hit him playfully with a tea towel and told him firmly she was glad Sam was happy and that he should be too.

I accepted the promotion and the house offer eagerly. After Mr Lumb departed for Bridlington, Ellie and I looked round our home. Ellie gabbled away at how this room should be, how that room should be decorated and we set about the place every spare moment we had. The kids loved the big rooms, especially as one was made solely into a playroom for them, they kept each other occupied in there for hours. Ellie's Mam had painted up Ellie's old rocking horse for them and Frankie announced he was going to be a jockey, when he was old enough.

Ellie and I moved in at the beginning of the Christmas holidays. Mam shed a tear as she waved us off from the flat. I knew she'd miss the kids. But Angela was playing a huge part in her life now. The little girl was almost a year old and was everything Mam wanted a girl to be. Our Ede was a tomboy, but Angela was dainty and liked all the girly things, Our Ede never did. Mam was quite happy looking after her while Ede was at work or college. Mam also looked heaps better, which stopped us all worrying about her.

Dad was dead chuffed with my promotion, yes, he still had a grumble about Ede doing a man's job, one not fit for a lady. You call Our Ede a lady, Dad? I would tease. Dad would huff and puff, and bury his head in his newspaper. Mam and I would laugh quietly to ourselves.

After living with Ellie in West Kirkby, for just a month, I got down on one knee and proposed. She was surprised and kept saying over and over. 'Ike are you sure, are you really sure?'

Well, I'd never been more sure in all my life. At one time I thought I would never get over losing Lily, I would never love another woman, as I'd loved her. Oh, how wrong can you be? Ellie and I fit together in ways Lily and I never had.

I wanted Ellie in my life always and not just as a girl-friend, 'I want you to be my wife,' I told her. 'Not only that, how would you feel about adopting my kids, so you can be a real Mother to them?'

Ellie made my day when she kissed me gently and whispered, 'Oh Ike, yes, and that's a yes to both questions.'

DEVOTION
DANCE HALL
DEVOTION
DANCING